Virginia Blackburn was brought up in the United States, Germany and Britain and read English Literature and Law at Newnham College, Cambridge. She then turned her hand to a variety of careers, including the law, banking and public relations before discovering her true calling as a journalist. She now lives in West London. Her first novel, *Blonde with Attitude*, is also published by Corgi.

Also by Virginia Blackburn

BLONDE WITH ATTITUDE

and published by Corgi Books

SOPHIE'S SCANDAL

Virginia Blackburn

CORGI BOOKS

SOPHIE'S SCANDAL
A CORGI BOOK : 0 552 14516 5

First publication in Great Britain

PRINTING HISTORY
Corgi edition published 1998
Corgi edition reprinted 1998

Set in 11/12pt Garamond Book by
Phoenix Typesetting, Ilkley, West Yorkshire.

Corgi Books are published by Transworld Publishers Ltd,
61–63 Uxbridge Road, London W5 5SA,
in Australia by Transworld Publishers (Australia) Pty Ltd,
15–25 Helles Avenue, Moorebank, NSW 2170,
and in New Zealand by Transworld Publishers (NZ) Ltd,
3 William Pickering Drive, Albany, Auckland.

Printed and bound in Great Britain by
Cox & Wyman Ltd, Reading, Berkshire.

To my parents

1

Do you remember that sensational scandal last year, concerning the tycoon, the fund manager and the television star? You must have seen it, it was in all the papers. It had everything: money, sex, the humiliation of the great and good – laugh? I haven't stopped yet.

Well, the reason I mention it is that I was working for van Trocken and Co. at the time, to say nothing of being acquainted with some of the major characters in that particular little drama, and so I saw the story unfold from the inside. In fact, it affected me too. Up until the events I'm about to relate took place, my personal life had been as unsuccessful as my professional life, if that were possible.

Although I'd had no inkling of it, however, all that was about to change – partly, because of the monstrous Vladimir van Trocken, and so perhaps I have something to thank him for after all. Anyway, whether you're interested in my story or the shenanigans surrounding my erstwhile employer, I thought that to set the record straight, I would tell you about what really happened in the course of that notorious week. After all, I was there.

It all began one bright morning in October. I was sitting at my desk, with my back to the sun, which was streaming in through the smeary window behind me, nursing a hangover and smarting about a telephone call I'd just had with my boyfriend, Martin. He, the bastard, had informed me that I spent far too much of my time in fantasy land, and that I should wake up to real life, at which point he was called away yet again on some urgent and mysterious work commitment, which he felt was far too dull to bore me with. All very well for him, I muttered to myself, if I had a totally amazing job and earned squillions of pounds in a fund management firm I wouldn't have to spend my time daydreaming. To distract myself, I picked up a copy of *Vogue*. 'The English Rose Blooms Again!' shrieked the headline on the front, beside a picture of some washed-out looking member of the British aristocracy.

I shut my eyes and imagined the scene. A rapturous storm of applause greeted me as I sashayed out onto the catwalk. Strolling down towards the end, and blissfully unaware of the crowd's adulation, I drew a hand through my ash blond hair, which fell beautifully and glossily back into place. (My hair was actually mouse brown at the roots and sort of strawberry yellow throughout the rest of it, but who cares, this was my day-dream and I could be ash if I wanted.) Then I turned on one fabulously stilettoed heel and – 'Sophie, get your ass in here!' roared a voice from the next floor.

Oh no, what now. I leapt up, winced as a dull thud of pain ricocheted through my skull, grabbed my notebook and raced up the stairs to my employer's office.

'Yes, Mr van Trocken?' I panted resentfully as I skidded to a halt in front of a large mahogany desk approximately the size of your average battleship.

'What took you so long?' thundered Mr van Trocken. The huge black leather armchair, from which he schemed and plotted and generally made everyone's lives misery, was turned to the wall so that the only sign of his presence was a huge cloud of cigar smoke hanging in the air above him. Gradually, however, the chair turned round to reveal a large bearded figure, face flushed through a combination of claret and fury, cigar in one hand and hysterically waving a piece of paper in the other. 'Sophie,' said Mr van Trocken, his voice shaking with rage, 'I have been examining your time sheets. Look at this!' He thrust a piece of paper across the desk at me and jabbed viciously at yesterday's entry.

I looked down at the line in question and, just for once, saw nothing that would have produced such a fury. 'What's wrong Mr van Trocken?' I asked nervously.

Wrong question. 'What's wrong? *What's wrong?'* Accompanied by a revolting squelching sound as his leather trousers parted company from his leather seat, Mr van Trocken leapt out of his chair, surprisingly nimbly for such a large man, raced round to where I was standing and held the paper in front of my nose, where he shook it furiously.

'This is what's wrong, you idiot girl! Yesterday, you said that you came back from lunch at 13.55 and it was actually 14.02! I saw you myself! I saw you come in! I made a note of the time there and then and I said to myself, I know that little girl isn't going to cheat me! I know she's not going to pretend that she got

9

back on time when she was actually two minutes late! And what do I find? Not only have you lied to me but you are pretending you got back five minutes early!'

I thought fast. This was a sackable offence in the offices of van Trocken and Co., the company that published *Food for Thought*, a magazine devoted to the creative arts and modern English cuisine. Mr van Trocken, who was the owner, said the two went hand in hand these days and I worked as a welcoming agent and telephone intermediary – some people would insist on referring to it as a receptionist – fact checker and all round dogsbody. My employer, however, was one of those chaps who believed in creative tension, and was given to disposing of employees at the drop of a hat: just last week he had fired one of the graphic designers for arriving at the office twelve minutes late, and the week before that someone else had got the push for pilfering half a bottle of slightly sour milk from the office kitchen. 'I'm really terribly sorry, Mr van Trocken,' I said hastily. 'My watch must be a bit slow, it's just totally unreliable.'

'Let me see it now, Sophie! And if I find you are lying to me, you are out!'

I proffered a wrist. Mr van Trocken seized it, glared at the slim little band of silver on my wrist, a reconciliation present from Martin after one of our numerous break-ups, and compared it to his own monstrous Rolex. The Gods must have been on my side: after a moment or two of squinting, Mr van Trocken reluctantly gave me my arm back. 'Well, Sophie, so it seems you are telling me the truth,' he said suspiciously. 'Your watch is four minutes fast. Adjust it immediately. And I notice that even so, you were trying to give yourself three minutes leeway. I will not tolerate this sort of behaviour from my staff! It is only because I am in such a good mood that I am not sacking you on the spot!'

'Thank you Mr van Trocken,' I said, for want of any other inspiration.

'And another thing,' continued my employer, ignoring my gratitude, 'how can you afford such an expensive watch on what I pay you?'

'It was a present.'

'You are lucky to have such generous friends,' said Mr van Trocken, in a tone that could only be described as menacing. 'When I was a poor boy on the streets of Prague, I had no-one to give me such admirable gifts! Scavenge, that's what I had to do! Scavenge!'

'Er,' I began, uncertain whether this was a reminiscence or a command, but, not for the first time in my brief tenure in the offices of van Trocken and Co., I was cut short by the turn of events.

'What is that!' screamed Mr van Trocken.

'The doorbell,' I said sulkily.

'Well why aren't you answering it, you idiot girl? You're the bloody receptionist after all!'

'I'm not a receptionist. I'm a welcoming agent and—'

'Just answer the bloody door!'

I took this as a sign that our little chat was over and nipped hastily down the hall and back to my desk, where I pushed the intercom button. 'It's me, Irina, let me in at once,' purred a voice in a tone that brooked no opposition. I pressed the door opening bell – my desk was at the end of a long hall, with the front door at the bottom – and a second later Irina, Mr van Trocken's mistress, appeared.

As befitted her status as star of *Take the Money and Run* – not the Woody Allen film, but a Channel 4 soap opera about the lives and loves of the simple folk who run the National Lottery – Irina was, as ever, clad in furs, diamonds and very high heels, with a blond chignon to top it off. She was clutching a copy of the *Daily Telegraph*, which surprised me a bit: I thought she was more of a *Hello!* person. Mincing up the hall with difficulty on those heels, she tottered onwards towards the inner sanctum. 'Vladimir,' she murmured menacingly, 'we must talk.' The door closed behind her and a second later the sounds of hissing – venomous hissing – began in the background.

I plonked the time sheet, which Mr van Trocken had thrust into my hand, down on the desk and gazed sadly at the line with my own name on it. 'Sophie F. Brackenbury,' it said, and although the 'F' actually stood for Frances, more than one wit had commented in the past that really it should stand for Feckless. Sod the lot of them, I thought, I couldn't help it if I wasn't very punctual, and couldn't stick with a job more than a few months, ditto boyfriends, and Little Ant, my flat-mate, had long ago forgiven me for nearly setting fire to his flat. How was I to know that a candle that I had lit and placed at the window – a little welcome home on his return from work one day, inspired by my desire to ask him to postpone the payment of my rent for another week – was going to fall against the extremely flammable drapery when I was in the bath? He had needed new curtains, anyway.

There was nothing for it: I fumbled in my desk drawer, swallowed a few aspirin and relapsed back into dreamland. As the rock music thundered from the speakers I, Sophie Brackenbury, muse to the greatest designer in Paris, Alexander Galliano or whatever his name was, prepared to go on in the wedding dress, the traditional finale of every designer's show. I sucked in my tummy, tried to look taller than my five foot six inches (OK, so it was a bit short to be a model, but Kate Moss was only five seven, so why not?) and batted my tawny green (oh, all right, puddle grey) eyes.

'Maestro,' I murmured as Alexander gasped at my appear— I practically leapt out of my chair as a huge siren filled the air. At first I thought that a fire alarm had gone off backstage at the Paris fashion shows, before realizing it was just the telephone. I hoped to God it wasn't British Gas (I'd once, stupidly, given them my work number): as usual I'd forgotten to pay the bills in the absence of Little Ant, and now they were threatening to cut us off. He was expected back from a month's vacation driving around Europe, and he'd go spare if he returned to a cold flat. Even worse, it could be Petrushka Henderling, the editor of the rag, who rarely bothered to come into the office and who had been hired, as far as I could see, entirely because of her social connections. 'Van Trocken and Co.,' I said through gritted teeth.

'Hello, Sophie, it's me,' hissed the precise and clipped tones of Penelope Tang, my best friend. 'You sound a bit wheezy. Out on the town last night, were we?'

'Oh don't you start,' I said grumpily. 'Martin stood me up at the last minute, so I went out with Paul the

13

Gaul instead.' Paul was an old boyfriend of mine, who now lived in France, and who was passing through London. 'Anyway, what is it? Is something up?'

'I must talk to you straight away,' said Penny mysteriously. 'It's important. You free for lunch?'

'It's not about Martin, is it?' I demanded anxiously. As of three weeks ago, Martin and Penny had been working for the same firm.

'I'm sorry, Sophie, but I do not waste my time thinking about miniature fund managers,' said Penny coldly. She was not one of Martin's fans. 'No, it is a matter of much greater importance. Can you get away?'

'What is it?' I demanded curiously. It must have been something big, Penny, who was half-Chinese, only lapsed in to formal Oriental mode when she was really excited. I supposed it must be something to do with being inscrutable. Then again, Penny was frequently excited: her greatest mission in life was to shock her parents, who, usually anyway, steadfastly refused to rise to the bait. To Penny's intense annoyance, their enormous wealth was matched only by their equally enormous liberalism.

'I will tell you at lunch.'

'Well,' I said hesitantly. 'I'm not sure. Look, Penny, don't laugh, but I've had this totally amazing idea. What do you think about me being a model?'

'What!' shrieked Penny, losing all inscrutability on the spot. 'You! A model! Sophie, fond as I am of you, I must point out that you would have to grow five inches and lose three stone, and that's even before we start on the plastic surgery. Ha, ha!'

'Well, thanks a lot,' I said, aggrieved. 'Nice to have

14

a vote of confidence. *Vogue* says that the English look is back in, and I'm fairly pale and slim, well, slimish, and . . .'

'You know, I hate to tell you this, but when they talk about the English look, they don't mean the racing around in the fresh air appearance,' Penny butted in. 'They mean someone who looks as if they've spent years cultivating a heroin habit on the streets of South London, and have just had time to have a few pictures taken before they breathe their last. Sophie, really, this is getting ridiculous. Last week you wanted to be a marine biologist and the week before you wanted to be an archaeologist, and I think it was more than a coincidence that those particular career paths might just have been influenced by what you'd watched on video. *Indiana Jones and the Last Crusade* followed by *Cocoon*? I mean, come on. I told you, you should never have dropped out of law school.'

'Oh, don't you start, and anyway, you dropped out too,' I said fretfully. Law school was where we'd met. 'You sound just like my parents. Anyway, what did you want to tell me?'

'I'll tell you at lunch,' said Penny firmly.

'Look, it's difficult to get away at lunch, you know that,' I complained. Mr van Trocken didn't like his employees being where he couldn't keep an eye on them. 'I don't have time to get into the City and back and still have time to eat.'

'Don't worry about that,' said Penelope briskly. 'I'll come to you. Meet me at the Bibendum Oyster Bar at one. And Sophie, what I've got to tell you might be a bit of a shock. Please understand.' She hung up.

15

I wonder what it is, I thought darkly. Perhaps the family fortunes – Penny came from an extremely rich Hong Kong shipping dynasty – had collapsed and I, as befits a best friend, will have to support her. Or maybe it's just yet another urge to shock. Or maybe it really is something about Martin. Maybe she's found out that he doesn't really come from Hackney, but he's a Romanian prince – even I had to pause there, though. Although I didn't know that much about his past, there was absolutely no reason to believe that Martin was anything other than a self-made fund manager from the East End.

If there was, though, Penny was in the perfect position to find out: three weeks ago she had taken up a job at Haverstock and Weybridge, the fund management firm of which Martin was a director. Maybe he's earned a fortune at the firm and will now propose, I thought happily. Or maybe— 'Sophie!' roared a voice. I leapt up, was knocked over by the fast disappearing figure of Irina tottering swiftly down the stairs, staggered to my feet and hobbled hastily back up to the temple of doom, as Mr van Trocken's office was known among his employees. 'Yes, Mr van Trocken?' I asked.

The huge black leather chair again had its back to me. It turned round slowly to reveal the sight of my employer again, but this time sporting a half closed eye, which looked as if it had a very good chance of developing in to a real shiner. 'Oh Mr van Trocken,' I burst out unwisely, 'what happened?'

Wrong question. 'What happened? *What happened?*' screamed Mr van Trocken. 'What happened, Sophie, is that you allowed a severely unbalanced woman in to this office! I've a good mind to sack you on the spot!'

'But I thought you said that Irina was always allowed in straight away,' I protested.

'I've changed my mind!' bellowed Mr van Trocken. 'You should have realized that weeks ago, Sophie, but I was too kind to say anything! I'm too generous for my own good, I sometimes think, and let far too many people take advantage of me, starting with my employees! Yes, yes, what is it?'

This last was to Rory, one of the magazine's writers, and a complete creep, who had just made an appearance in the doorway. 'I've had enough,' he muttered in a tone that was even more menacing than Irina's. 'This is it, Vladimir, I'm leaving. I've given you every chance to come to an arrangement, and in return I've had nothing but insults. A person of my talents – and knowledge – should not be treated in this way. Goodbye.' He turned and stalked off.

I, for one, was delighted. Not only was Rory a pain, but he was an admirer of mine and I was getting thoroughly fed up with having to rebuff his advances on an almost hourly basis. It was bad enough being constantly confronted with a stream of undesirable exes. Mr van Trocken seemed to be taking a different viewpoint, though, probably out of pique that someone had actually managed to resign before they were officially fired.

'How dare you!' he cried, leaping to his feet and chasing out after Rory. 'Come back here this minute!' I backed against the door of the study as Mr van Trocken raced by, and gleefully watched Rory bounding down the staircase, taking three steps with every leap, followed closely by Mr van Trocken, who, I was pleased to see, was in his stocking feet. I hoped intensely he would cut his feet on the broken glass outside. Really, why was everyone so intent on making my life so difficult?

2

The door banged behind them, and about a second later the phone rang. I hesitated for a moment – it was Mr van Trocken's private line, which bypassed the normal switchboard – but hastily weighing the possible outcome of the two avenues open to me, decided that on balance Mr van Trocken would probably be more angry with me if I didn't pick it up. 'Mr van Trocken's office,' I said brightly.

There was silence for a moment, and then a man's voice said, 'Who's that?'

'Sophie Brackenbury, the rec— I mean welcoming agent and telephone intermediary,' I said irritably, although I was incredibly relieved this wasn't Mrs van Trocken. Her horrible husband had made me lie to her more than once in the past about his where-abouts, which had always made me feel awful, as I had met her a couple of times and liked her enor-mously. She was totally different from him.

'Oh, Sophie,' said the voice, sounding slightly relieved and sniffing heavily. 'It's Tony. Where's Vladimir, is he around?' Tony was Mr van Trocken's chauffeur and all-round odd job man, and seemed to have a permanent cold. I was sure he was a cocaine addict. Maybe he could become one of those new British models.

'No, he's just popped out for a moment,' I said.

'Oh. Well just tell him I got the stuff he wanted but I had to pay over the odds because of the, uh, rarity value,' said Tony, sniffing violently again. 'I'll bring it to the office later.'

'Rightie ho,' I said, putting the phone down and wondering vaguely what Tony was going on about. I assumed it must be an antique something. Mr van Trocken was a collector, which, despite the fact that people who knew about these things said that *Food For Thought* was loss-making, he could well afford to be. The magazine was only a small part of the van Trocken business empire – his real money came from the import/export company he'd set up about thirty years ago when he first arrived in the UK, and which now sold exotic goods from far away places around the world to chi-chi department stores like Liberty. The trouble was that the main business was now so well established that Mr van Trocken didn't really need to attend to it on a day-to-day basis, and had plenty of time to devote to his latest project, *Food For Thought*.

To be honest, it was really vanity publishing – you know the sort of thing, entrepreneur emigrates to England, makes a huge amount of money and then decides to ingratiate himself with the British establishment by doing something cultured, such as running an unprofitable but extremely élitist magazine. 'To think,' he would sometimes smugly confide, 'that I, Vladimir van Trocken, a poor boy forced to make a living on the streets of Prague, should now be a leading member of the English intelligentsia!'

I intensely wished that there would be a crisis in the rest of his company – like the British shopper tiring of buying genuine wooden eating bowls, as carved out by the shepherds of Outer Mongolia in said shepherd's massive amount of spare time, for example – so that he could stop being at the forefront of the cultural élite (not that a great number of them actually seemed to read his magazine) and could go and run his business and leave the rest of us alone. Then again, I supposed it was a bit hypocritical of me to complain. I had as much a reason for wanting to be at *Food For Thought* as Mr van Trocken: he wanted to mix in the circles of the great and good and I wanted to mix in the circles of the Groucho Club, home from home to the trendy media brigade. Working at a fashionable, if unreadable, magazine seemed to be the best way of going about it.

I glanced around the room and shuddered. Mr van Trocken might be physically absent from the room, but he had seen to it that everywhere you looked there were little – or rather enormous – reminders of his hideous presence in the form of a series of portraits. Behind the big black armchair was Mr van Trocken in impressionist mode, represented by thousands of black, grey and red dots (the red was used both for his bow tie and his complexion) and further along the wall was a series of Mr van Trockens in Andy Warhol mode, with that great big mouth, hooked nose, trimmed beard and suspicious eyes on show in six different frames and variously picked out in green, orange, purple and yellow.

Then over the fireplace was Mr van Trocken as portrayed by a devotee of the chiaroscuro method, in a black coat and a black hat (with a large scarlet

21

feather), and lit from underneath by a light source, presumably a candle, that was out of the picture. Just underneath it, incidentally, was one of Mr van Trocken's most prized possessions: a picture of him shaking hands with Prince Charles at a Buckingham Palace garden party.

There were a lot more pictures dotted around the place, but nauseated, I could take no more. I had never been able to tolerate men with beards, ever since that unfortunate episode with Dr Bernard Dickson. Bearded Bernie as he was known to his students (he was a lecturer in sociology and the anthropological significance of local government administration at Hammersmith University, formerly known as Sulgrave Polytechnic) and I had dallied briefly shortly after I moved to London. Our relationship had come to a very abrupt end the night I had discovered a brunette tress of hair caught up in his stubble, and I heard later that one of his more hopeless students had suddenly, and unexpectedly, received a first class degree. Yuck, I thought. Yuckety yuck.

I was about to leave the room, when I suddenly caught sight of the newspaper Irina had been brandishing, and a headline caught my eye. 'Czech benefactor makes £1 million donation to the Conservative Party', it said, and beside it was a picture of Marcus Aimsworthy, the Treasurer of the Tory Party, chattering vigorously to the unmistakable figure of my employer.

Extremely large, both vertically and horizontally, with his beard neatly trimmed and his grey curly hair clipped short, and sporting a pair of ludicrous dark glasses that he fondly imagined made him look like a rock star, the only difference from Mr van Trocken's normal appearance was that whereas he usually favoured black leather suits, he was on this occasion wearing a rather more conventional dark grey woollen variety. He was laughing uproariously, revealing a set of extremely large, straight white teeth that reminded me of a still from *Jaws*.

What really drew my attention, though, was what he was doing with his hands. One gripped a large cigar, which he was waving under Marcus Aimsworthy's nose, and the other was clasped around the waist of an extremely beautiful blonde, who looked vaguely familiar, but who was most certainly not Irina. The picture's caption referred to her as Apricot Bellissimo, again a name that rang a bell, but I could not quite place it.

Maybe that was why Irina was so angry, I thought, although if truth be told you'd have thought it was Mrs van Trocken who would have the grounds for complaint here. Then again, maybe the mysterious Apricot was a Tory MP. She was a bit on the glam side, but who knows? Stranger things had happened, especially in the offices of van Trocken and Co. I made my way thoughtfully back to my desk and shut my eyes. 'As the right honourable gentleman knows,' I thundered at the opposition benches, 'it is incredibly naff to wear black leather suits, especially when you are a lecherous old toad like Mr van Trocken.' Uproar ensued. 'Silence! Silence!' bellowed Madam Speaker. 'I will not have this House . . .'

There was a huge clanging, which I first took to be the division bell, and which I realized after a second was actually the front door bell. I pressed the buzzer and Mr van Trocken danced back in. 'Traitors!' he cried, leaping up the hall in what appeared to be one bound. 'I'm surrounded by traitors! Any calls while I was out, Sophie?'

'Yes,' I said and repeated Tony's message.

'He rang you to tell me that?' enquired Mr van Trocken, frowning slightly as I finished.

'No, it was on your private line in your study.'

'How dare you pick up that phone!' began Mr van Trocken. 'You're fired!'

'Well, I thought you'd have wanted me to,' I said, aggrieved. 'I didn't know what to do.'

Mr van Trocken paused and glared at me. 'Well all right, I will let you get away with it just this once,' he said reluctantly. 'I hope you realize how lucky you are to work here, Sophie. You are incompetent, witless and absolutely no good at your job, but I, Vladimir van Trocken, am a kind and merciful man and I will not throw you out on the street, much as you deserve it.' He turned, and as I thoughtfully digested this vote of confidence, strode purposefully back to his study.

A second later there was a further roar. At first I thought I'd committed yet another crime, before I realized he was talking on the telephone. 'How dare you,' he cried. 'Do you know who you are talking to? I, Vladimir van Trocken, will see you in court!'

The door of his study banged shut. At the time, I took no notice of this particular little outburst, assuming it was part of yet another typical day at the office. Mr van Trocken was prone to threatening people with legal action when he couldn't get them to do what he wanted, including, on one memorable occasion, the milkman when he delivered half-fat instead of the full-cream variety, but, as it turned out, I was wrong. Oh my word, I was wrong, and, happy to relate, dear reader, it wouldn't be too long before I found out my error.

But I'm getting ahead of myself. At that particular moment, far more important items were on my mind. I shut my eyes. 'Madam Speaker,' I cried, 'I demand that the right honourable gentleman be forcibly transported to Gieves and Hawkes, the bespoke gentleman's outfitters and shoved in to some slightly less disgusting day wear immediately!'

3

It was, however, with a spring in my step that, a couple of hours later, I pushed open the wide glass doors that led into the Michelin building. Mr van Trocken had not noticed that I had not got round to filing last week's letters and invitations (well all right then, last month's) which was unusual for him: he really must have other things on his mind. Not that I wasn't a really brilliant welcoming agent and telephone intermediary, of course, but these things did keep slipping my mind. Nor had he commented on the fact that I had forgotten to have the office windows cleaned, which I was supposed to do on the first of every month, or even realized that the monthly supply of glossy magazines had dried up because I had not got round to reordering them. I must remember to do that this afternoon.

I marched into the large tiled forecourt that had once been a garage and looked around. Straight ahead was the Conran shop, where I had spent many a happy hour window shopping (Penny had once snootily pointed out that I spent most of my time in dream land: either working out alternative careers for myself or racking up long shopping lists of clothes and furniture that I would never be able to afford to buy), and above us was Bibendum, a fearsomely expensive Conran restaurant, where Martin had taken me in the early days of our relationship.

I sighed. Those early days weren't that far in the past, actually, it was only six months ago that I had shot out of the office at speed, tripped on the bottom stair and sent Martin, who had happened to be strolling past at the time, flying. He had been terribly nice about it and taken me for a drink as I was feeling rather shaken, and that had been that. Love at first sight. Except that I was beginning to suspect that it had not been love so much as a distraction from the important business of being important as far as Martin was concerned, and as for my own feelings – well put it this way, Penny, who had once informed me that my future most certainly did not lie with a miniature fund manager, might just have been right.

Still, I had more important immediate concerns, starting with lunch. Despite my best efforts to cultivate an eating disorder, I was absolutely starving, and beside the Conran shop and below Bibendum, was the Oyster Bar. I shoved my way through the various marble topped tables and wicker chairs scattered around, and into the little eating area. With its cream tiled walls and arc-shaped steel bar, it had a slightly clinical feeling, which I found vaguely comforting. There was a murmur of civilized chat in the background, which blended in nicely with the sounds of clinking cutlery, while the smells of white wine and cigarette smoke drifted above the lunchers.

A waiter ushered me to a table, took my coat and looked slightly dubiously at my ensemble: a silky bright orange shirt from Jigsaw, which I could not afford and had bought yesterday, a black miniskirt and my absolutely favourite pair of shoes: black, with two inch soles and five inch heels. I'd got them at the weekend from Kensington Market, and I couldn't afford them either. 'Spritzer, please,' I said. 'Oh, look, my friend's just arrived, can you make it two?'

'Certainly, madam,' said the waiter with the lofty air of one who knows when they're talking to someone who was opting just for a salad down here rather than the full works in Bibendum upstairs. His attitude changed quite dramatically as Penelope glided up to the table though, because if there was one thing Penelope did not look it was poor. As I mentioned earlier, she was half-Chinese – her father, Peter Tang, came over from Hong Kong to Cambridge as a student, and liked the place so much he decided to stay – and total glamour, a trait that she inherited from her English mother, an ex-model. 'Right away, madam,' said the waiter officiously helping Penelope with her brown leather coat. 'Two spritzers coming right up.'

Penelope looked down her nose at him, a feat she accomplished with no problem at all, despite the fact that she was, if anything, even shorter than Martin. 'I think you mean champagne,' she said coldly. 'Please attend to it at once.'

'Oh, certainly, madam,' said the waiter, impressed by her rudeness. He bustled off.

'Honestly, Penny, how do you do it?' I complained. 'If I'd spoken to him like that, we'd be out on the street by now.'

'All men are the same,' said Penelope loftily, producing a compact out of an unbelievably smart Prada handbag and dabbing away a nonexistent bit of fluff from her cheek. 'Treat them as badly as you can and they'll just crawl back for more, a fact that you should take on board, Sophie, when dealing with that ghastly little man of yours. He's in bad health, I hope?'

'I don't know what kind of health he's in as it's so long since I've seen him,' I said irritably. 'Do you think he's taking me for granted?'

'Taking you for granted?' enquired Penelope, raising an elegant eyebrow. 'You know I don't like to upset you, but frankly, Bluebeard would have been a better choice of life partner than Martin. And you, I might add, are not the only one who wants to see him: there was quite a rumpus about something at work this morning, and no-one could find him anywhere, but I'll tell you more about that when *we're allowed a bit of privacy.*'

This last was said with emphasis, and directed at the waiter, who had just placed two glasses of champagne in front of us, and was shoving a couple of menus in our direction. 'Oh, anything you say, madam,' he said reverentially, gazing in awe at Penelope's diminutive but graceful diamond-incrusted fingers and backing off very much in the manner of slave graced by a glance from a sultan. The Tang family philosophy was that if you've got it, don't just flaunt it, but rub everyone's noses in it as much as you possibly could.

I had to admit, though, that in the middle of the surrounding English drabness – pinstriped suits and sensible shoes, and that was just the women – Penelope stood out like an exotic tropical bird. Her face, with its long oval eyes, olive skin and full mouth, was, as ever, immaculately made up and her long black hair was drawn up into a glistening ebony chignon. Her tiny but slim figure, today clad in a brown suit that I knew without any doubt at all was an Armani, was languorously draped over one of the Oyster Bar's stainless steel chairs. Diamonds were everywhere: on both hands, one wrist and both ears. Less is absolutely not more was another Tang family philosophy. You had to be careful when talking to Penelope that you wouldn't be blinded by the rainbow of lights that danced about her: it was like having a conversation with a partial eclipse of the sun.

Anyway, I had other matters to attend to, starting with the hair of the dog. 'Oh that's better,' I said after a sip of champagne. 'I've decided to start taking life more easy: I'm going to limit myself to just one hangover a week and just one evening with an ex-boyfriend.'

'And how is Paul the Gaul?' enquired Penny, feigning interest.

'He's finding himself,' I said with a sigh. 'Decided that life as a merchant banker has only limited appeal, and that he's going to go trekking in Nepal to rediscover his inner soul. This just happens to coincide with him coming into his trust fund. Bastard, if I knew he had that lurking in the background, I'd never have finished with him. That's why I had to drown my sorrows in drink.'

'He finished with you,' said Penelope rather unnecessarily in my opinion, producing a packet of Dunhill from her handbag and inserting one into a very long cigarette holder, 'and don't be so mercenary. And you drown rather a lot in drink, if I may say so. Anyway, as I was saying there was quite a stir in the office this morning but your young – or should I say, middle aged and lecherous – chum Martin was nowhere to be seen.'

'He's not middle aged, he's only thirty-seven,' I said defensively. I couldn't think of a way around lecherous. 'And I would have finished with Paul, he just got his retaliation in first. What sort of a stir?'

'It was about a company called Molehill Magazines,' said Penelope, offering me a Dunhill and lighting her own. 'The Stock Exchange said there was something strange about their share price movement, but I'm not sure exactly what. They've just been talking to everyone who dealt in the shares recently, and there seems to be some talk about Martin buying some for his fund, but I must say, much as I hate to defend Mini-Mart, I can't see that there would be anything strange about that. Molehill Mags is a very large company, but if you do see him, tell him to get in touch. Sir Jeremy Haverstock is keen to have a word. And you, Sophie? How about you? Any further thoughts on the way you intend to spend the next sixty years or so and I am not talking about modelling?'

'Actually, I was thinking about a career in politics,' I said irritably. 'No, that was just a joke, for Heaven's sake. You Oriental types are prone to taking everything so seriously.'

'And you Caucasians are far too tall,' said Penelope, apropos of nothing. 'Do you know how embarrassing it is to have a mother who is six inches taller than your father and a brother who takes after the Occidental side of the family? Of course, any offspring of yours and Martin would be sure to discover that one, too. Honestly, Soph, you've got to finish with him, you don't want your children to suffer the way I have.' She inhaled magnificently and gave a passing waiter a filthy look.

'Suffer!' I spluttered. 'It's not that I want to disillusion you, but you know most people wouldn't call their own flat in Swiss Cottage by the age of twenty-five and independent means absolutely the worst that life can throw at you. It's me that's suffered, not only did I have to push Paul in to finishing with me rather than vice versa just totally out of the kindness of my heart, but it's all my parents' fault for making me genetically incapable of deciding what I want to do in life.'

'Will you stop going on about Paul? And if I remember correctly, there's nothing genetic about it, your parents seem perfectly able to make decisions and stick with them,' said Penelope. She was quite right too, my parents, who lived in Cheltenham, had worked out and stuck to their own vocations early in life: my father running a small antiques gallery and my mother shopping. 'How many jobs is it since we dropped out?' went on Penelope, rather labouring the point, I felt. 'We left three years ago, and since then it's been' – she began ticking off on her fingers – 'television researcher, shop assistant, photographer, waitress, would-be acupuncturist, furniture restorer and electrician's apprentice, to say nothing of your current triumph as a receptionist.'

'You mean welcoming agent and telephone intermediary, and you forgot poet,' I said indignantly. 'Speaking of which, would you like to see my latest?'

Penelope sighed, but took it well – in the full knowledge, as we both knew, that I would be paying for this within minutes by listening to whichever saga she intended to relate – accepted a scrumpled bit of paper and, slightly to my horror, began to read out loud.

> Strange the way I had a dream
> About a year ago:
> London Bridge was built of cream,
> Litter bins did glow.
> Yesterday I met a man,
>
> He told me it was true,
> Yetis oft do roam the land,
> Cavemen dwell in London Zoo.
> Acrobats are really birds,
> Notorious for their acts,
>
> Voracious harpies live in herds
> Inside a telefax.
> Regent's Park's the only place
> Great fishes stalk on legs,
> Icicles crash down from space
> Night porters do lay eggs.
>
> Apples build the motorways,
> Cheese is made from chalk,
> Kitchens feast on used ashtrays,
> Buses often talk.
> Unknown to all
> Rain doesn't fall
> Nails use a knife and fork.

Penny put the piece of paper down and looked at me with concern. 'Sophie, you've got to get out more,' she said. 'Meet a few people. Enlarge your horizons. I hate to tell you this, but I would most definitely recommend not giving up the day job, even if it is working for your charming employer. And tell me, have you been eating properly? Getting enough sleep? Little Ant's not taken to seasoning your breakfast cereal with some funny sorts of sugar has he?'

'I think you've made your point,' I snapped, grabbing back my little offering. I was deeply hurt. 'It's not my fault if you're incapable of appreciating totally obvious genius when it's about six inches away from you. And actually, apropos the job side, I have made up my mind, you know, I really do want to work in the media. I'm not going to change my mind again, whatever you may think. I've had quite enough of working for mad Vlad.'

'Vladimir van Trocken,' said Penny thoughtfully. 'It doesn't sound very Czech, you know. I'm sure he made it up.'

'You're quite right there, Rory told me the other day his real name is Jan Hoch, but he changed it to something he thought was more impressive,' I said. 'Anyway, what is it that you want to tell me? Another poor sod is foolish enough to want to spend his every waking moment with the most glamorous fund manager in town? What's his name this time?' Penny was a notorious manizer – although I sometimes wondered if this was yet another of her little ruses to upset her parents – and this was not an atypical subject in our little chats. I had lost count of the number of chaps she had dallied with since we'd met.

'Well, you're on the right lines,' said Penelope, stubbing out her cigarette and shooting me a surprisingly coy look. 'But you're not quite there. The name is Charlotte, since you ask.'

'Cool,' I said.

34

4

There was a brief pause. 'I said,' repeated Penny slightly tersely, inserting another Dunhill in to her holder, 'her name is Charlotte. Not Charles, Charlotte.'

'Yes, I heard,' I said, nibbling at a piece of bread. 'Is she nice?'

Penny was beginning to look downright exasperated. 'Of course she's nice,' she said. 'But that's not the point, the relevant point is that she's a woman. I'm going out with a woman.'

'Penny, that's marvellous,' I said warmly. 'Lipstick lesbianism is just totally fashionable these days, I was really worried about the fact that none of my friends were doing it, but now I can bask in your reflected glory.' I really was pleased, it would give me tremendous kudos to boast that my best friend had a girlfriend. 'What gave you the idea?'

'Nothing gave me the idea, it just happened!' cried Penny. 'Honestly Sophie, here am I, coming out of the closet, and you're acting as if I'd said I had just decided to start buying Lacroix rather than Armani. Actually, I am thinking of switching, I think Armani's a bit too conservative for my new life, but that's not the point. Aren't you even a little surprised?'

'No,' I said truthfully. Nothing that Penny did ever surprised me: as I said, she lived her life to shock her parents, and had been doing so all her life, including that occasion after she dropped out of law school and moved in to an alternative vegan commune – not that that had lasted for very long, I might add. Penny had moved straight out again as soon as she discovered they didn't have a cleaner. 'Anyway, I think it's great. Have you broken the news to your father yet?'

'Well,' began Penny, 'I – yes, yes, what is it?'

'I just wondered,' said the waiter, who had staged a reappearance, in one of the most sycophantic tones I have ever heard, 'if madam has decided what she would like to order?' He looked at her pleadingly.

'Two chicken Caesar salads and do make it snappy, my friend's got to go back to work,' said Penny, ice dripping from every syllable. 'And I'd appreciate it if you wouldn't interrupt us in the middle of a private conversation.'

'Oh, no, madam,' said the waiter. '*No*, madam.' He backed off.

'Hang on,' I protested. 'I was going to have the vegetarian alternative.'

'Since when have you been a vegetarian?' enquired Penny.

'Oh, ages,' I said. 'I'm just a vegetarian who still eats meat.'

'Don't be silly, Sophie, that's like being a teetotaller who also drinks.'

'Yes, I'm that too,' I explained. 'Anyway, I want to know more about this woman. What's she like? Is she half Chinese too?'

'No, actually, she's Scottish,' said Penny. 'And she – oh please, do feel free to listen in to a private conversation.' This was to a second waiter, who had just turned up at her shoulder.

'Cutlery,' explained the waiter briefly, beginning to lay out the table before catching sight of the rainbow of colours emanating from Penelope's tiny right hand. 'Oh, that's beautiful,' he gasped, standing back and looking quite pale. 'Oh, I don't think I've ever seen anything quite like that. It must have been quite a man who gave you that.'

'Indeed,' said Penelope, radiating a blast of arctic cold air. 'Thank you, I think that's all we need, oh, apart from two more glasses of champagne, of course. Please be speedy.'

The waiter, looking humbled, backed off. 'So have you decided that you're just totally a lesbian?' I enquired.

'Yes, I think I am,' said Penny gravely. 'It's a very big decision, Sophie, I hope you realize that.'

'Oh, I do,' I said. 'And I expect Alan and David and John and Peter and Tom and Stephen and Jason to name but last week's intake alone will too.'

'Oh, don't be silly, Sophie, I told you there was nothing between me and Peter,' said Penelope irritably. 'And the others were just, you know, diversions. Anyway, I'm tired of watching my father shove eligible Chinese men under my nose who are one day going to take over their own father's shipping fleet and are just desperate to meet a suitable HKH.'

'HKH?' I asked.

'Hong Kong heiress,' said Penny, wrinkling her tiny nose.

37

'Yes, that must be utterly terrible,' I said unsympathetically. 'Anyway, you didn't tell me, does your father know?'

'Not yet,' said Penny rather gleefully. 'I think I shall wait until Sunday and make a big announcement when we're all having lunch. It's much better to get these things out in to the open. And Michael's just got back from Hong Kong, so I'm going to have to tell him, too.'

I quelled a few risen hackles – Michael was Penelope's brother and I couldn't stand him – and nibbled some more bread. 'That should kick the conversation off on an interesting start,' I said. 'Incidentally, how long has this been going on? And are you thinking of making some kind of public proclamation? At least half the single men under the age of forty in London are going to be very, very upset, you know.'

'Must you keep bringing that up,' said Penelope, wrinkling her nose again in distaste. 'Honestly Sophie, I really don't feel like talking about my exes, and anyway, I don't have half as many as you and anyway, you're one to talk. There's not only Paul the Gaul, but what about Bearded Bernie and Tommy the Trannie and Desperate Dan to name but a few? It's not so much footprints in the sand as far as you're concerned, as the combined forces of Britain and the Middle East tramping through the Jordanian desert.'

'Yes, yes, yes,' I said irritably. 'We all make mistakes. But this is far more interesting, switching sides halfway through the game. Anyway—'

We both fell silent as the waiter reappeared, bobbed respectfully in front of Penelope's rings, put down two bowls of Caesar salad, rechampagned us

38

and disappeared. Operation complete, I started hissing again. 'Anyway, how long has this been going on?' I asked again. 'Where did you meet her? What does she do?'

'Glad to see you're so concerned about her prospects,' said Penelope loftily, stubbing out her cigarette, spearing a bit of anchovy and consuming it. 'I met her a couple of days ago at a dinner party. She's been living abroad for a few years, and only just got back last week. She's taking a couple of weeks break and then she'll be working for Cunningham and Meither.'

'Cunningham and Meither!' I burst out. Cunningham and Meither was the name of a long established and well known law firm. 'She's a solicitor! How could you go out with a solicitor! Penny, how can you do this to me?' My pain was genuine. As I mentioned earlier, Penny and I had both dropped out of law school three years ago, when we decided we didn't want to spend our lives arguing about the finer points of tort, along with another student, Belinda Cuttlesnipe. Penny was now doing totally amazingly as a fund manager, though, and Belinda was an actress, while I – well you know about me. The less said about that the better.

'At least she'll be able to keep me in the style to which I am accustomed,' said Penelope. 'Honestly, Sophie, you don't object to her being a woman, but you are worried by her being a lawyer. Sometimes I think you can be very perverse.'

'Oh, don't worry, I'm sure your parents will take it badly,' I said. 'And what about Haverstock and Weybridge?'

'What about them?'

'Well, are you going to tell them about it?' I asked.

'Of course not, it's none of their business,' said Penny. 'Did you tell Mr van Trocken when you started going out with Martin?'

'Good lord, no,' I said. 'What an appalling idea. It's that I thought, you know, in the City they're sort of conservative, and I, er, wondered if they had to vet suitable partners or something.'

'Sophie, I work for some fund managers, not MI6,' said Penny. 'Not that that ever seemed to stop anyone in MI6, gay relationships were almost *de rigueur* round that lot, I gather. And by the way, don't worry, I don't fancy you.'

'Why not?' I asked indignantly, shovelling in a bit of salad. 'No, don't answer that. Gosh, Penny, this is fantastic. When most people fancy trying something new, they get a haircut or a new dress or something, not change the entire nature of their sexuality.'

'Just following your example,' said Penny cheerfully. 'I seem to remember you came jolly near to going out with a woman yourself, once, too.'

'Tommy was not a woman, he was a transvestite,' I said crossly. I could still remember the shock of going to Madame Jo Jo's one night and realizing halfway through the evening that Martin's predecessor but four was the very glamorous dancer Little Ant had been ogling all night. Little Ant was none too pleased either on realizing his mistake and as for Tommy the Trannie, as he came to be known – well, you'd never have expected an accountant to have such an unusual hobby, would you?

'Anyway, I gather from this reaction that you'd like to meet Charlotte?' enquired Penny.

I hesitated, mid-chomp. On the one hand I was jolly

curious, but on the other I was not quite sure what the etiquette was when it came to meeting your newly-outed best friend's girlfriend. 'Well OK,' I said eventually, having swallowed a crouton or two. 'If you really want me to. When?'

'I'm seeing her tonight in Boom Boom and I'll tell her there's someone I want her to meet.'

'You're sure she'll want to meet, um, er, one of your straight friends?' I enquired.

'Oh, don't be so silly, really, Sophie, you do have a lot to learn about the world,' said Penelope cheerfully. 'We'll be there about eight. Oh God, look at the time. Waiter!'

I glanced at my watch and gasped. It was nearly two o'clock. Penelope was fully aware of my time constraints and, presumably slightly guilt-ridden at putting my job on the line yet again, she acted fast. Within the space of two minutes she had shoved a bit of filthy lucre on the table to cover the bill (which it did so amply that the waiters became even more subservient), got herself into her brown leather coat and me into my faded bit of worsted, whisked us outside, summoned her dark blue chauffeur-driven Mercedes (yes, you read that right, and although it was financed by the Tang family coffers rather than her employers, it irritated the hell out of Martin), leapt inside dragging me in after her and barked a few instructions. You could say one thing about Penny, when she knew something had to be done, she didn't mess about.

A couple of minutes later, she dropped me off. 'See you later!' she cried. 'And don't forget! Boom Boom tonight at eight! Oh and Sophie, do try to find Martin and tell him I'm after his job. Ha, ha!'

'I will!' I yelled. 'And it was me that finished with Paul, you know, psychologically if not actually!' The car zoomed off with no reply. I stood looking after it for a minute and then, shaking my head, made my way up to the front door.

5

I was still feeling deeply impressed by Penelope's new way of rocking the boat as far as her parents were concerned when I got back to the office. OK, so that sounds a bit cynical, but we are talking about a woman who once sent out Christmas cards with a picture of her and four trust fund cronies posing starkers except for a row of handbags covering their bottoms – their backs were to the camera – and Penny later informed me that it was the fact that the handbags were from Marks & Spencer rather than Asprey that really upset her mother.

Anyway, it took me little longer than usual to start panicking about the fact I was late. Reality kicked in with a vengeance after a second or so, though, and after this morning's little lecture on timekeeping, I did not like the idea of another heart to heart with Mr van Trocken. Running up the steps and arriving at the imposing office door, I fumbled frantically in my handbag for the key, opened the door, and raced up the hall to my desk.

Please don't let him be in, I thought, tearing off my coat, shoving it under my chair, plonking myself down and glancing nervously in the direction of Mr van Trocken's office, please don't let him see that today I've actually got back at 14.07, please don't . . . there was a noise at the front door and a second later Mr van Trocken himself appeared. I held my breath to stop myself panting and hoped to Heaven he wouldn't look at the time sheet, which I had not yet filled in. The Gods were on my side. 'Sit up straighter,' instructed my boss, galloping past me at speed and ignoring my weak smile of acknowledgement, 'we don't want visitors to think we've got a bloody dishrag in reception. And get your roots done, they're getting far too obvious.'

His study door banged behind him, leaving me smarting with annoyance. I was fully aware that I wasn't looking just as totally blond as I liked to, I thought, scribbling 13.52 on the time sheet, but on the amount he paid me I couldn't jolly well afford to have my hair dyed as regularly as all his women friends, Irina, Apricot, or whoever he was with now. If only he had given me the job he'd actually promised me before I started – features writer on *Food For Thought* – and paid me accordingly, my roots would be no problem at all.

As an extremely rare silence descended on the office of van Trocken and Co., I sat back to digest what I had just learned. You had to hand it to Penny, she certainly knew how to surprise. But then the three of we law school dropouts, Penny, the loathsome Belinda and me, had all caused a few shocks in our time, starting with dropping out of law school in the first place. Penny had been pressurized into going by her parents, who were grooming her to help run the family businesses, and although they had been extremely angry when she left, she had since pacified them by becoming a City whizzkid.

I had no idea what Belinda's parents thought as, happily, I knew little about her background, but dropping out was the second shock she had caused, the first being a passionate and open affair with our tutor, Professor Marsden. I suspected that the real reason she left was that she was deeply thick, and had no chance at all of passing the exams, but her proclaimed ambition had been to become an actress – and, bugger it, she was succeeding.

And then there was me. I sighed. On mature reflection, dropping out was no surprise at all, as I'd never been able to make up my mind what I wanted to do. As the youngest of three sisters – Jane and Rosemary, two and four years older than me, had become, respectively, a teacher and a doctor – I'd been the baby of the family and my darling parents had never put any pressure on me at all. I had thus originally gone to Exeter University to read History of Art and then changed to French and German. Then after I graduated, I decided, Heaven knows why, I wanted to be a lawyer, and so had started the conversion course you take after university. Like the other two, I had lasted three months.

In the three years since then, as Penny had pointed out, I had turned my hands to a number of alternative careers, before finally deciding that what I really wanted, above all, was to be a trendy media type. My options, however, were limited. I didn't have the stomach to be a modern artist as these days it seemed to involve either pickling dead animals or taking casts from the corpses of dead people. Neither could I be a late night television presenter. For a start I didn't take loads of drugs (my attempt to become a junkie had failed miserably when I'd taken three puffs on a joint, didn't like it, did inhale, and promptly was sick in the bathroom) and I didn't have the alternative qualification needed in televisual circles, viz a doctorate in history from the University of Oxford and the kind of right wing views that would make the likes of Genghis Khan start to seem a very real proponent of the welfare state.

And so, what I considered to be my undiscovered poetic ability and everyone else considered to be my febrile imagination meant that a job involving pseudo-intellectual hackery seemed to be the obvious choice, hence my presence in the offices of van Trocken and Co. It had all looked so promising: in my interview for the job at *Food For Thought*, Mr van Trocken had brightly informed me that what the magazine really needed was young blood and fresh talent on the writing side. On my first day, however, I was plonked at the welcoming agent and telephone intermediary's desk, told to answer the telephone and open the front door, and my talent for the written word, such as it was, had remained totally undiscovered. The features job had never been mentioned since.

My continuing relationship with Martin stemmed from a similar desire to change my lifestyle: I reluctantly had to admit that I had more in common with Penny pre-Charlotte and Belinda than I liked to let on in that I'd had about two dozen relationships since leaving home, all of them complete disasters, and I felt it was now time to have a serious and committed relationship. Shame I'd picked Martin.

Bugger Martin and the media: I should have become a barrister, not a solicitor, that's where I went wrong, I decided. I shut my eyes, preparing to imagine myself in a wig and gown, and then jumped as the door of the study burst open again and Mr van Trocken reappeared, now clad in a black leather coat and vicious black pointy boots under his grey leather trousers.

'I'm going out again for a little while,' he cried, racing past me and leaping down the hall (no-one ever seemed to move at normal speed in the offices of van Trocken and Co.) 'and I may be some time. That fool of a wife of mine has said she's leaving me and I have to go and take immediate charge of the credit cards. To think that she could do this today, of all days! When it has been announced that a humble Czech boy like me has been honoured to make a donation to our friends in the Conservative Party! To think that I can help our great politicians makes me very proud.' He produced a very large handkerchief, and blew his nose emotionally. 'Now we've got the ABC figures coming in later, if they haven't arrived by four, find out where the hell they've got to. Tell Tony I've taken a cab.'

The door banged behind him. For such a monster, Mr van Trocken was surprisingly indiscreet. Everyone (including Barbara, his wife) knew about Irina, knew when poor old Barbara, a rather meek and unassuming woman from the home counties, finally had enough and walked out, and knew about the combination of flattery and bullying he used to get her back again. At least, I thought shuddering, no matter how bad things get, I'm not Barbara and I'm not married to Mr van Trocken and from that *bon mot* about the credit cards I assumed it was going to be bullying tactics on this occasion, especially if he was going to take a taxi rather than wait for Tony. And what on earth was he going on about the alphabet for? Sometimes the workings of Mr van Trocken's mind were far too much for ordinary mortals to understand.

I shoved a few pieces of paper around on my desk in order to decide which chore to put off till last – sending a few *Food For Thought* covers to be framed to hang on the staircase, ringing round the more fashionable public relations firms to make sure Mr van Trocken was on their invitation list for forthcoming jollies or typing up an angry letter from my boss to one of our contributors, who had been half an hour late with his copy – when there was a commotion at the front door. At first I thought it was Mr van Trocken trying to get back in and so pressed the buzzer, but a second later, to my intense surprise and slight horror, none other than Martin lounged into my field of vision. 'How's my little popinjay?' he enquired as he sauntered up the hall. For some reason he seemed momentarily more interested in the wall beside my desk, which was blank, before bringing his attention to bear on me. 'Oh, you look fresh as a daisy, Sophie, reminds me of when I was as young as you,' he went on, before leaning over the desk (with a bit of difficulty – Martin was all of five foot four), and giving me a graceful peck on the lips.

'Oh, I'm fine,' I said resentfully. I still hadn't entirely forgiven him for that day-dreaming remark this morning. 'And Martin, what's going on? I had lunch with Penny and she said the whole of Haverstock and Weybridge is trying to track you down.'

'Of course you're fine darling, why shouldn't you be fine?' drawled Martin, ignoring my question, leaping up to sit on my desk (he achieved this manoeuvre with a bit of a hop) and producing a packet of cigarettes. 'You don't mind if I' – he cocked an eyebrow – 'light up?'

'Oh, must you?' I said tetchily. I was a nicotine fiend myself, but smoking was strictly forbidden in the offices of van Trocken and Co., unless you were Mr van Trocken himself, of course, in which case you were allowed to smoke extremely fat cigars all day long, or Petrushka Henderling, in which case you smoked extra long Silk Cut in a silver and ebony cigarette holder. 'If the monster finds out, there'll be all hell to pay. And why are you here and what's going on?'

'Couldn't bear to spend another second away from my little heart's desire,' said Martin, again ignoring both my request and my question, clicking open an extremely expensive gold lighter and inhaling deeply. Slightly on the chubby side, he was wearing his usual dark blue pinstriped suit, with a blue and white striped shirt and a very vivid red tie. A matching hand-kerchief tumbled out of his jacket pocket, which presented an unfortunate contrast to his bright red cheeks. He had sparkling little brown eyes which, when I was in an uncharitable mood after one of our many rows, I considered to resemble the fruit element in a currant bun. Short brown hair which needed washing completed the appearance.

'Oh, and I happened to be in this part of town on business, went out just after we spoke earlier, so I thought I'd pop in to see you, little day-dream believer,' continued Martin. (I suppressed a slight irri-tation at this one, I was a good two inches taller than him in stocking feet.) He paused and shot me a hot look. 'No chance of slipping out of the office for half an hour I suppose?' he went on.

This was typical Martin: always propositioning me when there was no chance at all of getting up to anything and then disappearing off the face of the planet when I actually had a bit of free time – like in the evenings, for example. 'You know I can't,' I said increasingly irritably. 'And if you're not going to tell me what's happening, please go, Mr van Trocken will go ballistic if he thinks I'm entertaining friends.'

'Well I hope I'm a bit more than a friend,' said Martin, exhaling an expert smoke ring. 'Learnt that trick in Marrakesh,' he went on, unable to avoid a boast or two, 'and that wasn't the only trick I learnt there either.' He winked. 'Well little dream boat, if you're going to reject my advances, I'll just have to look around elsewhere.' He slid off the desk and prepared to slink off.

'OK, go,' I snarled. 'Go and find someone else, I don't care. I have plenty of alternative offers too, you know. And don't worry about telling me about Haverstock and Weybridge, I'm sure Penny will be able to fill me in.'

'Only playing, my pretty little poppet,' said Martin, emphasizing the Ps. 'And I'm not at all sure I approve of junior staff gossiping about me in my absence. Of course they want to see me, I'm one of the most important members of the firm, unlike your little friend Penny. I don't suppose she said any more?'

I was eyeing him closely. For all the casual nature of his remarks, Martin was definitely sounding a little strained, which was most unlike him. He had even forgotten to cock an eyebrow. 'Something about some company, Molehill Magazines, I think,' I said.

'Oh, is that all?' said Martin coolly. 'If you ever bothered to read the papers, my darling, you'd see that I'm quoted talking about Molehill in the *Telegraph* today. Old man Haverstock probably just wants to congratulate me for bringing his antiquated little outfit some much-needed publicity. Now look darling, I'm far too important, I mean busy, to chat with you all day, but I've brought you a little present. Something to remember me by when I'm away.' He flicked open a very smart black briefcase and produced a package. 'Cover it with kisses and keep it on your desk,' he went on smoothly, handing it over. 'One day – perhaps – I'll do the same for you. Bye darling, lots of love.' He blew a kiss in my direction, and glided off down the hall.

Everyone's in the *Telegraph* today, I thought, fishing around in the pile of newspapers under my desk. Now feeling slightly mollified, although I still thought there was something odd about Martin's manner, I wanted to wait a moment before opening my present, to build up the anticipation. I hauled out the paper. I had left Irina's copy where I had found it – if Mr van Trocken had thought I'd touched anything in his study, his anger would have known no bounds – but we had all the papers delivered every day, and after Mr van Trocken was finished with them, they went to me.

I pulled out the *Telegraph* and turned to the business pages and the piece in question, which was indeed about Molehill Magazines, which had just announced their profit, or rather loss, figures. 'It's a fine show from an outstanding company, and the only reason the loss was incurred was due to turbulence in the foreign exchange markets,' said Martin in business mode, before going into a lot of guff about the dollar's performance against the pound. It seems that the company, which already owned loads of glossy lifestyle magazines on this side of the Atlantic, had been expanding into the US at a very bad time.

I dropped the paper back onto the floor and looked at my present, which was wrapped in that highly fashionable brown paper that looked a bit like normal wrapping paper, and was actually watermarked and cost about fifty times as much as the non-chic variety. It was tied with muslin. I undid the tie, tore open the tissue paper inside and squeaked with delight. It was a totally amazing picture frame, almost certainly solid silver, and inside was a photograph of Martin, dressed in full white tie and tails. His dark brown hair was sleeked back, his dark brown eyes were glittering with pleasure, he was beaming and he was raising aloft a glass of champagne. As it was only him in the foreground of the picture, you couldn't tell how short he was, although I did wonder where this was taken: he looked as if he was standing in some country house somewhere, and you could see other people milling around in the background.

Never mind, this was probably taken before he and I had met. What a sweet thing to do, I thought, my mood lightening immediately, maybe he's not so bad after all. I propped the picture up, threw the wrapping paper away, and shut my eyes. 'I'm sorry,' I said, peeping above my fan at the Duke of, um, Westmoreland (that didn't sound right, but whatever), 'I'm afraid my dance card has been filled already. So many waltzes and so little time!'

I spun round in my ravishing one-shouldered scarlet ball dress, cut perfectly simply and yet emphasizing my height and figure (or not, as the case may be) and fluttered my fan. My long painted nails perfectly matched my Gucci gown, and a slim bracelet – a string of pearls, with a ruby in the middle – adorned each wrist. As the music began to fill the room, Count Lorenzo di Lorenza, my dashing Italian admirer, swept me onto the floor. 'Your beauty overwhelms me,' he murmured as— I nearly went through the roof as a clarion filled the room. At first I thought it was trumpets announcing the arrival of carriages, before I realized that it was, yet again, the bloody doorbell.

With very bad grace I pressed the buzzer. At first what appeared to be a walking canvas made its way through the door, before I realized that it was Tony, bearing a very large painting. 'Vladimir?' he called. 'Is he here?' he continued as he staggered up the hall and skidded to a halt in front of my desk.

'No, you've just missed him, he's gone to persuade Barbara not to leave him,' I said. 'He said to tell you he's taken a cab.'

'Hmm,' said Tony, thoughtfully rubbing his chin and setting the canvas down with its back to us to lean against the turn in the stairs leading to the second floor. Of medium height and rather wiry, although with very muscular and tattooed arms, Tony, alone except for Petrushka, was allowed to address Mr van Trocken by his first name and, also like Petrushka, wasn't afraid of him. He'd been with Mr van Trocken for donkey's years, and no-one knew much about him, apart from a rumour that he'd had to leave the army in disgrace, although that must have been decades ago. 'Hmm,' he said again, sniffing violently. 'Well that's very unfortunate, Sophie, because I've got this to give him and he's asked me to go and collect another new painting

53

for his study this afternoon. Do you know when he'll be back?'

'No, that's all he told me,' I said.

Tony hesitated a moment. 'Is it the thing you were ringing about earlier?' I asked.

'What?' said Tony, looking sharply at me. 'How did you know I rang earlier?'

'You told me yourself,' I protested. 'You know, I picked up the phone.'

'Oh, yes,' said Tony, still looking suspicious. 'Well, don't you ask too many questions, my girl. You know what curiosity did to the cat.' He sniffed violently. 'Want to see it?' he went on.

'Yes please,' I said meekly.

Tony heaved the large canvas up and turned it around to show me. 'Oh, my good lord,' I said before I could stop myself. I looked open-mouthed at the painting. It was, needless to say, of Mr van Trocken, but in a guise I had certainly never seen him in before. Actually, it was the one they reproduced in all the newspapers, but if you were one of the lucky few to have missed it, allow me to present you with a description.

He was dressed as Zeus, for Heaven's sake, in lots of flowing robes, which failed to disguise a very large stomach, and some kind of crown on top of his head, which looked ludicrous against his black and grey curls. His beard, which was also black and grey, had been trimmed very short and framed very large red lips, which in turn surrounded a grimace that I think was meant to be a smile, but just terrified the viewer by revealing those awful gleaming shark-like teeth.

On top of that, his complexion was represented as brown rather than the reality, which was mottled red, his arms and calves were deeply tanned and muscly and he was holding some sort of sceptre. Worst of all, not only was he represented as standing on top of a globe of the earth, but two scantily clad nymphs were circling around him and clinging on to either arm: one with poor Barbara's drawn and unhappy features, which even this sycophantic painter had failed to conceal, and the other with the unmistakable smirk that Irina always displayed when she'd just received a present of the 24-carat and diamond variety.

'The seductress and the crone,' said Tony unpleasantly, leering at the painting. 'It's quite something, isn't it?'

'It certainly is,' I said, gazing at it in a horrified daze, and it wasn't just the subject matter that appalled me. The style had a certain horrible familiarity about it. 'Where's it going?'

'On this wall beside you,' said Tony briskly, levering the canvas up and placing it carefully against the wall beside my desk. 'Something for you to look at. Careful you don't trip over it, Vladimir paid a pretty penny for this. It's by that Alan Cotswold geezer, he's all the rage these days, and if Vladimir gets back before I do, tell him I'll put it up later.'

'Uh, yes. I mean right,' I said, controlling myself with difficulty. Not only was I going to have to look at the monster all day, but Alan Cotswold, or Alan the Artist as my chums referred to him, was an ex of mine. We'd split up after I discovered the dreadful Belinda had been doing some modelling for him, and I leave the exact type of modelling she did to your imagination. When I discovered the results in his studio one day, it certainly left nothing to mine.

'Well, I'm off now,' said Tony, turning back to the door. 'See you.'

He seemed to take the whole hall in just one leap. I shut my desk drawer as the door banged. What a truly strange man, I thought, attempting to ignore the large portrait beside me. And if he's not an out and out coke fiend (and I have to admit, it seemed unlikely) he should get those sinuses seen to. He's always sniffing. Anyway, where was I? Oh yes. I shut my eyes, but before I could get on with the dance, the phone rang again.

'Van Trocken and Co.,' I said.

'Sophie, it's me,' said Penny. 'I do hope I'm not interrupting one of your more onerous chores, like sticking a few stamps on envelopes or something, but the situation round here is really getting a little tense. Sir Jeremy is going berserk, and all because he can't find Martin. I realize you are not your boyfriend's keeper, but are you sure you don't know where he could be? I think you'd be doing him a favour if you told him to get in touch, you know.'

I opened my mouth and shut it again. Penny was my best friend, but Martin was my boyfriend, and it wouldn't have felt right to go around telling tales out of school. Anyway, I was still annoyed about her pointing out that Paul the Gaul had finished with me rather than vice versa. 'No, honestly, I don't know,' I said eventually. 'But Penny, have you seen, there's a piece in the *Telegraph* quoting him, are you sure Sir Jeremy doesn't just want to talk to him about that?'

Penny snorted. 'Oh, I know about the piece in the *Telegraph*, we've all seen that, but I'm afraid, Sophie, that isn't going to help Martin's case at all. Quite the reverse, in fact. I shouldn't be telling you all this, but you are my best chum and Martin does seem to have got himself in to some seriously hot water.'

'Like what?' I demanded.

'I honestly don't know,' said Penny. 'I've only found out this much by eavesdropping.'

'Oh,' I said. 'Well, I'll pass on the message if I see him.'

'Jolly good,' said Penny. She sounded a bit strained. 'Still on for tonight, then?'

'Deffo,' I said, and hung up. To be honest, at the time, I didn't take Penny's call at all seriously – I just thought she was being melodramatic and over-reacting, a trait more commonly associated with me.

Even so, I felt a tiny bit uncomfortable, wondering what it was that he had really done this time. Maybe he had sold shares he shouldn't have (I didn't know that much about the stockmarket, so I was rather vague about why someone should have done this, but it sounded good), or got an offer from a rival firm or, perish the thought, had messed around with one of the secretaries – I shuddered and pushed that thought to the back of my mind, at which point my glance fell upon the picture he had given me earlier.

I picked it up thoughtfully and, don't ask me why, I shook it. For just a second, it sounded as if there were a couple of pieces of paper sliding around, but I assumed they were just bits of cardboard supporting the picture's mount. After a moment or two of con-sideration, I decided to take it home. I knew Martin wanted me to keep it on my desk, but if there really was a bit of trouble brewing, it might be better if no-one knew he'd come here.

I shoved the photograph in my handbag, shut my eyes and immediately returned to that far more pleasurable alternative paradise, where I spent so much of my time, only to be jerked out of it again straight away by the telephone ringing. 'Van Trocken and Co.,' I said.

'Please put me through to Petrushka immediately, this is Edwin de Peacock-Smythe,' said the nasally tones of the well-known restaurant and literary critic and cynic, who was a frequent contributor to our little magazine.

'I'm awfully sorry, Petrushka is out,' I said. 'Can I take a message?'

'Oh typical,' snorted Edwin. 'I've had the most brilliant idea for *Food for Thought*: mozzarella as a metaphor for the blank page. What about Vladimir? Is he around?'

'No, he's out too.'

'Well take a note and give it to Vladimir, if Pet does make it into the office she's bound to be too spaced out to appreciate my genius. Just think of it. There you have the virginal cheese, cocooned in the pseudo-amniotic fluid of invention, just waiting for The Creator to cut open its wrapping and smother it in the welter of creativity. As the writer begins to cover the page, so the chef – are you getting this down, young woman?'

'Yes, yes,' I said, hurriedly reaching for a pen.

'So the chef plucks the mozzarella from the hinterland of the subconscious or, in most cases, Safeway's packaging,' said Edwin dreamily. 'At first he is in agony – agony – but then yes! Eschewing the cliché of the avocado, the horizon of gastronomic possibilities begins to make itself felt. As the author reaches for an image here, a metaphor there, so the chef uses this blankness symbolized by the cheese to voice his own analysis of our frail and human condition. Braezola perhaps? Or roasted peppers? Or even'

– his voice became hushed – 'the anarchic possibilities of the mango?'

'Avocado, braezola, roasted peppers, mango,' I wrote industriously.

'Brilliant, don't you think?' enquired Edwin. 'The ultimate symbolism for our materially satisfied but spiritually bleak post-modern age?'

'Oh yes, very,' I said hastily.

'Give the message to Vladimir and tell him to give me a call,' said Edwin. 'Oh, and my last two invoices still haven't been paid, can you please tell Vladimir that I can not live on air and spiritual inspiration alone?' He hung up. That's odd, I thought. Mr van Trocken had told me off so frequently for forgetting to put invoices in his in-tray (or, on a couple of nightmarish occasions, losing them), that I had actually become quite efficient at that part of my job, and I was sure I'd put Edwin's through. I carried the piece of paper up the stairs, deposited it on Mr van Trocken's desk, returned to my chair and promptly forgot all about the invoicing situation. I was just about to return to the Count Lorenzo di Lorenza, when there was a scrabbling at the front door, followed by a very sonorous, 'Oh, God.' Oh, God, I thought myself, pushing the doorbell. I knew exactly who this was going to be.

'God, darling, did you have to make that so violent?' complained Petrushka, the editor of *Food for Thought*, staggering in through the front door. 'I'm feeling rather fragile actually, darling. God, just so much stress, so much to do. God, God, God.'

She began limping up the hall, clinging on to the wall for support. I had no idea how old Petrushka was – she could have been anywhere between

twenty-five and fifty-five underneath all that make-up
– but she looked as chic as ever, if rather the worse
for wear, and her stick-insect figure was clad in her
usual trademark black. A red chiffon scarf, exactly the
same shade as her lipstick, was swept expertly over
her blond beehive, and she was wearing dark glasses
which hid almost certainly bloodshot eyes. 'God,' she
repeated in that gravelly voice which was almost as
deep as a man's, coming to a halt at my desk. 'Darling,
you don't have any aspirin, do you?'

I scrabbled in my drawer and handed her a packet
of Nurofen. Petrushka produced a hip flask from her
handbag, used the contents to gulp down two pills,
handed the packet back and sighed. 'God, darling,
I've never had a hangover like this before,' she
continued, scrabbling in her handbag for cigarettes
and holder. 'Bloody, bloody bastard Conran. It's all his
fault for opening such fabulous, fabulous restaurants
and making me go to every first night. God, darling,
that could be a piece for the mag, restaurant openings
as performance art. What do you think, darling?
Bloody brilliant.' She inhaled deeply and perched
rather unsteadily on my desk.

'Cool,' I replied, looking enviously at her right
thigh, today clad in black jodhpurs, which was
scarcely thicker than my wrist.

'No, darling, it's not cool, it's bloody awful,' said
Petrushka, holding her head in her hands. 'It's bloody,
bloody bastard awful. You know what we should do
with Conran, darling? The ultimate in transport cafés!
Think about it, darling. Bibendum was the Michelin
garage, Bluebird was a car wash and that lot by the
river must have been bloody barges or something.'

'Um, they're by the river, not on it,' I said hesitantly.

'Well, bloody wharfs, piers, lighthouses, whatever,' said Petrushka petulantly. 'That's it, darling, we'll have Terence on the front of the mag with "A beacon of hope", as the headline. Bloody brilliant, eh, darling?'

Mercifully I was saved from answering by Petrushka's mobile phone, which went off so suddenly she dropped her cigarette holder. It was one of those incredibly irritating phones, which rang to the tune of the dance of the four signets in *Swan Lake*. 'God, darling, sorry,' she muttered as I poured a splash of coffee on the paper which had quietly started burning on my desk. 'What, darling? Who is that? Oh, God, tell him I'm on my way.'

She clicked her phone off and attempted to stand up straight. 'Don't be like me, Sophie,' she advised, making her way unsteadily down the hall. 'Don't touch tonic water, darling, it's a killer. I had so much tonic water last night I think my bastard bloody head's going to fall off. From now on I'm drinking vodka neat. *Ciao*, darling.'

'Um, Rory's resigned,' I called after her. She was supposed to be the editor of the rag, after all, and I thought someone should tell her the news.

'God, darling, lucky sod,' said Petrushka, attempting unsuccessfully to open the front door. 'Does Vlad the cad know?'

'Yes,' I said, pressing the buzzer so the door would open more easily. 'Can I tell him where you've gone?'

'No, darling, I don't want him ringing me in the middle of a massage,' said Petrushka, hiccupping slightly. 'Tell him,' she swung round, holding on to the door for support, 'tell him I demand more editorial freedom, darling! I'm tired of having his floozies on the cover. Tell him the future of the magazine depends on me!'

The door banged behind her. This was not an atypical exit line, but frankly the chances of me passing on her messages to Mr van Trocken were rather less likely than little green men visiting us from Mars. Oh, for a real job, I thought, settling back in my chair. Oh, for a chance to escape from Mr van Trocken, Petrushka and the whole bloody lot of them. I shut my eyes, and music swelled back into the room. 'Bellissima,' (now why did that ring a bell – no pun intended) murmured Count Lorenzo di Lorenza, 'your beauty overwhelms me!' We swept on to the floor and began to dance.

6

Needless to say, some much needed peace and quiet
was not going to be mine. You would have thought
that all of the day's events up until now would have
been enough excitement for one afternoon, but you
would have been wrong. This was the office of van
Trocken and Co., remember, where the bizarre was
the stuff of everyday life and your wildest imaginings
became reality. And if you think I'm over-egging it,
just look back to the newspaper cuttings after the
whole affair was blown wide open, and you'll see
that, if anything, I'm rather underplaying the whole
sorry story.

Anyway, there I was, day-dreaming away, when the
phone rang again. 'Van Trocken and Co.,' I said,
yanking up the receiver.

'Please put me through to Vladimir van Trocken
immediately,' said an unfamiliar voice.

'I'm sorry, I'm afraid he's out of the office,' I said.
'May I take a message?'

'This is really extremely urgent,' said the voice. 'I
was told by a member of staff in Poland Street that he
is usually to be found here.' Poland Street was where
the head office of Mr van Trocken's import/export

business was based. 'Does he have a mobile or a pager?'

'No, Mr van Trocken doesn't believe in living at the beck and call of mechanical instruments,' I said (or to be more accurate, I repeated what he always claimed – I suspected it was so that Barbara couldn't track him down when he was entertaining one of his numerous girlfriends), 'but he usually rings in. He's just totally in touch with his office. Can I ask him to call you?'

'Yes, you most certainly can,' said the voice. 'Please tell him this is Marcus Aimsworthy and I must speak to him immediately. This is very urgent, do you understand?'

'Yes,' I said. The receiver clicked. Cor, I thought. I've just spoken to the Treasurer of the Conservative Party. I wonder if Mr van Trocken is going to make another donation? Impressed as I was, though, I was becoming aware of further impending crisis – or in other words, an extremely strong desire to go to the loo. This presented a problem. The lavatory was at the top of the building, three storeys up, and although there were other people in the office – I could tell that by the sounds of gentle weeping in the background, a not uncommon means of communication around here – there was no-one to guard the door and person the switchboard in my absence, as the secretary who was usually supposed to do so had been sacked last week on the grounds that her nail polish clashed with Mr van Trocken's red tie.

There was absolutely no point in asking anyone else for, as Mr van Trocken had pointed out on more than one occasion, there was no problem when I went out at lunchtime – surprisingly for a man who insisted on driving his employees to the point of breakdown and beyond, he was very particular about the fact that the office was closed between 1 p.m. and 2 p.m., and that neither telephone calls nor visitors were to be received – and the rest of the time I was expected to remain in situ.

I hesitated for a few moments until I became aware of the fact that if I didn't do something fast, a terrible accident was going to occur in the offices of van Trocken and Co. On the other hand, if Mr van Trocken himself reappeared and couldn't get back in, he'd go berserk. There was nothing else for it. I leapt up from my chair, and, squirming slightly with discomfort, raced down the hall and put the door on the latch. Then I ran back up again, panting slightly as I got higher and higher, almost certainly due to altitude sickness, and not the fact that I hadn't done any exercise for a decade or so, before reaching the top storey, gratefully hurling myself into the tiny, freezing cold little cubicle and then squawking and hurling myself out again.

'Well excuse *me*,' said Jemima, the magazine's art director and more commonly known as Jim. 'I mean, do you mind?' She stalked out of the tiny loo, as did Henrietta, one of the few remaining secretaries in the place and more commonly known as Henry. Both of them looked me up and down and marched off down the wooden stairs. Wondering vaguely if I was dreaming, I peered cautiously round the door to make sure I wasn't disturbing anyone else before nipping in and locking the door.

A few minutes later, nature having been dealt with, I raced down the stairs again and to my horror, as I turned on the landing, I caught a glimpse of someone who must have walked in through the open door and was just reaching for the new painting. 'Hey!' I yelled. 'You can't touch that!' I'd like to say that I was thinking nothing of my personal safety at this point, but to be perfectly honest, it was precisely my personal safety that was uppermost in my mind: Mr van Trocken's wrath didn't even bear thinking about if anyone touched one of his horrible works of art.

The figure squawked, shot about a foot in the air and leapt round, at which point I squawked too. It was Martin. 'What on earth?' I demanded as I turned the final corner and leapt down the last flight of stairs.

'Ah, there you are!' cried Martin, embracing me. 'I knew you wouldn't be a moment!'

'What on earth is going on?' I demanded, disentangling myself, and going round the desk to sit down.

'Nothing, darling, I just thought I'd like to see you again,' said Martin, regaining his poise. He cocked an eyebrow. 'And jolly lucky I did, darling, anyone could have walked in. Naughty, naughty.' He reached across the desk and chucked me playfully on the cheek.

'I had to go to the loo,' I said. 'But, I mean, I don't understand, you saw me just a little while ago.'

'And I thought my pretty little *pomme d'amour* would be happy to see me again,' said Martin, feigning sorrow. 'Never mind, darling, another time. Drink tonight, perhaps?'

'I can't, I'm meeting Penny at Boom Boom,' I said sulkily.

'Another time then my lovely one,' said Martin. 'I'll call. *Ciao.*'

'Wait, Martin,' I said. '*Wait.*' I had been intending to repeat what Penny said on the telephone, but I was too late: he had gone, and there was no way, what

66

with unlocked front doors and hideous paintings, that I could desert my post. He had probably thought that I was going to start one of those long and intense conversations about our future together.

There was nothing for it: I sighed and nipped down the hall to relock the door. Why hadn't I listened to my mother? The one and only piece of advice she had ever given me about men was just before I set off for university and ran as follows. 'Avoid short men, dear,' she had hissed. 'They're a menace.'

I had always stuck to this policy and had never had any problems until Martin, who was slightly shorter than me in stocking feet and massively shorter than me in heels, a fact that he was constantly aware of and constantly neurotic about. He could be terribly aggressive about it, too. Must be all that testosterone in such a small package, I thought wearily, returning to my desk. Now where was I? Oh yes, the ball. I closed my eyes and nearly hit the roof as the phone started bellowing again. 'Van Trocken and Co.,' I said through gritted teeth.

'Well, Miss Brackenbury, how very nice to hear you,' said a voice. 'All is well with you and ill with your employer, I trust?'

'Little Ant!' I shouted with pleasure. Anthony Hurlingham, more commonly known in our circle of friends as Little Ant (he was six foot three), an architect and my flatmate and landlord, was finally back in town. 'How are you? How was Italy and France and everywhere? How fab to hear from you.'

'What a very nice reception,' said Little Ant. I could hear him lighting a cigarette over the phone. 'I had a tremendous time, thank you, and you were much missed, Heaven knows why, but you were, so there. And you'll never guess who I bumped into in Paris.'

'Who?' I demanded.

'Michael Tang!' said Little Ant. 'Isn't that a coincidence?'

'Oh, you're joking,' I said in horror. I had only met Michael Tang, Penny's brother, once before he'd buggered off to Hong Kong, at a big party thrown by the Tang family, and, as I think I mentioned, I couldn't stand him. 'Ugh, poor Little Ant, how yucky for you.'

'What do you mean?' asked Little Ant in astonishment. He didn't know about my Michael-related feelings as he'd been away the time I met the chap, and by the time he'd got back, I'd decided it was better to keep stumm about how loathsome Michael was for Penny's sake. Little Ant and Penny, who he'd met through me, got on very well. 'I thought he was a decent bloke,' he continued. 'Why don't you like him?'

A picture of the revolting Michael Tang reared up in my mind. Slightly shorter than Martin, he had wandering hands, thick spectacles and a big problem in the halitosis department. He even affected a slightly American accent, for goodness sake. How totally pretentious. 'Oh, I just don't,' I said lamely. 'Where did you meet?'

'He was sitting next to me in a café and we just got talking,' said Little Ant. 'I didn't know who he was, though, as he just said he was called Michael, but then we swapped business cards and after he left I looked at it and saw the surname. He said he was coming back to live in London, so we're going to meet up. I would never have guessed he was Penny's brother, though, would you?'

'Not in a million years,' I said firmly. I still couldn't

believe that the specimen I'd met had anything to do with my chic and glamorous friend. I hoped intensely Little Ant wasn't thinking of inviting him round.

'And where did you meet him?' enquired Little Ant.

'You know, when her parents threw that big party about two years ago, and you were away, so you couldn't go,' I said, wishing we could drop the subject. 'He just walked up and introduced himself and that was that.' It was more than that, actually, Penny had asked me excitedly if I'd met Michael when we were talking the next day and I had said yes and changed the subject.

'I'd have thought a chap like that would have appealed to you,' said Little Ant, for some reason sounding rather pleased.

'You must be joking,' I said. 'Anyway, tell me about the rest of the trip.'

'I'll do it in person,' said Little Ant. 'You busy tonight or can I expect you at home?'

'Well, I had arranged to meet Penny at Boom Boom and I can't really get out of that, but why don't you come along too?' I asked.

'To be honest, there's something I'd rather talk to you about alone,' said Little Ant. 'Shall we have a drink around there before you meet them? Say seven at the Market Bar?'

'Sounds fab,' I said. I really was intensely pleased Little Ant was back, even if he had made a few undesirable friends, as I'd missed him enormously.

'Good,' said Little Ant. 'What I've got to say might be a shock, to be honest, but I've got to tell you. Please understand.' He hung up.

Oh, good Lord, what now, I thought, hoping intensely this had nothing to do with the gas bill.

Then again, this was exactly what Penny had said when preparing me for her little bombshell, although I thought it was unlikely that Little Ant's news was going to be along the same lines. Was it to be forever my fate to be surrounded by madmen? Martin was behaving even more strangely than usual, my employer was stark, staring bonkers and now Little Ant was coming on all mysterious – they need help, I thought. They must get help.

I shut my eyes, gave up on the belle of the ball front, and decided to be a psychiatrist instead. 'So tell me Mr van Trocken,' I enquired, looking at the enormous figure stretched out on the leather sofa beside me, 'just how long have you been suffering from delusions of grandeur?'

Wrong question, even if it was my day-dream. 'Delusions of grandeur?' bellowed my employer. '*Delusions of grandeur*? How dare you, you insolent psychiatrist! I, Vladimir Napoleon Bonaparte van Trocken, a direct descendant of the noble King Wenceslas and Catherine the Great, the greatest philosopher and businessman who has ever emerged from that magnificent city of Prague and a close confidant of our own dear queen, will see you in court!'

7

It was with even more of a feeling of relief than usual that I pulled the door to behind me at six sharp a couple of hours later and savoured the thought of another fifteen hours of freedom before I had to be back in the office again. What a day, I thought. Mr van Trocken had not returned that afternoon and, unusually, had not rung in to make sure I was performing my duties properly, and so I had had no chance to pass on Marcus Aimsworthy's message.

Then the weeping fits from upstairs had become louder and more frequent, as the magazine's sub-editor Samantha, more commonly known as Sam, was very upset about something to do with Henry and Jim. She wouldn't tell me what was wrong, although after that little scene upstairs I thought I might have a pretty good idea, and I'd had to spend some time dispensing tissues, tea and sympathy, when she came down to sob on my desk, which had cut back on valuable day-dreaming time.

Oh, well, I thought, all bad things must come to an end, and the night was now mine to do with as I would. The only trouble was that it was still too early to go and meet Little Ant, but neither was there any real point in going home. I, or rather, we, lived in Edwardes Square, just off Kensington High Street. It was only a twenty minute walk from here, but as soon as I got there I would have had to go straight out again and anyway Albert, my cat, was liable to make a terrific fuss if I returned home in the evening and then deserted him again later.

It was with these thoughts and others in mind, that I decided to take a stroll through Hyde Park. It was still quite early in October, and the sky had turned that brilliant but deep shade of early evening blue that made all the trees and buildings stand out as if they were in a painting. The offices of van Trocken and Co. were on Gloucester Road, just round the corner from Kensington Gore, and so it was simplicity itself to nip across the road, through the huge wrought iron gates and mooch down towards the Serpentine.

As I looked around, I was briefly distracted from my woes. It was a lovely evening, a few stars were winking away, and there was a slight nip in the air as the onset of winter began to make itself felt. People were wandering around and looking quite normal, always a reassurance when you'd spent a day in the offices of van Trocken and Co., and I began to think that maybe the world wasn't that black after all. Martin couldn't have done anything that terrible, as he was, after all, a respectable fund manager in his late thirties, Penelope should be allowed to sleep with whom she wanted, Petrushka might hit the sauce rather more than was strictly advisable but brought invaluable contacts to the magazine and Mr van Trocken – well OK, I couldn't think of any redeeming features about Mr van Trocken, but who cares. The night was mine.

As I walked down through the flower beds, I began to muse about what I should really do with my life. I wasn't, it must be said, the outdoors type, but suddenly it struck me how fab it would be to be a landscape gardener. I imagined myself, hoe in hand, and looking rather fetching in a pair of old jeans and some wellies, relating to Sir Pelham and Lady Agatha Fotheringay, whose grounds I tended, the extensive improvements I intended to implement. 'There be time for mulching and time for squlching but I says to you my good lady and noble sir, this be time for gulching!' I declared. The stately couple gasped with delight. 'Truly,' said Sir Pelham to his spouse, 'this is genuine green-fingered genius. How we ever tended the grounds before—' 'Psst!' hissed a nearby bush.

'What on earth?' I demanded, skidding to a halt and looking wildly around. Sir Pelham and Lady Agatha were nowhere to be seen.

The bush peered suspiciously in either direction, and then parted to reveal the bedraggled figure of Rory. 'Don't say a word,' he muttered, hopping out, grabbing my arm and beginning to lead me down towards the lake. 'Just act normal. I don't want anyone to see me.'

'Well, I can understand that,' I said uncharitably, attempting unsuccessfully to remove my arm and fighting down feelings of fury. I had thought I'd seen the last of this particular irritant. Never a looker at the best of times, Rory was quite definitely not at his best today: the bush had deposited a few twigs in his lank, brown hair, which was parted in the middle and fell down to his shoulders, while his normal sprinkling of spots had got rather worse.

He was sporting a sort of khaki-coloured combat

gear, presumably in an attempt to blend in to the surroundings, which was rather spoiled by the black trainers at the bottom and the thick black rimmed National Health spectacles, through which he was peering at me with an expression that could best be summed up as barking mad. I had never liked khaki anyway, ever since my brief fling with Weirdo Will, who had once been in the French Foreign Legion, and who, I had heard, had recently been arrested on some obscure island off the east coast of Africa for his part in an unsuccessful uprising led by a group of mercenaries.

Anyway, that, thankfully, was another story. I cast another glance at Rory. In his free hand he carried a battered Europa shopping bag that I assumed contained his van Trocken and Co.-based worldly goods – a correct assumption, as it turned out, and rather more besides. 'What on earth do you think you're doing?' I complained, as he pulled me ever faster over the grass. 'All I wanted was to have a quiet walk. Let go.'

'No time for walks,' muttered Rory in a conspiratorial tone. 'I've got to talk to you but you must promise not to breathe a word of this.'

'Oh, for Heaven's sake,' I said crossly, digging in my heels and managing to pull myself to a halt. 'What is it Rory? Stop being just totally ridiculous.'

'I'm not being ridiculous,' hissed Rory. 'This is important. You've got to know before it all breaks, so that you can make sure you're not implicated.' He peered around again, and then leant forward to adopt a whispering position. 'Well,' he began, 'the thing is . . .'

It would be inaccurate to relate that Rory's words

of wisdom were to be lost for ever, as I found out exactly what he was going to tell me just a few days later. For the time being, however, I was to remain in ignorance as Rory chose this moment to leap about twenty feet into the air, squeal, 'Oh, no,' and then vanish into thin air almost as quickly as he had appeared. Well, not totally vanish, but you know what I mean, he just hared off incredibly quickly in the opposite direction from the one in which we'd been walking.

What on earth is it now? I thought. I mean I know the whole world's going mad, but even for a long-term inmate of van Trocken and Co. this was going a bit far. And what is going to break? One of Mr van Trocken's fine examples of Bohemian glass? Did Rory intend to stage a midnight mission to smash the place up by way of revenge? And what on earth made him shoot off like that? I couldn't see anything that looked remotely alarming nearby, there were just a few couples strolling hand in hand through the park, an au pair wheeling a pram, two teenage boys on skate-boards and an extremely glamorous looking woman talking into a mobile telephone.

I wish I looked like that, I thought, gazing at her wistfully. Even in the semi-dusk I could make out perfect blond curls, an elegant fawn raincoat and lovely sleek high heels, although they must be taking a bit of a battering on the grass. And she was sporting even more diamonds than Penny – I must have been gazing at her a bit too intensely as she looked up sharply and gasped. 'No autographs!' she shouted suddenly as I approached. 'Leave me alone! Even I must have my privacy!'

She burst into tears and raced off, managing, I noted

with respect, both to keep her heels out of the grass and to continue talking into her mobile phone. I stood and stared after her for a moment. Maybe it's me, I thought. Maybe I have a strange effect on people that will make them behave in a way that seems eccentric even by the admittedly peculiar standards of the people I spent my time with. And anyway, who on earth was she? She looked slightly familiar. Maybe – I froze. Lying on the ground in front of me was a copy of the *Evening Standard*. The pages had been blown open, and right at the bottom of page four, I saw a tiny snippet that arrested my attention. I picked up the paper.

'Beware the bouncing Czech?' I read. 'Senior figures in the City were today warning the Conservative Party to act with caution over a £1-million pledge' – it seemed the monster hadn't actually handed over the dosh yet – 'from the entrepreneur and self-made millionaire Vladimir van Trocken,' it went on. '"Who is this man and just where did he really make his money?" said a source in Borings Merchant Bank. "We don't even know where he went to school."

'But Conservative Treasurer Marcus Aimsworthy defended Mr van Trocken, chief executive of the import/export business van Trocken and Co., and publisher of the epicurean and arts magazine *Food for Thought*. "Vladimir is an outstanding businessman, and we look forward to a prolonged working relationship," he said. "I am only sorry that our colleagues in the City of London feel it necessary to denigrate the source of a Conservative Party donation that they themselves would be hard put to match".'

And that was it. There was nothing more, not so much as a hint about why anyone was worried about my employer, although frankly, I could have told the Tory lot that they were stark staring bonkers to take Mr van Trocken and his donations at face value. If there wasn't something in it for Mr van Trocken, then there certainly wouldn't be anything in it for anyone else. I wonder what it could be, though, I thought, dropping the paper and walking up towards Bayswater Road. It couldn't be a change of nationality: he'd obtained British citizenship years ago when he married Barbara (and when, incidentally, her father was a senior civil servant at the Home Office, Rory had told me that, I had no idea how he knew) and apart from even more money, I wouldn't have thought there was anything else he wanted.

Not that the paper seemed to be taking it that seriously either, or they wouldn't have shoved it in such an obscure spot. I glanced at my watch and squeaked. It was now 7.15 and it was much too far to walk to the Market Bar in a couple of minutes: there was nothing for it, my limited resources were going to be used, yet again, to fatten the wallets of London's taxi driving community.

About ten minutes later, I pushed open the big wooden doors of the Market Bar and stood blinking in the half light. There were a few electric bulbs here and there but the main source of light came from the small candles winking away at each table. Directly in front of me was the heaving bar, and to the right was a small area with tables and chairs. The vast majority of the clientele, many of them trendy media types of the kind I wished to become, sported black clothes, black hair, black nails and black eyeliner, and there was no way at all of telling the genders apart. They went well against the deep red walls, though.

I hesitated for a moment, eavesdropping on one of the local drug dealers making a call on his mobile phone, before I spotted Little Ant sitting at one of the tables at the back, looking better than ever after his month driving around in the sun. He spotted me at the same time and leapt up, after which we had one of those hugging scenes you see in slow motion when someone is advertising shampoo.

'Well, look at you!' exclaimed Little Ant, eventually, when he had put me down. 'Don't you look well. And what an absolutely lovely shirt. I haven't seen it before, have I?'

'Uh, no, it's new,' I said shiftily. Little Ant was only too aware of the state of my finances and prone to chide, so I decided to blurt out all my crimes as fast as possible. 'And I owe you a crate of wine. Actually I owe you two, and the gas might be turned off any day now.' I hastily changed tack. 'Honestly, Little Ant, you're looking fab too. A good time was had by all?'

'Indeed it was,' said Little Ant, taking my hand and leading me to the back, where he had been nursing a bottle of wine. 'I'll tell all in a moment, but let's sit down first. And don't worry about the wine and the gas, I'm sure you can make it up to me in other ways.'

'Cool,' I said in surprise following him through the bar. Generous at the best of times, this really was going it a bit. And he really was looking fab. Little Ant was very tall and very slim (he and Martin didn't get on, no prizes for guessing why), although with a slight muscularity in the shoulder area, and a few weeks in Southern Europe had bleached his normally fair hair until it was almost white. It was cut quite short, but flopped forward over two brilliant blue eyes and an extremely haughty nose, which, like the rest of his face, was dark brown. Today in casual gear – black jeans, black shirt and black loafers – he looked positively swoony.

The funny thing was, though, that I could never look on Little Ant in an amorous light. I tended to think of him as the brother I'd never had, as I had known Little Ant all my life. He was actually ten years older than me, but his parents lived opposite mine in Cheltenham, and they were all great friends. That meant that whenever we went over to their place, I was brought along too, first as a baby and then a little girl. I must say, though, that even though I had known him all that time, there had been a fairly big break from when I was eight, and he went away to university, to when I was twenty-one and moved to London. We had seen one another in the holidays, of course, and always got on fine, but because of the age gap you couldn't have said we were really good friends until three years ago, when, knowing that I needed accommodation, Little Ant had offered me a room in his flat. I had lived there ever since.

'As I was saying,' said Little Ant, as we plonked ourselves down, 'it was a great month. I'm beginning to feel I know Tuscany like the back of my hand. Great wine, great food, what more could you ask for?'

'Great women?' I enquired, slurping gently at the glass that Little Ant had thoughtfully filled up.

'Well, there were certainly some beautiful Italian girls around,' said Little Ant, shooting me a look that I couldn't quite make out. 'But I'm beginning to think the English rose type has something going for it. You know, I – yes, yes, what is it?'

79

'Great ganga, man,' said a dreadlocked individual companionably. He had seated himself at the table, and looked as if he wanted to join our little chat. 'Really great, and good price too. You want some for you and your lady? Best prices in West London, man. You won't do no better.'

'No, thanks, we've got plenty at home,' said Little Ant briefly. The dreadlocked individual, looking hurt, moved on. 'Anyway, as I was saying,' continued Little Ant in a slightly exasperated tone, 'I've been thinking a lot over the last few weeks. I'm getting on, you know, Sophie, I'm thirty-five.'

'That's not that old,' I said, slurping again. 'Martin's thirty-seven and he doesn't feel old, quite the opposite, in fact. Sometimes I find it hard to keep up with him, actually.'

Little Ant shuddered at the mention of Martin's name. 'Oh yes, him,' he said dryly. 'The only reason you find it hard to keep up with him, Sophie, is that he's more elusive than the Loch Ness monster. You mark my words, he's trouble.'

'Actually, I saw him twice today,' I said defensively. 'And I've told you before, I'm tired of floozying around with every man in town. I'm trying to be grown-up. Anyway, what's brought on the cranky old age talk? This isn't like you.'

'Oh, you know,' said Little Ant dreamily. 'You get away for a few weeks and suddenly your perspective changes. There's more to life than working eighteen hours a day in an architect's firm, and there's more to life than working for that monster you have to put up with. We should both just chuck it all in and run away.'

'You're not serious, are you?' I said in horror. I had

80

no intention of chucking anything in, but if Little Ant did, this would raise serious questions about my housing situation. 'Anyway, I thought you were looking forward to the new job.'

'Oh, I am, but anyone can dream,' said Little Ant, wistfully refilling my glass. 'But look, Sophie, I honestly have been – what now?'

A colleague of the dreadlocked individual had appeared on the scene. 'I've been watching you, man, and you know what? We met before, man,' he said conversationally in a strong Jamaican patois. He took a seat. 'Remember? At de car-ni-val, man. You was not with your lady, you was with another woman. Oh man, she was a looker and den some. Oh-ee!' He roared with laughter.

I could tell Little Ant was intensely annoyed at the interruption, but no-one else would have been able to notice his mood. Incredibly polite on all occasions, he even managed to force a smile. 'Yes, I remember,' he said, feigning enthusiasm. 'Yes, we had a great time, although unfortunately this is not my lady. Anyway, it's been great to meet you again—'

'Oh, man!' shrieked our new friend, who did not seem to be taking the hint. 'Come here, woman, I want to introduce you to de ar-chi-tect.' A very stylish young girl dressed, of course, in black approached our table. 'Dis guy,' continued our chum, 'dis guy I met at de car-ni-val. What a man! He was rockin' and rollin' wit de most beautiful woman! More beautiful dan you! Though not' – here he obviously felt keen to avoid any domestic fracas – 'as beautiful as dis yong girl here. What is your name, darlin'?'

'Sophie,' I said, beaming at him.

'Sophie,' said our chum. 'I'm Thomas, man. Why

dis beau-ti-ful girl not your lady, man?' he continued, turning to Little Ant. 'She has such lovely dimples when she smile. She wit' another man? You don't want to let no looker like dis get away from you now, man.'

I couldn't suppress a giggle. Poor Little Ant, who had obviously been keen on a private tête-à-tête, was now explaining to Thomas that yes, I was with another chap. More of Thomas's friends were gathering round and while I was thoroughly enjoying meeting so many new friends, I had a feeling the same could not be said for my flatmate. Anyway, I thought, taking another sip of wine and basking in a few more compliments, we have plenty of time to chat at home and we wouldn't have had time for an in-depth conversation now anyway, as I was meeting the others at eight. Speaking of which – I glanced at my watch and squeaked in horror. It was five past, and Boom Boom was still a bit of a walk from here. 'Look, I'm really sorry, but I've got to go,' I said, leaping to my feet and dragging on my coat.

'Oh, man, and we was just getting acqu-ain-ted,' said Thomas, looking genuinely regretful. 'You going to walk out on old Thomas just like dat?'

'I've got to,' I said, taking a quick last slurp of wine and stubbing out my cigarette. 'I'm meeting some people and I'm already late.'

'Oh, Sophie,' said Little Ant, standing up likewise, 'do you really have to go? There really is something I want to talk to you about. Can't you see them another time?'

'I really can't, I promised,' I said. 'And Penny wants to introduce me to her new girlfriend.'

'I always thought she spent more time with

boyfriends than girlfriends,' said Little Ant, following me to the door. 'And so, I might add, do at least half the single men under forty in the whole of inner London.'

'Well times have changed,' I said, waving to Thomas and his pals. 'It's her girlfriend, as in I'm Martin's girlfriend. At least, I think I am.'

Tête-à-tête forgotten, Little Ant began to laugh. 'So that's this week's ploy, is it?' he asked. 'Her parents will be pleased. And do Andrew and Neil and Gerald and Ian and Robert and the Spaniard Gabriel know about it yet?'

'Oh, there was nothing between her and the Spaniard Gabriel, that was just a rumour,' I said airily. 'As for the others, well yes, but don't ask me. Anyway, you do see, I really must go.'

'Indeed I do,' said Little Ant. 'But look, Sophie, if we can't chat tonight, what about dinner tomorrow? Let's have a proper reunion since I've been away such a long time: I'll take you to The Collection.'

'Sounds fab,' I said. I happened to be free, as per usual, as I was hoping Martin might take me out, but equally, as per usual, any definite time at which we might see one another had not been arranged. Anyway, it would probably be more fun to see Little Ant. We threw our arms round each other, did a bit of double pecking, and I sped off into the night.

8

I needn't have worried about being late. It was quarter past by the time I shoved open the huge steel doors of Boom Boom, but there was no sign of Penny at all. Another Tang family philosophy was not just leave them wanting more, but keep them waiting – sometimes for hours – in the first place.

Still, I was in no hurry. I liked Boom Boom: outside it still looked like the old spit and sawdust pub it once was, while inside it boasted a glittering steel interior that wouldn't have been out of place in a space station. I walked over to the long oval bar that ran about three-quarters of the way down the vast room, and deposited my coat on a bar stool. 'Kir please, with not too much cassis,' I said to the barman, who smiled and began fiddling with wine glasses.

I do hope she's not too late, I thought, I want to meet Charlotte and hear all the latest news. Even though I'd known Penny for some years now, the Tang family were a constant source of fascination to me. There was her minute father Peter, who looked like a miniature Oriental version of his namesake, Peter Ustinov, and had started his daughter's business education early on: he had her reading the *Financial*

84

Times at the age of four, and took out a subscription for *The Economist* for her when she was sent away to Cheltenham Ladies School. That, unfortunately, backfired: Cheltenham was just the first of the many schools Penny managed to get herself expelled from, in this case by starting a bonfire in the dorm with said copies of *The Economist*, in order to hold a midnight feast composed of stir fry Chinese food. Typical of Penny not to stick with the usual sandwiches.

Then there was Benenden, from which she was expelled at thirteen for writing a satire on girls' boarding schools, which was published in *Private Eye* and promptly traced back to Penny, Heathfield, where she was expelled at fifteen for a less original sin, harbouring boys in the dorm, and then Roedean. Her parents were pulling some serious strings by now to get her in to a decent school and were apoplectic when Penny penned a Communist manifesto, declared that all property was theft and forged a letter to *The Times* in the headmistress's name calling on the Government to close down all private schools. 'Well, you'd have thought my parents would be pleased I managed to make so many contacts in the old girls' network even before I finished school,' said Penny in aggrieved tones when telling me about this.

Godolphin & Latymer was last on the list, not least because it was based in London and so Penny could live at home, and this time Peter and Pamela told her in no uncertain terms that one more expulsion meant no more trust fund. And so, true to form, Penny finally pulled herself together and promptly infuriated all her old schools by getting in to University College, Oxford, to read Classics. 'Revenge is a dish best eaten cold,' she had said happily. 'Did I tell you my English mistress at Benenden told my parents that I'd be lucky to get to GCSE standard in needlework?'

Penny's mother Pamela, however, a very tall and graceful English woman who had been both a model and a débutante in the late 1950s, had done her own rebelling in her time by running off with Peter. Penny had once told me that her mother's family, a rather conservative lot, had been none too pleased about the Far Eastern alliance, until they had been exposed to first, the quite overwhelming charm of Peter Tang, and second, his even more overwhelming bank account. It was quite obviously a love match, though: the two of them still behaved like lovesick teenagers after all these years, which was a constant source of embarrassment to Penny. 'They were holding hands in public *again*,' she was prone to hissing down the telephone when describing the events of the previous evening.

And then there was Michael. I just couldn't see how he could be so different from the rest of them. Small, weedy, with all the charisma of a wet fish – ugh. I shuddered. After that meeting at that party, Penny obviously realized that we hadn't got on, and had mentioned him only twice since then: once to tell me he'd gone to Hong Kong, and the second time, earlier today, to tell me he'd come back. Double ugh.

It was at this point that I became aware of a tall chap of Italian appearance, who was standing across the bar from me. I looked away hastily and then peered back cautiously when I thought he'd turned away. Wrong. The chap smiled at me. I blushed furiously and looked away again, mentally kicking myself for behaving like a five year old, and then turned slightly and surreptitiously examined his reflection in the mirror behind me. He really was extremely dishy: about six foot two, with jet black hair, dark eyes, olive skin and a very full mouth. Like so many of the people I'd bumped in to today, he also faintly reminded me of someone, although I was sure we hadn't met before: this chap was not the sort of chap you forgot in a hurry.

I quite suddenly realized he was walking round the bar towards me. Oh, bugger, I thought, what am I going to do now. And on closer inspection he got even better: broad shoulders and a slim waist, and dressed in jeans, a denim shirt, blue blazer and black loafers, just like Little Ant's. I noticed the latter bit, by the way, as I was staring rigidly at the floor when he approached. 'Hello,' he said. 'I think you've dropped something.'

He bent down and picked up a piece of paper that had indeed fallen out of my handbag. It took me a moment to realize what it was – another of my little poetic efforts – by which time, to my stunned horror, he had begun to read it.

> I wandered lonely as a hill
> On which no rain would fall,
> And chatted to a window-sill
> Which made a caterwaul;
>
> I dived into the oceans deep
> But there not long did tarry,
> For all I saw to earn my keep
> Was Neptune's cash and carry;
>
> I soared on wings of painted silk
> To lands not far from here,

And shuddered as the sky of milk
Was watered down with beer;

I met a strange and wond'rous beast
With flowers for a nose,
When asked, he said, 'It's just the least
Flamboyant way to pose';

I dallied with the weary moon
And quoth, 'I like your style',
He said, 'You've got here far too soon,
Could you back off a while?'

And when at last I came to quell
The mountains of the mind,
I learned a simple witch's spell
Is better left behind,
And so I sought a wishing well
And there did solace find.

'Oh please,' I said in agony, grabbing the piece of
paper back, 'that's just a bit of nonsense. It's not
meant to be taken seriously.'

'Sensational poem,' said the chap. I couldn't quite
place his accent, it wasn't Italian, but it wasn't quite
English either. 'What's it about? Twentieth-century
alienation?'

'Uh, yes,' I said. Actually it was about last week's
shopping trip to High Street Kensington, when I
couldn't find a thing to suit me, but whatever.

'I love exciting, intellectual thingummies,' said the
chap. 'It's much more fun than the black propaganda
I have to read during the day.'

'Oh, really?' I demanded, intrigued. There was only

one explanation for this: he must be a spy. 'What is it that you do?'

'I work in the City,' said the chap cheerfully. 'Is there anyone personning the bar round here? I could do with another snifter and I'm sure you need topping up.'

'Oh, no thanks, I'm fine,' I said, as the barman traipsed over. Penny was bound to turn up in a minute and I rather felt I should pace myself.

'Thanks for popping over,' said the chap. 'Another Becks please. So what's the day job then, or are you a full-time poet?'

'I work for a magazine,' I said cautiously. I didn't really feel like admitting what my real job was.

'Like it, like it,' said the chap. 'Are you one of those journalists who scurry around in flashers' macs doorstepping old grannies and persecuting innocent members of the Government for doing a perfectly respectable spot of arms dealing? No, of course, I can see you're not. Go on then, what was today's scoop? Something excitingly xenophobic, I hope. All the best journalism is, these days.'

I burst out laughing. 'Actually, today's scoop was between seeing mozzarella as a metaphor for a blank page, or Sir Terence Conran and his penchant for turning petrol stations into restaurants,' I said. 'Actually—'

There was a ringing sound from inside the chap's pocket. 'Buggeration, do excuse me,' he said, taking a bleeper from his pocket.

'Oh, by all means,' I said. 'Actually, would you mind watching my drink for a second? I must just nip to the loo.' And with that, I nipped.

Well done, Sophie, well done, I thought, running

my hands under the cold water. I was beginning to hope that Penny was going to be seriously late, and while I didn't want to tempt fate too much, things were definitely looking up. 'Well done!' I shouted out loud, gazing at myself in the mirror. 'Well done!'

I'd thought that I was the only inhabitant in the loos: I was wrong. A woman dressed all in black, with long straight red hair, emerged from one of the cubicles, gave me a very strange look and disappeared. I looked after her with deep embarrassment and then looked back at my reflection. Mr van Trocken was right, my roots did need redying, especially after this little encounter. I dragged a comb through my hair, which was touching my shoulders and needed a good trim, put a bit of blusher on my face, which was looking even paler than usual and touched up my mascara. On a good day my eyes looked dark blue: they were currently still puddle grey.

Having composed myself, and after taking a few deep breaths I emerged to see – nothing. With a thud of disappointment I realized that the chap had disappeared and the barman had assumed guard duty over my glass of kir. He grinned at me as I approached. 'That bloke,' he said as I reached the bar, feeling just totally fed up, 'you know the one standing here?'

'Yes,' I said glumly, reaching for the kir and taking a hefty gulp. It must have been something I said. I was feeling just totally fed up.

'He said to tell you he was very sorry but he had to go,' said the barman. 'And it was true, you know, he wasn't making it up.'

'How do you know,' I said glumly, taking another gulp.

'Because it was his bleeper, right?' said the barman.

'I saw it, didn't I. His bleeper bleeped and he pulled it out and he looked at it, right? And then he beckoned to me and said he had to go, but would I tell you, right? And then he said, would I tell you that he'll be coming in again on Monday.'

'Really?' I asked, brightening up considerably.

'Or was it Tuesday,' said the barman thoughtfully. 'No, no it was Monday, he definitely said Monday, because I thought, right, I'm in on Monday, so's I'd remember to tell you.'

'Actually,' I said glumly, suddenly remembering that I was not supposed to be a free agent, 'I have a boyfriend so there's no point anyway.'

'Shame,' said the barman. 'He's a nice looking bloke. Your bloke look like that?'

'No,' I said briefly. 'But he's got a very strong personality. Anyway, I do not particularly like strange men approaching me in bars. It's just totally out of order.'

The barman gave me a sceptical glance, as well he might, and turned to answer the phone behind the bar. Honestly, I thought staring at myself in the mirror and noticing that a streak of mascara had created a smudge on my cheek, why can't I get a grip? Every time I attempted to be suave and sophisticated, I just ended up tripping over my feet or my tongue, depending on which would cause the maximum embarrassment at the time. I should leave Martin, resign from van Trocken and Co., find a proper job on a magazine that did not entail answering the phones all day long, stop behaving like an idiot when handsome men attempted to get to know me and—

'You Miss Brackenbury?' asked the barman, interrupting my train of thought.

'How did you know?' I demanded, rather startled.

'You fitted the description,' said the barman snickering and handing over the phone. 'She said you'd probably have make-up running down your face.'

I took a deep breath and was about to aim a blast at the receiver, but, as ever, Penelope got there first. 'Just a joke,' she said brightly, before I had a chance to say anything. 'Honestly, Sophie, you've had no sense of humour since you started working at that ghastly place.'

'I think my lack of a sense of humour owes more to the inability of friends to meet me on time,' I snapped. 'Honestly, Penny, I've been here for ages. Where are you?'

'In my car on the way over,' said Penny icily. 'Really, Soph, it's not that late. Anyway, I was held back a bit at the office, so I thought I'd call and let you know I'm on my way. I won't bother in the future.'

'But what on earth has kept you so late?' I demanded. 'I thought you finished work hours ago.'

'I usually do,' said Penny. 'But you know how it is when you have a high-powered job. Oh, no, of course, I'd forgotten, you don't. Joke, joke! Oh, it was just about this Molehill Magazines thing, you know, I mentioned it earlier. Martin still hasn't put in an appearance, by the way. Anyway, see you in a bit.' She hung up. I passed the phone back to the barman and took another broody sip of kir.

'Not your night, is it,' said the barman conversationally. 'Been stood up, have ya?'

'No, no, she's on her way,' I said irritably. This barman was becoming altogether too accurate in his assessment of my situation. 'Can I have another kir?'

'Certainly, as soon as I've served these gentlemen,'

said the barman cheerily, turning to two young men standing at the opposite side of the bar.

'Gentlemen?' roared one of them, who I suddenly realized was Jim. 'How dare you.'

'Can't have had his eyesight checked for years,' jeered the other, who I suddenly realized was Sam. She was looking a lot more cheerful than she had been for ages.

'Sorry ladies,' said the barman hastily. 'What can I get you?'

'A pint of bitter and a pint of Guinness, and make it snappy,' said Jim. 'We've worked up quite a thirst, eh Sam?' She pounded Sam, who was agreeing enthusiastically, on the back. I couldn't help but stare – what with those crewcuts, lack of make-up and muscly arms, I could quite understand the barman's confusion – until the two women noticed my gaze. Both ignored my feeble attempt at a smile, looked me up and down, and then stalked off to one of the little oval tables lining the walls, where they both started muttering.

The barman raised his eyebrows at me, clinked the money into the till and walked back over. 'A kir was it?' he enquired. I nodded, waited until I got my drink and then went off and sat at one of the little oval tables at the opposite side of the bar from Jim and Sam and lapsed into thought about the attractive chap at the bar. Boom Boom suddenly melted into a casino. I was wearing a shimmering cream silk sleeveless number, with pearls embroidered at the top, matching cream silk stilettos and diamond and pearl earrings. Bored with the mêlée at the gaming tables, and bored with my life in the jet set, I wandered outside onto the balcony, and gazed moodily at the sea, when

suddenly, a tall dark and handsome figure material-
ized beside me. 'The name's Tang, Michael Tang,' he
said.

I shuddered violently and nipped back to reality
pronto – what with Penny having told me her loathsome brother was back on these shores and Little Ant
meeting him too, the name must have been on my
mind – before returning to the tropical scene in the
South of France. 'I mean, the name's Gloucester-
Harding, Alexander Gloucester-Harding,' said the
chap. 'I have been watching you all evening and you
are quite simply the most ravishing woman on the
Côte d'Azur. May I?' He uncorked a bottle of champagne and handed me a glass (fortunately he'd carried
two out with him). 'To . . . the future,' he whispered.
We clinked and sipped. 'So tell me,' he continued,
'what brings you to this balmy beach? Surely, you
must be a model.'

'Well I was,' I explained modestly, 'but now I do a
bit of scribbling – a piece here, a piece there. I'm sure
you won't have read my stuff – the name's Sophie
Brackenbury.'

'Sophie Brackenbury?' enquired the handsome spy.
'*The* Sophie Brackenbury? But of course I know your
name. You are one of the trendiest writers in Britain
today, and to think' – he raised his glass again – 'you
are beautiful too. Oh, Sophie! Sophie! Sophie!'

I blinked. 'Yoo-hoo, Sophie,' called the voice again.
I blinked again and looked around me. Boom Boom
suddenly reappeared, along with an exceedingly
unwanted addition. Oh no, I thought, but it was too
late.

'Yoo-hoo, Sophie, it is you!' exclaimed Belinda, the
old cow who Penny and I knew from law school, in

surprise. To my complete horror, I suddenly realized she was sitting at the table next to mine. This was absolutely not turning out to be my night. 'How totally amazing!' she went on. 'Meet Gerard and Simon!' She swept an arm out to encompass the two men sitting with her, who looked like twins: both slightly solid looking, with light brown hair and outdoor complexions. Both were also dressed in cords and stripy shirts and both grunted in a friendly manner by way of introduction. 'Gerard and Simon are polo players,' continued Belinda. 'Isn't that great? But listen, how are you?'

'I'm fine,' I said heartily, eyeing her up. So far our little meeting was progressing entirely as usual: Belinda was accompanied by at least two good-looking men and was making me feel totally inadequate. She was as small and as slim as Penny, but whereas Penny gave off an impression of glamour mixed with intrigue, Belinda somehow conveyed an image of fragility. You got the feeling she would break in two if treated harshly, and this vulnerability was accentuated by her face: a huge mouth that seemed permanently on the verge of quivering, tiny little pearl like teeth, a small straight nose and big brown eyes.

This impression, incidentally, was entirely illusory: she was one of the hardest women I knew. Her fair brown hair was straight and shoulder length, and she had a habit of running her hands through it when under stress, after which it would invariably fall straight into place. And she wore the kind of clothes that would look downright galumphing if I wore them: today it was black hipster trousers, a brown silky shirt that matched her hair and little black boots.

'Amazing,' said Belinda, gazing at me earnestly. 'Honestly, Soph, you look just the same every time I see you! No, just kidding, you look great, you really do. But listen, someone told me you were working as a receptionist! That isn't true, is it?'

'No, actually I'm a welcoming agent and telephone intermediary,' I said, trying and failing to quell feelings of hatred. 'But it's just for a little while until I get myself sorted out. I'm actually planning a career in the media. And what about you? What are you doing now?'

'Oh, God, it's so embarrassing!' gurgled Belinda. 'I mean, it's incredible.' She ran a hand through her hair, which fell perfectly back into place. 'Well believe it or not, I've just landed this amazing new role in *WestEnders*, you know that new soap the Beeb's going to be doing with Apricot Bellissimo? I've got a part in it too! God, I just can't believe it, I'm going to be a soap star!'

I could perfectly well believe it. After deciding she wanted to be an actress rather than a lawyer, it was just a matter of time before Belinda landed some plum role, and it went without saying that her path would be littered with the aspirations of a group of far better but not quite so pretty thespians who would have been passed over in the past. Not that I was jealous, of course, I had far loftier ambitions than appearing on television and becoming incredibly rich and famous. After all, I was deep. 'That's fantastic, Belinda,' I said, attempting to sound sincere. 'I mean, that's totally wonderful.'

'Belinda!' shrieked Belinda, clapping her hand in amusement to those large and trembling lips and rocking backwards and forwards. 'Oh, God, I can't believe you haven't heard! The producers of the show thought that sounded too Sloaney, so they've made me take a new name and guess what it is! Tiffany!'

'Tiffany?' I demanded.

'Yah, Tiffany!' shrieked Belinda, or Tiffany as I supposed I must start to think of her. 'Isn't that just the greatest? Tiffany Day! Amazing.'

'Not Cuttlesnipe?' I enquired nastily – bloody Belinda's surname was the only decent thing about the woman – but I was drowned out. One of the blond men, I wasn't sure if it was Gerard or Simon, had snorted loudly at this point, as a prelude, I assumed, to a contribution to the conversation. I was correct. 'Right, we thought,' he began, choosing his words with care, 'I mean like we said to Tiff' – Belinda, I mean Tiffany, shrieked at this point while the other blond man made a noise that sounded like a constipated horse crying out in pain – 'that, right, it was good news they didn't call her Cartier! Cartier! Do you know what I mean? *Cartier!*'

'Ha ha,' I said dutifully, as my three companions all collapsed in hysterical laughter and pounded one another on the back.

'I mean, isn't that just the greatest?' demanded Bel— Tiffany after she had recovered. 'I mean, isn't that just hysterical? And God, Soph, to think that three years ago we were all going to be lawyers! You know, I really envy you. I wish I was like you and just sort of had an easy life and a job you could leave behind when you go home. But you've always been like that. I remember Professor Marsden telling everyone that you were so easy going and just didn't have the ambition of someone like me!'

I had had enough by this point. I remembered very well Professor Marsden making just such a statement, although admittedly that was after I had put in some quality time spreading the news about him and Belinda, I mean Tiffany or whatever the hell she was called, and despite the fact that Penny was bound to be furious with me – she disliked Tiffany even more than I did – I was going to have to leave. 'It's really been lovely to see you,' I said, scrambling to my feet, 'but I must be off. I have a horrible feeling I've come to the wrong place and I'm actually meeting my friend at—'

'Sophie!' said a voice behind me. 'Darling! I'm so glad to have caught you, but where's Penny? I thought you were all meeting here.'

There was nothing for it: I turned round and looked down and there, looking even more pleased with himself than usual, was lover boy himself. Absolutely typical of him to turn up out of the blue when I was least expecting him – and talking to someone who I had to admit was universally considered to be an incredibly attractive woman. 'Just what are you doing here?' I asked.

'Darling, I would have thought you would have been pleased to see me,' said Martin reproachfully. 'You told me you were going to be here, remember? – and I wanted a little chat. Well, hello,' he continued, catching sight of Tiffany. 'I'm Martin.' He took Tiffany's outstretched hand and brushed it with his lips in a gesture of gallantry that would have put the three musketeers to shame, nodded at the chaps and drew up a chair.

'How lovely to meet you,' he went on, emphasizing the 'L'. 'You're a friend of Sophie's, are you? She's certainly' – he paused, cocked an eyebrow, produced a packet of cigarettes and a gold lighter, offered one to Tiffany (and not me), lit his and hers and clicked the lighter away, all in one fluid movement – 'been keeping you under wraps.' He exhaled dramatically. 'You must tell me all about it.'

As Tiffany quivered and began a wide-eyed recital of our little history – including, I might add, that I was certain to fail all the mock exams at law school – I sat back and looked at Martin. His complexion was more flushed than ever, his short brown hair really did need washing and he kept pushing his square-shaped glasses up his little nose with one of his pudgy little hands. I tried, and totally failed, to remember what it was that I had first seen in him.

'Sophie, I didn't know you had such interesting friends,' he purred when Tiffany had finished filling him in on our time together and her current success. 'But listen, I know you actresses, never making plans for the future. It just so happens that I'm a fund manager, though. In fact' – as if from nowhere Martin produced a copy of today's *Telegraph* – 'this will show you my credentials!' He whipped it open to the relevant page and Tiffany, the old cow, pretended to be suitably impressed.

'Now look,' Martin continued seriously, fumbling in his jacket pocket and producing a card, 'give me a call some time. We should have lunch and I'll give you some advice about investing for the future. It's a cold world out there you know! And listen, you should give Sophie some advice. She could do with a friend like you to get her out of her current rut.'

'Oh, any time,' said Tiffany, thrusting the card into her handbag and failing not to look triumphant. She avoided my gaze, possibly fearing, and with good reason, that I might clock her one. 'Amazing,' she went on. 'Look, now, it's been just great to meet you and I'll definitely give you a call. God,' she consulted a small metallic watch that, minute as it was, still looked far too heavy on her tiny wrist, 'we're really, really late.' Her two friends leapt up and began pulling on tweed jackets and muttering farewells.

'Amazing,' said Tiffany again, turning round and kissing Martin on both cheeks – ever the gentleman he had leaped up for the group's departure and could hardly control his joy that she was even shorter than he was – and then turning to me. I extremely reluctantly started double pecking activity myself, and was rewarded with a mouthful of hair. Tiffany never kissed women: rather she just proffered a cheek and rather made you feel as if the whole thing was a bit of an honour. 'Look Sophie, give me a call. We must meet up. I'm still in Kensington Park Road and we should do a catching-up session. Oh, and it would be great if that friend of yours, what's her name, came too?'

'Penny,' I said through gritted teeth. Frankly I would rather have swum the Atlantic naked than see Tiffany again in a hurry, and I had a funny feeling Tiffany was the last person with whom Penelope would have wanted to share her little bit of news.

'Ya, Penny,' said Tiffany dismissively. 'OK, look. It's been great.' The blonds grunted in unison. 'Call me. *Ciao.*'

The trio moved off. 'What a charming girl,' said Martin, making a great play of swirling his red wine round in the glass, sniffing at it and then taking a gulp. 'Bit sharp, but what can you expect,' he went on.

'Really, Sophie, I didn't know you had such nice friends. I mean Penny is all right in her way, but Tiffany did you say her name was? She's delightful.'

'Yes and I'm sure that she'll be on the phone to you any minute now,' I said bitterly and truthfully (Tiffany would have had to have a major personality transplant if she were to miss an opportunity for one-upmanship like this). 'Anyway, what on earth are you doing here?'

'Well, darling, I told you, I just can't keep away from my little ray of sunshine,' said Martin. 'Come on, darling, why don't we' – he shot me a hot look – 'slip away now. I want to ravage you now, my darling. Wouldn't you like that, my pretty one?'

A few weeks ago, even a few days ago, the answer might have been yes. Part of Martin's appeal had been not only that he was older and more sophisticated than me, but that he was always suggesting amorous encounters at inappropriate moments. At the time I considered this to be the sign of a passionate nature: I was now beginning to suspect that it was so he could keep his evenings free for his many other women friends. And this 'ravage' business was beginning to drive me up the wall: I wanted to shout, 'ravish, you silly oaf! It's ravish, not ravage!' All a sign that love really had died, but wimp that I was, all I said was, 'You know I can't, Martin. I'm supposed to be meeting Penny.'

'Don't be such a spoilsport,' murmured Martin. 'You know what I thought we could do? We could go to your office and' – he re-cocked his eyebrow – 'take it from there. You have a key, don't you? We could let ourselves in and', his voice dropped to a whisper, 'no-one would ever know.'

I did indeed have a key, as I was required to open the office in the morning if Mr van Trocken was not around, but if there was one location in the world that would have put me off the erotic arts, that was it. 'You must be joking,' I said.

'Darling,' said Martin, his tone somehow becoming a touch harsher, 'I'd really like to go there *now*.'

'Well, I wouldn't,' I protested. 'I have to spend the whole bloody day there, I certainly don't want to spend my nights there as well.'

'Look, darling,' said Martin, his tone harsher still, 'I was thinking this would be a good opportunity for us to be together. But to be honest, I must go there tonight anyway. I left something in the office when I saw you earlier, and I need to get it back now. Now if you don't want to come with me, just give me your key, and I'll bring it back later.'

I was feeling taken aback to put it mildly: although we had had frequent rows in the past, I had never heard Martin use this tone before. It was, however, nothing to the tone that Mr van Trocken would use if he found that I'd let someone in the office out of hours. 'What did you leave?' I asked reluctantly.

'Oh, nothing important, just a few papers that I need for meetings tomorrow,' said Martin rather coldly. 'Now come on, Sophie, this is getting tiresome.'

I had been on the verge of giving in, but the tone rankled. 'You know I can't, I'd be fired,' I said firmly. 'You can collect them first thing in the morning.'

'No-one would know,' said Martin. 'Look, Sophie, stop pissing around and give me that key.'

Do you know, I was beginning to feel quite nervous. Gone was the bonhomie, the suavity, the flirtatiousness – even his eyes had stopped twinkling. Instead, there was a black look of absolute fury. 'I said, give me that bloody key,' he repeated.

Penny – where was she, bloody woman – had told me truculence was one of my failings: in this case, it leapt to my rescue. 'No, I bloody won't,' I said. 'And how dare you talk to me like that.'

'You?' repeated Martin. 'You? Just who do you think you are? Some small-town receptionist from the sticks, and you think—' I think he must have suddenly realized what he was saying, as he pulled himself together in about one second. 'I'm sorry, my lovely one,' he said hastily, his tone softening massively. 'I didn't mean it, you know that. But darling, you know how much pressure I'm under at work. Now, my little angel, don't be such a tease. Give me the key, darling, and I'll have it back in no time, and you know what? I think I'll be paying a little visit to Cartier tomorrow to buy a gorgeous present for my gorgeous girl.'

It was too late, though. I had not forgotten that black look of fury on his face, and all the mention of Cartier did was to remind me of his behaviour towards Tiffany. 'I'm not going to and that is that,' I said firmly, and who knows where it would have ended up were it not for the appearance of two further players in our little drama. I didn't see them at first: all I was aware of was that Martin had suddenly dropped his briefcase and gone white. 'You!' he said.

9

I turned round hastily to discover the cause of the commotion, and was not even remotely surprised to find Martin addressing an extremely pretty and slim girl. She had shoulder length blond hair, lips that really were in the shape of a heart, the old cow, and dark blue eyes. Probably one of his exes, I thought sourly, before coming out with a 'You!' myself, for standing behind her was Penny, looking even more dashing than usual.

'What in God's name are you doing here?' demanded Martin, and after a second, as the mists of confusion thickened considerably, I realized he was still addressing the blonde and not Penny. The latter, incidentally, was regarding him with a very black look indeed.

'Well, why shouldn't I be?' demanded the blonde in a slightly Scottish burr, glaring at Martin. 'I've just moved back from the States and I've come to meet ma wee friend's friend here, and I assume it must be you.' She turned to me at this point and extended a paw. 'Charlotte McPherson,' she said.

'Sophie Brackenbury,' I said, shaking her hand. 'Wotcha, Penny.' Penny leaned towards me and did a bit of double pecking and then, regarding Martin with increased distaste, threaded her way through the chairs to the opposite side of the table and sat down. Charlotte followed suit. Martin, to my intense annoyance, sat back down as well. Typical of him to attempt to bugger off when we were alone and then remain in situ when I wanted a private chat with someone else or, in this case, two someone elses.

'Well, well, well,' he continued, gazing at Charlotte. 'This is a surprise. I haven't seen you since, oh when was it?'

'July two years ago, as well you know,' said Charlotte coolly. 'I didn't know you numbered Martin amongst your friends, Penny.'

'I don't, he's with Soph,' said Penelope bluntly – in fact, rather more bluntly than was wise, considering she and Martin worked in the same firm and he was senior to her – before casting a rainbow of diamond-inspired colours across the room as she reached up to relieve the waiter of a bottle of champagne and three glasses. She'd obviously ordered them on the way in. 'We need another glass,' she added to the waiter rather reluctantly.

'Oh no, I mustn't stay,' said Martin who, nonetheless, showed absolutely no signs of moving. He was still staring at Charlotte. 'You're looking well. And who's the lucky woman in your life at the moment?'

Charlotte hesitated, but Penny, as ever, rushed in where angels feared to tread. 'I am, actually,' she said, taking another glass from the waiter, who had reappeared, and splashing more champagne in to it. 'We met a few days ago, and we're very happy together, right Charlotte?'

'Oh, yes,' said Charlotte, in a rather strained voice. 'Yes very.'

'You?' demanded Martin, turning to Penny and looking even more taken aback than I had been when confronted with the news. '*You?* But what about—'

'Yes, yes, yes,' said Penny hastily. 'Charlie knows all about that, but I've turned over a new leaf, haven't I, Sophie? I was telling you so earlier.'

'Uh yes,' I said, attempting and failing to keep up with events. My main emotion, if truth be told, was actually one of faint pleasure. Not that I had ever felt threatened by the allegedly numerous exes in Martin's life, of course, but meeting this one and learning that we were, in fact, in a totally different ball game, was not going down badly at all.

Martin's reaction, however, was not quite what I'd expected. 'And does Penny know?' he asked calmly, turning again to Charlotte.

'No,' said Charlotte. 'And do you?' she continued, turning to me.

'Know what?' I said blankly and slightly irritably. This tendency of people to behave as if they were actually barking mad when they were around me was really beginning to get on my nerves.

Charlotte sighed and looked at Martin. 'Well, I didn't think it was that important,' said Martin coldly. 'It certainly doesn't matter to you anymore.'

'Will someone tell me what the hell you two are talking about?' Penny butted in rudely. 'I mean, I don't want to sound impolite, but two of us seem to be at a disadvantage in this conversation.' I was rather pleased at Penny's interruption here: the conversation was definitely getting a bit abstruse for me. And on top of that, I wanted to find out how Charlotte had gone from being Martin's ex to Penny's current. Something didn't seem to be adding up here.

'Well go on then,' said Martin to Charlotte. 'You tell them.'

'How long have you two been together?' enquired Charlotte, turning to me.

'About six months, I think,' I said. 'Why?'

Charlotte didn't answer and instead turned to Martin. 'You two have been together longer and anyway I've only seen Penny a few times so I haven't had a chance to explain yet,' she said. 'But you two are different. Six months means a steady relationship.'

'Listen,' said Penny heatedly, rising to her feet and drawing herself up to her full height of five feet and two inches, 'will someone please tell me what is going on?' She sat down again and glared at Martin. I did, too, partly to be supportive, partly because I was getting increasingly fed up, and partly because I enjoyed having the chance to glare at Martin.

'Go on then,' said Charlotte. 'Tell them.'

Martin cleared his throat and looked at me. 'Well, you see the thing is,' he began. 'I mean, it's not very easy to tell you this Sophie, but I've been meaning to for some time and, well, the thing is, I mean, I really hope you don't mind and there's honestly nothing to mind about, but you see, well we, I mean Charlotte and I, well the thing is, um, actually—'

'Oh, for Heaven's sakes,' said Charlotte irritably. 'We're married.'

Well you could have knocked me down with a feather, and the same goes not only for Penny, but also for the barman, who was lurking nearby and pretending to pick up glasses at the next table. 'Married!' I burst out.

'Married!' echoed Penny.

'Married?' demanded the barman, abandoning all pretence at doing his job. 'You? Married to a lovely bird like that?'

He got such an array of glares that he retreated hastily, but his interjection had given Martin a moment to regain his composure. 'Well, yes, married in the sense that we haven't actually got divorced yet,' he began.

'I would have thought that would have described most marriages,' said Penelope coolly. She was twisting her diamonds, always a sign that trouble was in the offing.

'Well, yes, but I mean no,' said Martin. 'I mean we're married in name only, we separated years ago, when we both lived in New York.'

I was only just beginning to get to grips with this one. I mean, I knew Martin was unreliable, and I knew he'd had plenty of girlfriends, but I didn't actually know any of his set as he'd never introduced me to them. In fact, the only person I knew who knew him, apart from other friends of mine who he'd met, was Penny. 'Married?' I repeated again incredulously. 'You're married?'

'Yes but I told you, we're not really,' said Martin irritably. 'We haven't even spoken for years, and it's just that neither of us have had the time to get divorced.'

'Oh right, yeah, meetings, meetings, meetings,' I said. 'Why I find I'm so busy myself that I scarcely have time to put my make-up on of a morning, let alone get divorced when I've got the odd free lunch hour and of course, I've never even got time to mention past or present spouses to my current girl-friend because I really wouldn't have thought they'd be interested. I know just how you feel.'

The rest of the quartet ignored my little attempt at irony. 'Why didn't you tell me you were married to someone in the same firm I work for?' enquired Penny, calmly taking another sip of champagne, and fixing Charlotte with a beady eye. I noticed with respect that despite the drama, her scarlet woman lipstick remained unsmudged. 'It's the sort of thing I thought might have come up in the conversation.'

'She doesn't know I work there,' said Martin patiently. 'I only moved there a year ago myself, and as a matter of fact, I was still labouring under the happy delusion that Charlotte was in the States.'

'Happy, was it?' enquired Charlotte, who seemed to have a temper on her to match Penny's. 'Well believe me, sonny boy, happiness is just going to be a distant memory if you start behaving again like you did last time.'

'What did you do?' I enquired of Martin, but as usual, I was drowned out by the ensuing chorus.

'Me behaving?' protested Martin. 'So it was my fault, was it? I mean I'm not the one who ran off with another woman, well OK, I did, but only after you'd done so first and you say it's my fault?'

'Honestly, Martin, I can believe it. I mean, you're so difficult in the office I bet you're a nightmare to live with,' said Penny bluntly, making yet another ill-advised contribution to the conversation. 'But I never thought you'd be a member of the AA.'

'AA?' demanded Martin, momentarily nonplussed.

'Ageing adulterers,' said Penny smugly. 'I'm compiling a list for when I publish my memoirs, one day.'

Martin glared at her and opened his mouth to make

a suitably cutting rejoinder, but was drowned out by Charlotte, who had regained centre stage. 'I was bisexual until I met you, Martin Silverspoon,' she hissed. 'It was you that turned me totally to women. Ma mother always told me to stay away from wee men and very good advice it was too.'

'Really? So did mine,' I said, fascinated to learn that Charlotte and I had so much in common. Luckily no-one heard me.

'I am not wee!' insisted Martin jumping to his feet, a move which, unfortunately, rather belied the point he was making.

Charlotte ignored this. 'And another thing, Martin Silverspoon,' she continued, rising to her feet and towering over him, 'it's one thing to go off having affairs, but with ma bridesmaid? The day before the wedding?'

'Well how was I to know you and she were still an item,' protested Martin. 'I thought it had ended months before. Now look darling' – this was to me – 'you mustn't listen to any of this. It was all a long time ago.'

'Penny's wee friend should be warned, old habits die hard,' said Charlotte firmly. 'Which reminds me, what about the preacher? Don't try to tell me there was nothing going on there.'

'The *preacher*?' I protested, finally managing to make myself heard. 'Martin, don't tell me that you, uh, have friends of both sexes too.'

'Of course I don't, it was a female preacher – not that I'm saying that anything went on there,' added Martin hastily. 'I can't help it if the poor woman threw herself at me. She'd obviously never met anyone as cosmopolitan as me before, poor child. I was just trying to be kind.'

Penny and I looked at each other open-mouthed. Martin obviously had an altogether jollier background than either of us had realized before. It put Penny's attempts to raise the parental eyebrows quite into the shade.

The same thought had obviously occurred to Martin, along with the realization that the only way to stop this flow of reminiscence was to skedaddle, which he duly prepared to do. 'Well, I mustn't sit around chatting all night,' he said cheerily, picking up his briefcase. 'Lovely to bump in to you again, Charlotte, we must do lunch. Now look, Sophie darling, I really must rush. We'll talk about this tomorrow, yah? Lots of love.' He darted off.

'My word,' said Penny after a moment. 'There was I, thinking we'd all have a nice little chat, and I hear a story that would fit rather neatly in to the latter excesses of the decline of the Roman empire. Is it something they put in the water over there?'

'Och, it wasn't really that bad,' said Charlotte sitting down again and patting Penny's hand. 'We met in New York when we were both working there about five years ago. It was just a bit of a shock to bump in to Martin like that, and you know how it is when you still have an unfinished history with someone.'

'Unfinished how exactly?' I enquired.

'Unfinished since we haven't divorced yet,' said Charlotte reassuringly. 'This was all a long time ago. It was a bit of a whirlwind romance, you see, I'd just gone out there and I didn't know anyone, so after we got chatting in a bar, it sort of gathered speed from

111

there. We were only together for a few months in all. He's ma ex in all but name. But, er, Penny, were you quite wise to talk to the wee man in the way you did? I can't vouch for him now, of course, but in the past he was a wee horror when he thought people were being rude and you, er . . .' She trailed off.

'Oh, don't worry about him,' said Penny calmly. 'I can deal with him. Which reminds me, bugger, bugger, bugger, I should have told him he's the world's most wanted man as far as Haverstock and Weybridge are concerned.'

'Oh, really, why?' asked Charlotte rather sharply.

Penny hesitated. I think that she had already been regretting mentioning the Molehill Magazines row to me, as it was all supposed to be hush-hush company business, and I got the distinct impression she felt that Martin's estranged wife was not absolutely the best person in the world to tell. She hadn't known Charlotte that long, after all. 'Oh, just little things, like the fact that he's never around, for a start,' she said after a moment, tucking a wisp of stray black ebony into her chignon. 'They call him the invisible man in the office, you know.'

'Och, that rings a few bells,' said Charlotte, returning to good humour. 'He always thought he was a wee bit too grand to work the same hours as ordinary mortals. You know, there are quite a few things more I should tell you about him, Sophie.'

'Like what?' I asked resignedly. If the fates were trying to tell me anything through the course of the events of the last few days, I felt I was beginning to get the message.

'Well,' began Charlotte, lowering her voice confidentially, 'he—'

'Let's talk on the way out,' interrupted Penny. 'Come on you two, I'm starving. I booked a table at The Sugar Club for nine, I just hope they haven't given it away yet. We're terribly late and we can find out about Martin's murky past then.' She grabbed her Prada handbag and skedaddled. Charlotte raced after her, leaving me to gather my belongings. A moment later my attention was caught by the barman, who was hovering round the adjacent tables and collecting yet more glasses. 'That your bloke, was it?' he enquired, fascinated.

'Yes,' I said sadly.

The barman paused for a moment and gave me an appraising look. 'You know, nice girl like you, you could do much better than him,' he said. 'You just remember Monday. Or was it Tuesday?'

'Are you working Tuesday?' I enquired.

'Nah, it's me night off, innit,' explained the barman.

'Monday then,' I said, dragging on my coat. 'Might see you then. Tara.' I made for the door.

10

It was another beautiful day. The cold nip in the air was making its presence increasingly felt, but the sun was streaming in through the smeary windows behind my desk and all was well with the world. Or rather, all was well with the world with the major exception of the bit of the world that was inhabited by van Trocken and Co.

Even more than usual, I was at an absolute loss to work out what on earth was going on. The morning had started as usual: I had breakfasted in our large sunny sitting-room with Little Ant and Albert, my cat, who was completely furious with me. Despite the fact that he was a neutered tabby of dubious parentage, no-one could play the role of outraged aristocrat like Albert: he had refused point blank to be petted by me when I staggered in at God knows what hour last night, and he was still being extremely standoffish this morning.

It had been a bit of a heavy session, if truth be told, what with all the tales Charlotte had to tell about Martin – which were actually just amusing little anecdotes about his frequent tendency to show off – to say nothing of a rather extended conversation about changing the nature of one's sexuality in one's mid-twenties, a very serious discussion about which I could remember precisely nothing. In fact, the main reminder of last night was a dull throbbing feeling around the temples. My resolution to have only one hangover a week would have to be put off until tomorrow.

Usually these breakfast-time discussions put me in a good mood for the rest of the day, even if it was to be spent in the offices of van Trocken and Co. Not only did I get on very well with Little Ant, but I loved his flat, especially this room. On the west side of Edwardes Square, it had windows looking out onto the square itself, with enormous deep gold velvet curtains cascading down onto the wooden floor. You could scarcely see the floor, however, as Little Ant had covered it with battered antique rugs he had picked up all over the world. White painted book-shelves were everywhere, absolutely crammed with everything from cheap airport thrillers to learned discourses on architecture. Little Ant's mother was Russian, and he spoke a smattering as well, which meant there were also volumes of Tolstoy, Dostoevsky and Gogol in the original, as well as shelves full of books about art, Victorian novels and Elizabethan poetry, which Little Ant absolutely adored.

Photographs and mementoes stood in front of the books and on the mantelpiece of his great stone fire-place, Little Ant's pride and joy, which had two great lions carved out on either side. The little remaining wall space was filled with pictures – oils, line draw-ings, watercolours, you name it – while the room was filled with great big squashy sofas and chairs, a large nineteenth-century globe and a huge round mahogany table, at which we were sitting, and which had been the scene of innumerable chaotic dinner parties in the past.

Little Ant, however, was being even more unfriendly than Albert. Normally the most jovial of flatmates, he had listened in cold and unsympathetic silence as I told him that I was worried Tiffany was about to make a play for Martin, who, incidentally, had a wife. 'Oh, for Heaven's sakes, just finish with the bloody man,' he snapped at the end of my tale, wandering over to a little mahogany sidetable set against the light gold walls and beginning to mop up some water. I realized with a thrill of horror that I must have knocked over a vase on the table when I'd blundered in last night: there were flowers all over the floor.

'I mean what do you expect if you go out with a little jerk like him? And at least you can start alliterating him the way you do all your other boyfriends,' he continued. 'Married Martin. And this table is going to need revarnishing.'

'I'm sorry,' I said looking down, 'I'll pay for it. And you don't need to be quite so horrible, I didn't know he was married, you know. It's a bit of a shock to me too.'

Little Ant's mood softened considerably. 'I'm sorry too,' he said, wandering over and ruffling my hair for a second, 'I know you didn't. And don't be silly, you can't possibly afford to pay for that. Honestly, Sophie, you are hopeless, you need a good man to look after you.'

'So I've just been saying,' I muttered, picking at my floaty floral blouse. It was a high-street version of

Dolce & Gabbana, which I had bought to celebrate my last paycheck, and which, even if it was just high street, I couldn't afford. I had teamed it with a pair of brown trousers which I didn't really like wearing as I'd bought them over six months ago, and a pair of brown suede boots. Martin had given them to me last month, to make up for the fact that he had been incommunicado for the previous week, and had refused point blank to tell me where he was. I shuddered at the recollection, reached out to stroke Albert who, having finally forgiven me, had just jumped on to the table in a gesture of solidarity, and knocked over Little Ant's mug of coffee.

'Come on,' said Little Ant, as I squawked, leapt up and began hastily mopping it up with the nearest piece of cloth to hand, 'I'll drive you to work. It's very sweet of you to clean up, Sophie, but that is my best shirt, you know.'

It was jolly lucky he did give me a lift: I was thirty seconds away from being late as the soft top dark blue BMW screeched to a halt outside my office, thirty seconds that were sure to be deducted from my salary by Mr van Trocken if he was already in situ. The Gods were on my side, though: I fell out of the car, waved goodbye to Little Ant, who yelled, 'Don't forget tonight!' before zooming off, raced up the steps and charged to my desk, trying not to pant.

It was some minutes before my boss stormed in with a face like thunder, which gave me a chance to swallow my morning aspirin and lie on the time sheet – 8.56 – which he didn't even glance at as he marched into his office. 'What the hell is this bloody recipe doing on my desk?' I heard him demand, presumably picking up yesterday's message from Edwin. 'Sophie, get your ass in here!'

This is really no way to live my life, I thought, grabbing a pencil and paper, and whizzing up the stairs. Mr van Trocken was sitting on his leather throne, lighting a cigar and resting his feet on a pile of as yet unopened newspapers on his desk. He was sporting, I realized with a thrill of horror, a new pair of red leather trousers.

'Tasks for the day,' bellowed my employer, choking slightly on the cigar smoke, and preparing to issue commands. Excessive proprietorial interference in the magazine was not a concept that unduly worried my boss. 'Number one: call Petrushka and tell her I'm hosting a small soirée at my house two weeks from today, and I expect her to be there. We've got some prospective advertisers coming along, and she's bound to get pissed and suck up to at least four of them, which should help sell a few pages. No, don't write that bit down, you idiot girl! Just tell her I want her to be there, and write out these invitations. Here's the guest list.' He shoved a piece of paper at me.

'Number two: we're now planning the seafood issue. Tell Jim to set up a photo shoot for the cover based on Venus rising from the waves. Apricot Bellissimo will be the model' – (this was typical of Mr van Trocken, getting his latest girlfriend on the cover of the mag) – 'and I want a bloody supermarket at her feet! Got that?'

'Er, you mean a building?' I enquired. This was also typical of Mr van Trocken – getting me to relay his instructions to other staff so that the recipient couldn't argue with him, and he could blame me if it all went wrong – but even I was finding it difficult to envisage Apricot and Tesco on the same front cover.

'No, you idiot girl, I mean food!' roared Mr van Trocken. 'I want oysters, I want crabs, I want mussels, I want anything that has a shell and lives in the bloody ocean, and I want them gathered at her feet! I said, it's the bloody seafood issue!'

'Oh, right,' I said truculently.

'And then,' said Mr van Trocken, adopting the particularly silky tone he used when trying to pull the wool over anyone's eyes, 'I am going to do you a great honour, Sophie. I am going to allow you to be involved in the running of our great magazine.'

'Oh, gosh,' I exclaimed in delight. 'You mean you want me to write something?'

'Don't be ridiculous,' snorted Mr van Trocken. 'We have professionals to do that sort of thing. No, Sophie, I am going to allow you to correct the page proofs.'

'Oh really?' I asked, trying to look alert and responsible. 'And what do they prove?'

'They don't prove anything, you idiot girl!' yelled Mr van Trocken. 'What I mean is that I want you to proofread final drafts of the pages before they go to the printers! Ye Gods, how long have you been working here now? They're lying over there. You may go now, I wish to read the papers. Shut the door behind you.'

Smarting, I picked up a pile of page proofs – well, how was I supposed to know what they were – and marched back down to my desk, slamming the door behind me as hard as I dared. A moment later Sam and Henry appeared together, today sporting matching new dark red Doc Martens. They both ignored my mumbled greetings, looked me up and down and disappeared upstairs. Jim came in a few minutes later with a black look on her face and black Doc Martens on her feet. She similarly ignored my good wishes, received the Venus rising from the sea instructions with exceptionally bad grace and stomped upstairs. A moment later the sounds of gentle weeping began again.

Oh, sod the lot of them, I thought, and shut my eyes. I really had been impressed by Little Ant's car – a new one, to go with his new job. 'They're revving up for the start of this year's Morocco' – or was it Monaco? – 'Grand Prix,' said the announcer. 'Newcomer Sophie Brackenbury, driving the latest in technology from the Ferrari workshops, is looking to give the other contestants the race of their lives.' I settled into my seat, with my faithful mechanic hovering over me. 'Wheels?' I said. 'Sorted,' said he. 'Engine?' I said. 'Sorted,' said he. I picked up my helmet and just before I put it on, I blew a kiss to a tall, dark and handsome type who looked very much like the chap from the night before, and who was watching from the grandstand. The crowd roared.

Then I – I shot out of my chair as there was a sharp bang, which I first took to be my car backfiring, and then realized was the sound of Mr van Trocken's study door opening, followed shortly by Mr van Trocken himself, who was carrying his black leather coat under one arm. The red of his trousers loomed bright, but it was as nothing compared to the red of his complexion. I had worked here long enough to know when a storm was brewing, and let's just say this: it was time to invest in a brand new brolly.

Mr van Trocken marched down to my desk, and slammed down a copy of the *Daily Telegraph*. As I said before, he was surprisingly indiscreet in front of members of staff. 'Traitors!' he roared after a moment of breathing deeply. As you might have gathered by now, self-control was not Mr van Trocken's forte. 'Traitors! My wife, my useless employees, and now the gutless, spineless, legless creatures you English choose to rule over you!' I was distracted for one second by trying to imagine such a being, but without success.

'I have done everything for this country!' continued Mr van Trocken at some volume. 'I have given you the benefit of my wisdom, my expertise and my presence in your great city, and this is how I'm repaid! I will sue the lot of you! I, Vladimir van Trocken, will not be treated like this!' He banged my desk so hard that the whole building shook.

It would not have taken a genius to work out that Mr van Trocken was feeling a little put out, and so, unwisely, I attempted to sympathize. 'Um, what's wrong, Mr van Trocken?' I asked.

Very definitely the wrong question. 'What's wrong? *What's wrong?*' shrieked my employer. 'I'll tell you what's wrong, Sophie! First that fool of a wife of mine has me chasing up and down the country looking for her, and then she has the gall to ring and tell me just now that she is staying at the Savoy. The Savoy! Spending money on a suite at that hotel when we have a five-bedroom townhouse and an estate in Wiltshire for her to go to!' (I know that sounded a bit like estate agent speak, but Mr van Trocken was prone to boasting about his properties when he was particularly angry.)

'How dare she! I, Vladimir van Trocken, will make her pay for this! And then' – he paused for breath. I was getting quite worried, I thought he was going to have an apoplectic fit if he went on like this, but Mr

121

van Trocken was without fear for his health. 'And then,' he continued, 'this!' He banged my desk again, or, to be more accurate, the copy of the *Daily Telegraph*. 'How dare they!' he shrieked, louder still. 'How dare they! I am Vladimir van Trocken and I will have' – there was a short pause as he summoned the full might of the van Trocken lung power – 'VENGEANCE!'

With that, he turned on his heel and stalked off down the hall as the word bounced off the walls and rolled up and down the office. The very air was throbbing as the door banged behind him. I sat for a moment in stunned silence. Even by van Trocken standards, this was quite a temper tantrum. 'Sophie?' said a trio of voices. 'Are you all right?'

I looked up. Jim, Henry and Sam, the latter with a tear-stained face and clutching a tissue, had appeared at the top of the stairs. This really was quite something: they usually seemed so absorbed in their own little worries, that the behaviour of Mr van Trocken rarely seemed to impinge on their consciousnesses. 'Yes,' I said a little shakily. 'I think so.'

The trio, thus reassured, nodded curtly at me and stomped off upstairs again. My glance fell on the copy of the *Daily Telegraph*, but before I had a chance to look at the offending item in the paper, there was a further piercing yell from outside, of the kind that my bank manager had recently made when I accidentally set foot in my own branch.

I was absolutely certain that it must have something to do with Mr van Trocken, and so didn't dare to bound down to the front door and peer outside, rather, I raced up to his study and attempted to watch the proceedings from the window. Not that I was nosey, of course, but I felt it was my duty to look after the well being of my employer. To my astonishment, Mr van Trocken seemed to be on the verge of murdering a perfectly innocent looking but increasingly enraged tourist. He first clocked the chap, and then grabbed his camera and pulled a reel of film out of it, at which point the tourist began leaping up and down and shouting even louder. I saw Tony laboriously get out of the Rolls, which was parked nearby, and join in. A moment later a mounted policeman appeared and the quartet began yelling at one another.

As entertainment goes, it was certainly a lot more interesting than sitting at my desk and laboriously filling out invitations in my best Gothic script for the little soirée Mr van Trocken was supposed to be hosting in two weeks' time, but at that point the phone began to ring and so I was forced to race back down the stairs. 'Van Trocken and Co.,' I said, snatching up the receiver.

'Where is Vladimir! I must speak to him immediately!' shrieked a voice. The message was familiar enough, and the voice also rang a bell, though I was pretty sure this wasn't Irina, and I hadn't been told about any possible replacement. 'I'm sorry, he's just popped out,' I said, at which point the caller began to sob. 'Just at the moment when we should both be celebrating our triumph, we are undone!' she cried, and at that moment must have gone into a tunnel, for her phone, which was crackling the way that only mobiles do, suddenly went dead. I replaced the receiver and looked at it in astonishment. Never mind, if it was urgent, she was sure to call back. Mr van Trocken's women friends always did.

Taking advantage of this extremely brief lull in the proceedings, I picked up the paper. On the front was a tremendously large picture of a very beautiful woman with blond hair, who looked puzzlingly familiar. 'Last night it was confirmed that Apricot Bellissimo will be taking the lead role in the new BBC drama series *WestEnders*,' said the caption. 'Full story – Page 3.' I looked at the rest of the page. At first I couldn't see anything that could have given rise to such fury, but then I noticed the news-in-brief column. 'Row grows over Tory donation,' it said. 'Last night Labour MPs were accusing the Conservative Party of shielding another Asil Nadir. See Page 5 for full story.'

I practically ripped the paper apart in my haste to get to Page 5. 'There was turmoil in the Conservative Party last night as allegations of fraud emerged over one of its leading benefactors,' I read. 'Just hours after it was announced that Vladimir van Trocken, the Czech entrepreneur and self-made millionaire who runs an extensive import/export business was to donate £1 million to the Tories, it emerged that the Department of Trade and Industry is believed to be investigating the flamboyant tycoon, who also owns the magazine *Food for Thought*. Full details of the investigation have not yet emerged, but it is believed to centre on unusual price movements in the shares of Molehill Magazines.

'And last night, a Molehill Magazines spokesman confirmed that the company had been in talks with Mr van Trocken, regarding the potential purchase of *Food for Thought*. Blue-blooded fund management firm Haverstock and Weybridge last night also confirmed that it had been asked to participate in the investigation. "We are all very shocked, and will be making a further announcement as soon as it is practicable," said chairman Sir Jeremy Haverstock.

'But Cheltenham MP Bob Snoutfoot, Labour Party spokesman for sleaze, was jubilant. "You'd have thought that the Tories would have learned their lesson about getting involved with dubious businessmen after the Asil Nadir affair," he crowed. "I'd love to see how they're going to talk their way out of this one." Mr van Trocken and Conservative Party Treasurer Marcus Aimsworthy were last night unavailable for comment.'

Well you could have knocked me down with a feather. No, you could have knocked me down just by looking at me. Mr van Trocken? Fraud? And, far, far more to the point, Haverstock and Weybridge and Molehill Magazines?

For a moment I was so stunned that I just sat there, frozen. After a moment or two, though, a ringing sound began to penetrate my consciousness, which I eventually realized was the telephone. 'Van Trocken and Co.,' I said automatically.

'I'll tell you Sophie, this is too much!' shouted an extremely familiar voice. 'He's gone too far this time, I don't care whether he is going out with you or not but I'm not taking this lying down. I tell you, I'll make him pay for this if it's the last thing I do!' Penny slammed the phone down. She's not the only one, I thought bemusedly. I was still not thinking straight, but even I had worked out that Haverstock and Weybridge may be talking to the DTI, and that Martin worked for Haverstock and Weybridge. And Haverstock and Weybridge had been looking for Martin. I just couldn't work out why Penny was taking it so personally.

My question was answered about one second later, when the phone rang again. 'Why haven't you called me back?' cried Penny. 'How could you leave me to worry like this? Honestly, Sophie, I'm distraught.'

'You're distraught?' I said. 'You are? How do you think I feel! Not only have I discovered that my boyfriend is married to your girlfriend, but now I gather he might have committed some kind of fraud as well!'

'Fraud is not the only thing that self-satisfied young, or rather, middle-aged and lecherous individual has committed,' said Penny. She was speaking in precise and clipped tones again. 'You can now add slander to the list. Have you spoken to that pathetic imitation of a real man you spend so much of your time with?'

'No,' I said. 'Penny, what on earth is going on?'

'I gather you've seen the papers,' said Penny through gritted teeth.

'Yes.'

'Well, Sir Jeremy is even more anxious to speak to him now than yesterday,' said Penny. 'Of course that *creature*' – she spat the word out – 'hasn't actually turned up here. But what he has done is leave a message on Sir Jeremy's answerphone to the effect that because of the degenerate state of my personal life he doesn't think I should be allowed contact with any of the clients and, furthermore, he harbours doubts about whether I should be permitted to stay on at Haverstock and Weybridge at all.' She burst into tears.

I was terribly shocked, both at the fact of Penny crying, which I had never heard her do before, and at the fact that Martin could be quite this treacherous. It was one thing committing fraud, it was quite another trying to get my best friend kicked out of her job. 'Oh Penny,' I burst out. 'Oh, I'm so sorry. But are you sure? Couldn't he just have made a bitchy remark and it's got blown up out of proportion?'

It was then that I learned the tears were of fury, not upset. 'I'll blow him out of proportion!' cried Penny. 'I'll teach him to mess around with the Tang family! When I've finished with him he's going to regret the day he met me and Michael's back now so he'll be able to help! I'm sorry, Sophie, I know you don't like him, but he is my brother and blood is thicker than water and I'll tell you, there's going to be blood on the carpet, the walls and just about everywhere you could think of when I've finished with him! Moral degenerate, huh? The board of Haverstock and Weybridge doesn't know the meaning of the words but let me tell you, they will do when I've done!' Another Tang family philosophy, incidentally, was first to get incredibly mad, and then to get really well and truly even.

'Look, Penny,' I said, 'are they going to pay any attention if he really is in trouble?'

'He is still a director of the company, and they don't know for sure he has done anything,' said Penny, calming down slightly. 'No-one seems to know quite what has happened. How's your estimable employer, by the way?'

'Very, very angry,' I said. 'And also, mercifully absent. Look, Penny, what are you going to do?'

'Nothing at this exact second,' said Penny, sounding clipped again. 'I will give the matter some consideration. No-one has said anything to me formally, it's just Sir Jeremy's secretary who told me about the message, and they seem to have a few other things on their mind at the moment than talking to me. I will let you know when I've decided. But I'll tell you, Sophie, if that man dares to show his face in here, I won't be responsible for my actions.'

'I know how you feel,' I said with feeling. 'Shall we talk later?'

'Indeed,' said Penny. She hung up. I replaced the receiver and looked thoughtfully at the phone, but before I could think about what to do next, there was a soft scrabbling at the front door. I held my breath and braced myself for the reappearance of my employer, but just as I was about to press the intercom and demand to know who was there, the door swung open. I opened my mouth likewise, shut it and sat very still as the pale and shadowy figure of Barbara van Trocken came slowly in to view.

'Hello, Sophie,' she said.

11

How totally unexpected. I hadn't been so taken aback since I'd gone on a blind date during one of my break-ups with Martin, and the chap concerned, Daniel, had proposed to me after the first half hour. I had referred to him ever since as Desperate Dan, and – come to think of it, Little Ant might have a point about that alliteration business.

Anyway, that was another story. It took me a second, but I finally, mercifully, pulled myself back together properly and leaped up. 'Hello, Mrs van Trocken,' I said. I was quite appalled. I had met her a couple of times before, just after I started working for that monster of a husband of hers, and she was already looking gaunt and unhappy then. Now, however, she looked about a thousand times worse: her clothes, which were well cut and obviously expensive, but of the elegant variety rather than the style sported by Mr van Trocken's mistresses, were absolutely hanging off her, there were great big caverns where her cheeks should have been and black hollows under her deep set grey eyes.

Her brown hair, which was stained with grey and which should have curved round her face down to the level of her chin, hung limply behind her ears. She was trembling slightly, and although she was only in her early forties, she looked about ninety. 'Please sit down,' I babbled on as she reached the top of the hall, caught sight of the portrait of my employer in the guise of Zeus and the two nymphs and shuddered. 'Can I get you a coffee or something?'

'Thank you, Sophie, that would be very nice,' said Mrs van Trocken in a near whisper. She slipped off a grey suede coat, which only emphasized her pallor, to reveal a grey woollen dress underneath, and sat down. I raced up to the little kitchen on the next floor, where luckily the percolator had just produced a fresh pot of coffee, poured some into a mug, splashed in milk and carried it carefully down again, all the while praying that Mr van Trocken would not choose this moment to stage a re-entrance.

Mrs van Trocken stretched out two boney hands – free, I noticed, of wedding and engagement rings, although in her current state they'd probably have fallen off – and took the mug as I got back to the desk. 'It's all right, Sophie, he won't be back for a while,' she said softly, obviously reading my thoughts. 'I don't know what that business with the police was, but I waited till he'd gone to come in. You see, I rang Tony on the car phone after they'd driven off and said I was still at the Savoy, so we have a little while.'

'Oh,' I said. 'Um, how are you?' Not that I was thrown at having my boss's wife turn up out of the blue, of course, but you know how it is, it's difficult to know what to say at times like this.

'Not very well, Sophie,' said Mrs van Trocken. 'Not very well at all. Has he told you I've left him?'

'Er, yes,' I said, looking down. 'I'm really awfully sorry, Mrs van Trocken.'

'Well, I'm not,' said Mrs van Trocken, her voice suddenly sounding rather stronger. 'It's a long overdue move. Oh, and you should call me Barbara, Sophie.' She took a long draught of coffee.

'Yes, Mrs, I mean Barbara,' I said, looking up. 'Thank you.'

Barbara smiled at me, the first time I had ever seen her do so. 'And how about you, Sophie,' she continued. 'Are you happy here?'

'Oh, yes, very,' I said heartily.

Mrs van Trocken snorted gently. 'He doesn't deserve such loyal employees,' she said. 'Or such a loyal wife. Now tell me how he's been treating you.'

'Well, I'm really happy here and really enjoying the job,' I said, deciding now was the time to take the plunge, 'but, you know, I don't think he's really up with it himself. I mean, just yesterday he was saying something about the alphabet, going on about ABC figures! And then there's Petrushka, I just can't understand why he lets her do the job. I mean, she's never here.'

Mrs van Trocken smiled sympathetically. 'Actually, dear, the ABC figures relate to the magazine's circulation,' she said gently. 'And Petrushka is a special case. But he should have told you all this himself, rather than expecting you to know about everything. Now tell me, what did he tell you you were going to do when you started here? Something a little more interesting than this job, I suspect.'

'He said I was going to be a features writer on *Food for Thought*,' I said resentfully. 'And I've got such brilliant ideas, I mean I suggested to him the other day that Jean Pierre van Jones should be our chief book critic, and he didn't even answer!' I was still feeling miffed about this. Jean Pierre, who hailed originally from Birmingham, was one of the celebrity chefs around at the moment, and I thought he would be the perfect bridge between the worlds of literature and cuisine.

'That's a brilliant idea,' said Mrs van Trocken warmly, 'but I think the trouble is, dear, that Jean Pierre can't actually read. I hear that there were terrible problems when he was asked to do a cook book last year, because no-one told him he was actually going to have to write the recipes down, but never mind. I think you have the potential for much better things than this.' She got to her feet. She was slightly hunched up, even when standing, although not from the cold: rather she looked a bit like a long-term invalid. 'Now look, dear, will you come with me to Vladimir's study? I want a witness for what I have to do.'

'Yes, of course,' I said, rather taken aback.

'Thank you, dear,' said Mrs van Trocken. We walked up the stairs, and into the temple of doom. Mrs van Trocken hesitated for a moment, and then went to one of the pictures on the near wall – an abstract portrait of Mr van Trocken, executed in dashes of red, grey and white – which she shoved aside. This turned out not just to be a very understandable piece of art criticism, but a deliberate move as well: there was a safe behind the picture.

'Did you know, Sophie,' said Mrs van Trocken companionably as she began to turn the lock, 'the company doesn't actually belong to Vladimir?'

'No,' I said blankly. 'Who does it belong to then?'

'Me,' said Mrs van Trocken, with a little chuckle. The safe door opened, and she took out a bundle of documents. 'All his companies belong to me,' she went on, shutting the door again. 'All this stuff about a self-made millionaire – he's never made a penny in his life. He was just lucky to find a very rich and very gullible wife, although according to the papers, he does seem to have got himself into a bit of bother now.' She chuckled again. 'You would have thought, wouldn't you Sophie, that even a man with an ego like Vladimir's wouldn't actually parade his mistresses across the newspapers if he happens to be married to his only source of income.'

'To you?' I said blankly. 'But I thought he'd made millions, everyone says so. I thought – I mean, I don't understand. How can he not be rich?'

'Very easily,' said Mrs van Trocken, sitting down on a nearby chair. 'Van Trocken and Co. is a private company, you see, which means that they don't have to make anything like as much information public as they would if it was quoted on the stockmarket. And yes, it is profitable, but there's only one shareholder and you're talking to her. Vladimir didn't build it up from nothing as he always claims: he was running a very small and pretty unsuccessful business when he met me, and it was only by using my capital that he really began to get things going.'

'But how come he didn't make you hand over the ownership?' I asked rather tactlessly.

'Well, he certainly tried,' said Mrs van Trocken, sighing. 'I shouldn't really be telling you this, dear, but I don't suppose it's going to matter now. When we got married, my father was a rather senior figure in the Home Office. Vladimir had been making a nuisance of himself in Britain for a couple of years, once he got out of Czechoslovakia, and he was absolutely desperate to stay in this country. Then we met and got engaged, and Daddy had a quiet word in a few ears, and not only was Vladimir allowed to stay, but was granted British citizenship as well. I'm sure that's why he married me – that and my inheritance, of course.

'Daddy loathed him.' She sighed again. 'But he was a sweet man and was devoted to me, and I was adamant that Vladimir was the man I wanted to marry. I was only fifteen when we first met, you know, our wedding was on my sixteenth birthday. Anyway, Daddy agreed to help us, but on one condition. In return for releasing quite a substantial sum from my trust fund, the ownership of van Trocken and Co. was to be in my name only, and Daddy had a document drawn up that said if ownership ever changed, the company would have to be broken up, sold off and all the proceeds would go directly to me. So Vladimir's always been tied to me, you see.'

'Gosh,' I said. I was totally amazed. 'But he's always seemed so, you know, rich.'

'Oh, he's always been paid a very handsome salary,' said Mrs van Trocken. 'And Vladimir's not stupid, I'm sure he's managed to salt away a very nice nest egg for himself, but unless he was prepared to sacrifice the whole company and make it clear that it all really belonged to me, he had to stick with van Trocken and Co. And it is a big company now, dear, and Vladimir's always been very keen on money, so I don't think he'd have wanted to do that. Of course there's the pride issue as well: I don't think he wanted to destroy the myth that it had all been built up out of nothing.'

'Did you know that *Food for Thought* might be sold?' I asked.

'Oh, yes, Vladimir can't sell company assets without my permission,' said Mrs van Trocken. 'I was so down-hearted by everything, dear, that I didn't really care. But I didn't know about this business with the DTI, and I tell you Sophie, I'm jolly well going to find out what's been going on.'

'And what about that Tory Party donation?' I asked.

'Oh that,' said Mrs van Trocken, stuffing the papers in her handbag and getting up. 'That was typical Vladimir. Making a big announcement to the press without telling me, and then assuming I'd go along with it afterwards. And I must admit, I have done that often enough in the past, but those days are over. I think it's time someone taught Vladimir a lesson.'

'Cool,' I said, deeply impressed. This was more like it, Mrs van Trocken taking on the monster. This was really girl power in action: first my best friend starts sleeping with them and then Mrs van Trocken, although admittedly a long way from being a girl these days, starts throwing what little there was of her weight around.

Mrs van Trocken pulled the picture back across the safe, and we walked back down the stairs together. She really was terribly pale. 'Mrs, I mean Barbara,' I burst out suddenly, 'are you going to be all right? I don't mean to interfere but you're not looking at all well. Shouldn't you see a doctor or something?'

Mrs van Trocken looked at me and smiled again, this time a really wide smile. I could suddenly see she must have been quite beautiful when she was younger. 'You are very, very sweet, Sophie,' she said. 'But I don't need a doctor. What I need is a lawyer, and I'm happy to say that I've got a very good one. I've had enough, Sophie.' She put down her bag and began struggling with her coat. I leaped to help her. 'You know,' she went on after a moment, beginning to do up the buttons, 'all I care about is getting out of this marriage, and I'm about to do it, so you mustn't worry about me. I'm stronger than I look. Now I've got rather a busy day ahead, but I want to have a little glass of champagne to celebrate my impending release from prison this evening. Would you like to join me for a celebratory drink?'

'Oh, I'd love to,' I said, and then stopped, struck by a terrible thought. 'Blow it, I'm supposed to be having dinner with my flatmate.'

'Well, why don't we all have a little drink before dinner and then you and he can go off afterwards?' asked Mrs van Trocken. 'Where are you meeting him?'

'At The Collection,' I said. 'There's a bar there, but it can be a bit of a scrum.'

'I know it,' said Mrs van Trocken, beginning to move off. 'Shall I see you both there at eight?'

'Yes, that would be lovely,' I said. 'Goodbye, I mean, *au revoir*.'

Mrs van Trocken paused at the bottom of the hall. '*Au revoir*, dear,' she said. 'I'll see you later.'

The door closed softly behind her. How on earth did he ever persuade a woman like that to marry him? I wondered, sitting down behind the desk. There really was no accounting for taste. I closed my eyes. 'We are now approaching Planet Gaga,' I informed mission control, as I carefully manoeuvred the space ship in to land. My co-pilot, who looked very much like the tall, dark chap from last night, smiled at me.

'I see signs of life, Houston,' I went on. 'A very strange creature with a grey beard and red leather legs is scuttling on the face of the planet. Houston, we have found life! There is life in outer space, and we've found it here on Planet Gaga!' A rustling sound began, which I at first took to be the space ship's radio acting up, and then realized was someone tapping on the window behind me. 'What on earth?' I said, whirling round.

Well, of all the peculiar ways to make an entrance, even for him. 'What on earth are you doing?' I demanded, as I raised the sash.

Martin, who had been leaning languidly against the outside ledge, hopped in as soon as the window was open. He was not looking remotely his usual suave self: his sparkling white shirt was sporting a few window-sill smudges and there were some chips of paint on his bright red tie. 'Hello, darling,' he said, reaching up to give me a graceful kiss and brushing the dirt off his jacket. None of last night's bad humour was in evidence. 'How's my little angel face this morning?'

'A little bit surprised to see you leaping in through the window,' I said. 'What's wrong with the front door?'

'I'm having a few problems at the moment that I won't bore you with, and so I didn't want anyone to see me coming in,' said Martin smoothly. 'And the gate to the garden was open, so I thought I'd come in this way. I rather enjoyed it, actually, made me feel like a boy again. Now where is it?'

As Martin had been explaining himself, he had been doing something that even I, used to the lunatic behaviour of the inhabitants of Planet Gaga or rather, van Trocken and Co., found odd: he had gone over to the big portrait of Mr van Trocken and the nymphs, and had been running his hands behind the frame. 'Where is it?' he repeated, lifting the picture off the hook and beginning to examine the back.

'Martin, put it back,' I implored. I knew Mr van Trocken was trying to track down his wife, but he had a very nasty habit of turning up when he was least expected, and I didn't even dare think what he'd make of this. 'And what's happening? What was all that stuff in the papers this morning?'

'Where is it!' said Martin, ignoring the question. He whirled round and looked at me. 'Have you got it? Give it to me at once!' he demanded.

I suddenly remembered that last night he said he'd left something in the office, but behind the picture? 'What are you looking for?' I asked.

'The envelope,' said Martin through clenched teeth. 'The envelope that he said he'd leave here. Where is it!'

'I don't know,' I said blankly.

Martin looked wildly around, and then focused on my desk. 'The photograph!' he said. 'Where's it gone!'

'I took it home,' I said. Actually, it was still in my handbag, but I had a strange feeling it might be better not to mention that.

'Home?' asked Martin. 'But you were supposed to leave it here! On your desk!'

I didn't say anything.

'Of course!' said Martin. 'If he hadn't received the – where is he?'

'Who?'

138

'Vladimir! Where's Vladimir?'

'At the Savoy, I think,' I said.

Martin looked dubiously at the front door, and decided to leave by the alternative route. 'I must find him!' he cried, scrambling out of the window. 'I must find Vladimir!' He disappeared from sight.

Vladimir? I thought, shutting the window and sitting down. *Vladimir?* I had no idea they knew one another, Martin rarely mentioned my employer, and only then to sympathize when I was moaning about him, and Mr van Trocken had certainly never mentioned Martin.

What ever was going on, I quite seriously wanted to know about it, and fast. I rummaged in my handbag for the photograph and eased the back off the frame. Inside was a piece of paper. I unfolded it and stared at it in complete horror. It was a note from Martin – to my employer, of all people! Not that I wasn't completely cool and in control at all times, of course, but my hands were shaking so much I could hardly read it. When I eventually did, I saw it ran as follows. 'Vladimir – I've bought the number of Molehill shares that we agreed – I almost went higher, but decided too risky. They should double tomorrow. Please leave the banker's draft as planned and we'll sort out the profit in a day or so. M.'

My first thought was to hide everything. I shoved the bit of paper back inside the frame, closed it up again, and crammed the lot into my handbag. I know it sounds idiotic, but I was honestly worried that I was going to be implicated in whatever it was they had done.

My second thought was to ring Penny and ask her what to do, but before I could do so, the phone rang.

'Van Trocken and Co.,' I said, clearing my throat.

'Hello, darlin',' said a male voice. 'Vladimir around, is he?'

'I'm afraid he's out,' I said. I honestly thought I might be talking to the police. 'May I take a message?'

'Out, is he?' enquired the voice. 'Out wiv one of his ladyfriends, is he?' This was followed by a rather unpleasant noise, that sounded like someone wiping their nose on the back of their hand.

'I'm afraid I am unable to reveal to you Mr van Trocken's whereabouts,' I said self-importantly. 'To whom am I speaking?'

'I bet you are darlin',' said the voice, sniffing unpleasantly. 'Revealed anything else to Vladimir, have ya? Quite a lot of you ladies have done, I hear tell.'

'No, I jolly well haven't,' I said, outraged. 'Who is this?'

'Me name is Melvin Micklemouse, just call me Melv,' said the voice. 'I am a senior investigative journalist at the *News of the World*. Heard of the *News of the World*, have ya?'

'Yes,' I said, feeling rather shocked. Then again, I had been in recent communication with the Treasurer of the Conservative Party, so I suppose the *News of the World* was bound to follow on soon.

'Well, we've been hearing quite a bit about your Vladimir down here,' said Melv, 'and we'd like to have a little chat. He's been quite a busy boy, by all accounts, got women comin' out of his ears, and now he's got all his posh friends in the Tory Party too. I'm sure they'll be very interested to know what your Vladimir's been gettin' up to.'

I wasn't quite sure what to say, I didn't know how

one addressed *News of the World* reporters. 'No comment,' sounded stupid, and anything else was bound to cause trouble. 'I really don't know anything about it,' I said eventually. 'I'm just the welcoming agent and telephone intermediary, although I'm bound to be promoted soon, of course.'

'Are ya, darlin',' said Melv companionably. 'Now look. If your Vladimir comes back to the office, you tell him we'd like a little word, right? I'll give you me number, and just say, I think it would be better if he called. We'll get him one way or the uvver, and it would be easier for him if he came to us. Oh, and mention we know about Buck Palace. Got that, darlin'? Good. I'll be speaking to ya later.' He hung up.

I looked at the piece of paper on which I'd scribbled down the number, and then wrote above it, 'Mr van Trocken – Melvin Micklemouse from the *News of the World* rang. Something about Buckingham Palace. Please call back.' I took the message up the stairs, deposited it on Mr van Trocken's desk, and sat down to mull over the situation. In the past twenty-four hours of what, cigarettes and whisky and wild, wild men aside, had been a fairly conventional existence, the following had happened.

My best friend had come out as a lesbian and was dating another woman. Said woman turns out to be married to my boyfriend, who in turn appears unexpectedly to know my employer. My boyfriend and my employer seem to have got themselves implicated in iffy business dealings, involving the firm where my best friend works. Well that seems to have brought it full circle, I thought, satisfied that I had managed to create a neat pattern out of events, until remembering that Mrs van Trocken wanted me to help her do her husband down, the ghastly Tiffany had crawled out of the woodwork and was chatting up Martin, and I had just met a very dishy stranger about whom I knew absolutely nothing. It would have to be a Venn diagram rather than a circle, I thought fretfully. Did everyone have to make life so complicated? I vaguely wondered if it was all actually a conspiracy to confuse me – and then, having returned to Planet Reality, prepared to call Penny and ask her what I should do.

12

She was in a meeting, of course, Penny was always in meetings when I needed to talk to her. I sat back, looked around me and tried to start making sense of it all. Beside me on the wall Mr van Trocken, as portrayed by Alan the Artist, leered horribly, but outside the sun was shining, birds were singing – everything looked almost normal. I thought perhaps that I should get on with my normal duties, presuming, of course, that the walls of van Trocken and Co. didn't actually start collapsing around me, which I half expected them to do.

I sighed, forced myself to calm down, went down the hall to collect this morning's pile of post, which was still scattered all over the floor, returned to my desk and opened the first letter. I was just supposed to slice the top of the envelope, but I frequently couldn't resist having a quick glance inside. 'Dear Vladimir,' I read. 'I am writing to complain about the very offensive manner of your receptionist. When I rang the other day, it took at least two minutes before she answered the phone, after which she sounded downright annoyed when I asked her to take a message. Then she . . .' There was about another page of this stuff, which I dealt with easily by tossing the lot in the bin.

The next missive smelt of perfume, and was written on very expensive notepaper with very large, curly handwriting. 'Darling Vladimir,' it ran, 'I can't tell you how much I enjoyed our little supper at The Ivy last week – and afterwards was even better! Are you really thinking about running a picture of little old me on the cover of *Food for Thought*? I thought your idea of draping me with winter fruits and nothing else was just fabulous although you know, darling, I think everything about you is just fabulous, too. Can't wait to see my big, bad Vlad again, darling, please, please, please call soon. Love and hugs and kisses and much, much more than that when we meet – Caprice.' I wouldn't have had the courage to do this before, but after that little session with Mrs van Trocken earlier, I knew just where my loyalties lay now: that one went into the bin as well.

There were a couple more love letters, both of which also mentioned the cover of *Food for Thought*, one from a Tara and one from a Tamara, which also ended up in the rubbish. Then there were the usual numbers of invitations – Mr van Trocken had been nothing if not assiduous in cultivating members of the British establishment – a couple of ideas for exciting new features from hopeful writers and, rather to my surprise, several reminders for unpaid invoices. Mr van Trocken was notorious for late payment in his business dealings, but he was usually pretty good where writers were concerned – mainly, I suspected, because the vast majority of them had double, if not triple barrelled surnames and the monster wanted them as much for their social cachet as their literary skills.

I gathered the letters into suitable piles, took them into the study and went back to my desk. There was usually a second round of letters that arrived in the mornings as a lot of post went to the main offices of van Trocken and Co. in Poland Street, and the urgent or important bits were biked round, but it hadn't appeared yet. I wondered what to do next. There was a huge pile of faxes building up on the machine beside me, most of which were articles for future editions of the magazine, and which it was my job to type into the system, but I had decided to adopt a work to rule philosophy, and anyway, I couldn't be bothered to look at them just yet. There were also those pages to be proofread, and I felt even less keen to attend to that. I was also feeling increasingly anxious about the contents of my handbag, but a second call to Penny just elicited the information that she was still in a meeting. I rang home but Little Ant wasn't in: I left a message for him to call as soon as possible, and then settled back into my chair.

I wonder what it's like to be a detective in the Fraud Squad, I thought dreamily. I shut my eyes, pulled my trench coat around me and strode into the dark, murky bar, deep in the heart of Soho, which was said to be the headquarters of one of the most notorious criminals of our time. It was the kind of place where even a cockroach would complain about the dirt and I knew I stood out like a condom in a convent. 'Slug of whisky and make it snappy,' I said in a suitably husky voice to the barman.

He gave me a glance. 'Bit blond to be in here on

your own, aren't you,' he rasped. 'Look, kid, I'm telling you this so's others don't have to. Stay out of this place kid, you're dealing with a desperate man.'

'I said I wanted a slug of whisky,' I rasped back, 'and I want it now. There's nothing that can frighten Sophie Brackenbury, not after all the, er,' I thought hard, 'frauds I've been after in my time.' I dug deep in my trench-coat pocket for reassurance and yes, it was a gun, and I wasn't just pleased to see him. 'And tell The Roach that I'm here,' I went on. 'There's unfinished business between us and no-one leaves business unfinished with Sophie Brackenbury.'

The barman shrugged. 'Have it your way, kid,' he said, reaching under the bar, producing a chipped glass and filling it half full with amber nectar. 'But don't say's I didn't warn you.'

I downed the liquid in one, and turned around. At the back of the bar was a staircase, and at the top of the stairs, beside the cracked windows, you could just see an absolutely enormous figure in red leather trousers lurking in the shadows. 'So Vladimir,' I said quietly, 'or should I say, The Roach, we meet again. I've been looking for you for a long time now, and . . .' I nearly went through the roof as the sound of a pistol shot rang in my ears, which I suddenly realized was the phone ringing. 'Van Trocken and Co.,' I snapped.

'Hi, kiddo,' said a voice. 'It's taken me quite a while to track you down, but I finally got hold of your flatmate this morning and he said I could get you here.'

I looked at the phone blankly. For a second I thought it was the bartender in the sleazy dive. 'Who is this?' I demanded.

'Just as well you didn't recognize me,' said the voice quietly, 'it'll make it all the easier to say what I have to say. It's Bernard. Bernard Dickson, although I can't believe that even you could have forgotten all about Us, Sophie. You were a really great girl – and I don't want to hurt you.'

What on earth was Bearded Bernie doing ringing after all this time? As I think I mentioned, he was my first London boyfriend but there had been, shall we say, rather a lot of water under the bridge since then and if there was one thing I could do without today, it was lecherous lecturers staging a reappearance. 'Of course I remember you. What's up?' I demanded.

'Well, Sophie,' said Bernard self-importantly, 'I have a lot of respect for you and for all my girlfriends, and so I just wanted to tell you all myself rather than having you hear about it from a third person. I'm getting married, Sophie. I hope you understand, and I hope you don't suffer too much. I could never have married you, Sophie, you were too young and imma- ture and frankly you're a lousy cook, but I just want you to know I'll always value you as a person. Don't despair, Sophie. There's someone out there for you too, you know.'

I opened my mouth and shut it again. Bernard had never had a big problem in the insecurity stakes, but to ring after all this time and – 'Have you been drinking?' I asked.

'Sophie, don't say that!' cried Bernard. 'Don't go into denial! Accept the fact that I am lost to you for ever and cry in the wilderness and express love and suffering and humility and pain and dig deep in to the heart of your very soul and say one day, maybe not for years or even decades, but one day you will recover and one day – perhaps – you will learn to love again. For God's sake, Sophie, don't let me down now! I need to know you can be strong and be there for me and spare some strength for yourself and—'

'Who on earth are you getting married to?' I enquired, lighting a cigarette and inhaling deeply. I knew I wasn't supposed to but frankly, that didn't seem to matter now.

'Oh, an ex-student,' said Bernard vaguely. 'Nice girl. Now look, Sophie, I want to be there with you now, I want to physically suck out the anguish from your body, I want to take you as a lump of clay and shape you into strength and resolve and courage and valour and above all, Sophie, above all, I don't want you to be bitter. Fancy a drink tonight?'

'*What?*' I demanded.

'A drink,' said Bernard with a self-conscious laugh. 'No reason we shouldn't, I mean I'm not married yet, and anyway, even when I am, Cordelia and I have an understanding so there's no reason I can't see a few of my old friends.'

'No bloody way,' I said, exhaling again.

'Why not?' asked Bernard, sounding hurt.

'Because you're a prat,' I said spitefully, giving vent to feelings that I had felt since our break-up, and finally had the chance to share with my ex. 'And a bearded prat at that. And while we're on the subject I'm not suffering, I just feel deeply sorry for Mrs Bernie-to-be. Anyway, I wouldn't want to see you even if you were as free as a bird. Getting a bit bored with just seeing one person all the time, are you?'

'Of course not,' protested Bernard. 'I just like to share my feelings and experiences and values with so many people, and just empathize and communicate and hey, just hang out. And I know why you're talking to me like that, Sophie. You're just trying to conceal and deny your inner pain.'

'I am sharing my outer disgust and I've got to go,' I said firmly. There was a beep on the line which meant another call was waiting and frankly, although I genuinely couldn't care less about Bearded Bernie any more, I was getting a bit fed up with being reminded of yet another disastrous love affair. Why couldn't I be like normal people and meet someone nice?

'Sophie, you can't go, not like that,' said Bernard. 'There's so much I have to say and be and feel and—'

'Bernard, I'm sorry, I've really got to go,' I said irritably. 'I'm very happy for you. Have a good life.' I clicked the receiver and the phone rang again immediately. 'Van Trocken and Co.,' I said.

'Ah, Sophie,' said Penny. She was sounding a lot calmer now. 'I gather you rang.'

'Yes, look, I have to talk to you urgently,' I said.

'I'm terribly sorry, Sophie, but I can't now,' said Penny firmly. 'The place is in pandemonium, although I am happy to say that Sir Jeremy has apologized to me personally for Martin's message. No sign of the little chap, I suppose?'

'Yes, that's what I must talk to you about,' I said. 'Look, Penny, I think Martin's trying to make me the fall guy.'

Penny let out a snort. 'Sophie, this day-dreaming business is becoming a problem,' she said. 'How on earth could Martin mix you up in all this?'

'I'm not day-dreaming!' I cried. 'Penny, really, this is serious! He left a note to Mr van Trocken in the back of a picture frame and gave the frame to me!'

'Oh, Sophie, *please*,' said Penny in a pained voice.

149

'This isn't a spy thriller, you know, why on earth should Martin be leaving notes in picture frames? Why not just telephone?'

'Maybe the phone's bugged,' I said, at which point we both stopped talking abruptly.

'I doubt it,' said Penny cautiously, after a moment.

'You know what he's like,' I said.

'Um,' said Penny uncertainly. 'To be honest, Sophie, I always thought you were exaggerating a bit. Is he really that bad?'

'Yes, his wife, look I can't talk,' I said. 'And Penny, I think Martin may be in serious trouble.'

'I think you may be right,' said Penny gleefully. 'And it couldn't have happened to a nicer chap. All right, look, Sophie there's such uproar here I don't know if we'll be allowed to leave the building, but if we can I'll see you for lunch at one. Joe's Café all right with you?'

'I can't possibly afford it,' I said fretfully.

'Oh, don't you worry, Sophie,' said Penny with a meaningful laugh. 'If this has anything to do with that repellent specimen, I will be only too happy to stand you lunch, dinner – you name it. If you don't hear from me before, I'll see you in a bit.'

'All right,' I said and hung up. The phone rang again. 'Wotcha, Soph, me,' said Little Ant. 'What's up?'

'Have you seen the papers?' I demanded.

'Absolutely not, until I return to the world of the gainfully employed next week, I have no intention of touching them,' replied my flatmate. 'Any particular reason?'

'Oh, only that Mr van Trocken seems to have committed some kind of fraud and that Martin's caught up in it,' I said, forgetting that I wasn't supposed to be talking over the phone. 'Little Ant, what am I going to do?'

'Oh, really?' said Little Ant, sounding amused. 'Why on earth should Martin have anything to do with it? And what kind of fraud?'

'I'm not sure but,' my voice sank to a whisper, 'I think it might have something to do with *insider dealing*.' I hadn't the faintest idea what insider dealing was, but it sounded good.

Little Ant laughed indulgently. 'Sophie, are you sure this isn't one of your little fantasies?' he enquired. 'Insider dealing is the sort of thing you see in the movies and I noticed you'd left the video of *Wall Street* in the machine.'

'No, I mean it!' I cried. 'Honestly, Little Ant, something's really wrong! The *News of the World* has been on the phone. Go and get a copy of the *Telegraph* and you'll see!'

'The *News of the World*?' demanded Little Ant. 'Look, Sophie, are you feeling all right?'

'Yes!' I said. 'Why won't anyone believe me? Please, Little Ant, get a copy of the paper.'

Little Ant sighed. 'Well, I'd been thinking of going for a drive before our date tonight, but if you insist,' he said. 'By the way, some character who said he was an old friend rang just after I got back, and I gave him your number. I hope that was OK.'

'Ha!' I said. 'I'll tell you about that later, but honestly, Little Ant, you owe me dinner for that alone. Oh, by the way, about tonight, we're having a drink with Mrs van Trocken first, I knew you wouldn't mind.'

'Mrs van Trocken?' demanded Little Ant. 'Sophie,

have you gone mad? First insider dealing, then the *News of the Screws* and now you're consorting with the boss's wife?'

'No, honestly, she's totally different from her husband,' I said. 'It's just a quick drink, but she wants to celebrate being let out of prison. Look, go and get the *Telegraph*. You'll see.' I hung up, felt nervously in my handbag – the picture was still there – and looked around wildly. The Fraud Squad hadn't marched in, but I was beginning to feel it was only a matter of time. What am I going to do? I thought – and the answer was simple. I settled back to do what I always did in moments of crisis and shut my eyes. The prairies of the Wild West loomed up in front of me. It was hot, damn hot, but the blood coursing through my veins was hotter still. I adjusted my Stetson, and leapt up onto my trusty steed, Minesa Double, who reared up in anticipation of the chase. I flourished my shotgun and set off at a gallop after the enormous figure who was riding into the sunset. 'It's no good, Vlad my lad!' I yelled as I began the pursuit. 'We know what you're up to! You can run, Vladimir, but just remember this. There's nowhere to hide!'

13

OK, OK, so it was running away from reality, but it was certainly the only light relief I got that morning. The next hour or so was a nightmare – not only was my love life lying in ruins, but my chances of using *Food for Thought* as a stepping stone to a media career weren't looking that hot either. The phone hardly stopped ringing: more newspapers called and Marcus Aimsworthy left another two messages. After that it was Petrushka's turn. 'God, darling, it's just busy, busy, busy,' she said when I passed on the party invitation. 'I really shouldn't go, you know darling, editors shouldn't mix with advertisers on principle, but if that bloody bastard Vladimir insists, I suppose I'll have to. Now look darling, I've got lunch at Le Caprice and I just must pop in to Harvey Nicks afterwards, but I'll try to make it in later. *Ciao.*'

Then the woman who had rung earlier in tears rang again and said that Vladimir should ring Apricot immediately, my bank manager rang to tell me they were about to start bouncing my cheques – it seems that for some reason I had not been paid the previous month – and then, absolute horror of horrors, Mr van Trocken himself phoned in.

'What took you so long to answer!' thundered the unmistakable tones of my employer as I picked up the phone. 'And sound more enthusiastic, you idiot girl, it could have been one of my friends in the Conservative Party – one of those who has not yet betrayed me, that is. To think that I, Vladimir van Trocken, a poor boy from Prague who now regularly rubs shoulders with the great and good should have to tolerate staff as incompetent as this!'

'Er, yes indeed,' I said.

'I am ringing,' continued Mr van Trocken, ignoring my little contribution to the conversation, 'to tell you that I will not be back in the office until late this afternoon. That idiot wife of mine is not at the Savoy and I demand to know where she is! I will teach her to lie to the likes of Vladimir van Trocken! I don't suppose the traitorous fool has rung in to the office?'

'No, no, she hasn't,' I said truthfully.

'Hmm,' said Mr van Trocken, extending the word to at least four syllables, and imbuing it with the kind of menace that would make your average viper think twice before biting. 'Any other calls?'

'Quite a few, actually,' I said shakily clearing my throat. The thought of what the Mr van Trockens of the past did to the bearers of bad news was making itself uncomfortably uppermost in my mind. 'Er, Marcus Aimsworthy wants you to ring him, someone called Apricot does too and at least five newspapers have been on the phone, including the *News of the World*. Something about Buckingham Palace. Oh, and a friend of mine, Martin Silverspoon, is looking for you too.'

My best friend and my flatmate might have treated

my revelations with disbelief but my employer seemed more than willing to give me the benefit of the doubt. A howl of fury came down the line. 'You tell your friend Martin that he has let me down badly, and I will make him pay for this!' he yelled. 'Those who cross the path of Vladimir van Trocken know what it is to feel the might of avenging fury!' He paused and then changed tack dramatically. 'And I suppose Martin has told you all about our little business arrangements?' he enquired craftily.

'No, Martin doesn't tell me anything, he's my boyfriend, you see,' I explained.

'I know he is,' said Mr van Trocken silkily. 'Nothing? He's never even mentioned a few investment plans we might have spoken about?'

'No, nothing,' I said. 'I didn't even know he knew you until he turned up here this morning.'

'Did he indeed,' said Mr van Trocken. 'Well, I suggest you tell your friend Martin to stay away from me if he knows what's good for him. And you say newspapers have been ringing in too?'

'Er, yes.'

'Well, say nothing,' said my employer somewhat unnecessarily. 'I will deal with them, Sophie. Mark my words, they will learn what it is to take on the likes of Vladimir van Trocken. And get on with that proofreading, I can tell you have done nothing so far. I may not be in the office, Sophie, but I can still sense you are being lazy!'

He hung up. I did likewise and briefly wondered how my boss was going to manage to blame me for his wife running out on him, the papers writing whatever it was they were about to write and Martin for being Martin. Oh, God, I thought, why is the whole world deliberately out to get me? I put my head in my hands. I felt confused.

About twenty minutes later, however, I was feeling a lot better. There had been no further call from Penny which meant that lunch was still on and I was using the last of my limited funds – that reminded me, I must find out what had happened about my salary – on a taxi. We were speeding down Gloucester Road, towards Joe's Café on Draycott Avenue, an uneventful journey except for the fact that we nearly ran over Henry and Jim, who were strolling hand in hand across the road. They must have been taking a long lunch break too: I had certainly decided that I would. I didn't even care whether Mr van Trocken rang in again while I was out.

Joe's Café felt like paradise on earth after the stormy offices of *Food for Thought*. The ultimate in urban chic, quite incredibly trendy-looking waiters and waitresses were chatting to favoured clientele and giving at least a semblance of being pleased to see the rest of us. Slightly to my surprise, I saw one particularly glamorous waitress, who was taller and rather fuller in the chest than the rest, give me a very strange look, followed by a wink. Never mind, nothing could surprise me now.

I was led through the minimalist field of chrome, stiff white linen and elegant glassware to a table on the raised dais to the left of the restaurant, over-looking the scene below. A waiter took my long white flannel jacket, rather better quality than the rest of my clothes since I had pinched it from my mother, an order for a glass of kir, and disappeared. I looked around. The place was filled with stick-thin women, pushing a piece of lettuce around their plates, and sipping glasses of champagne. Everyone, without exception, was blond, tanned and glossily made-up.

Gosh, it must be nice to be like that, I thought dreamily. Why do I worry about having a career, why not just find a wealthy man with a house or four, a fleet of cars and servants to take care of the important things in life, like peeling grapes and wrapping up my clothes in special acid-free tissue paper to hang in the little mews house next door that I intended to use as a wardrobe. The restaurant faded into the background. 'I'll have that suit in white, brown and cream, oh, and any other colours you might have in stock,' I informed the sales girl at Emporio Armani, extending my no-limit ultra-exclusive platinum credit card, as issued only to the absolutely stinking rich.

Thor, my Swedish personal trainer and bodyguard, who had accompanied me on my shopping expedition, and to whom I gave little gifts, looked petulant. 'Oh, and throw in a couple of shirts for Thor,' I said. 'Something to show off his muscles. Now do get a move on, I'm having my legs waxed in half an hour for next week's little jaunt to the K club in Barbuda, then I've got my manicure, and then I just must look in at Prada, I haven't been there since yesterday. Then I've got my masseuse coming to the house at four, shopping is just so stressful, and then there's that film première tonight, and we'll be going on to a party with Tom and Nicole, so I just must look my best. What a fabulous dress, why not throw that in too, and no, I don't have time to try it on. If it doesn't fit, I'll give it to Oxfam.'

A crowd of shop assistants raced off to start carrying out my demands. I blinked, and focused on the restaurant again, as what seemed to be most of the

staff actually did rush to the doorway and start grovel-
ling to someone who had just walked in. 'I am
meeting a friend,' said Penny haughtily, in tones that
could be heard across the restaurant. 'Please take me
to her table at once.'

Clearly regretting not giving us a table centre-stage,
the waiter escorted Penny over to the table. 'A kir for
you as well, madam?' he enquired.

Penny wrinkled her tiny nose, and flashed a
diamond-inspired rainbow across the room as she
rubbed her cheek. 'I would really prefer champagne,
wouldn't you Sophie?'

I nodded and the waiter, taking Penny's unbeliev-
ably smart Dolce & Gabbana coat, whizzed off.
Underneath was a lovely lilac two piece, with large
Chanel buttons. 'Nice suit,' I said.

'Yes, I like the London look,' said Penny vaguely.
She had long ago told me that tai-tais (rich chicks,
as they were known in Hong Kong) always rushed
out to buy the total London look as soon as they
hit England and Penny, despite the fact that she had
been born here, was no exception. 'Now, I have
something to tell you, Sophie, but I must – yes, what
is it?'

The waitress who had winked at me earlier had just
appeared at our table. 'Just came to say hi,' she said.

Penny prepared to start radiating arctic blasts, but
to my intense astonishment, took one look and burst
out laughing instead. 'Well, hello,' she said. 'You've
certainly changed a lot since we last met.'

Penny consorting with waitresses, even very
fashionable ones? I looked blankly from one to the
other, and then realized both were grinning at me.
'You recognize me don't you, Sophie?' asked the wait-

ress. 'We certainly saw enough of each other in the past.'

Actually, now she came to mention it, there was something very familiar about her. The heavily made-up eyes rang a bell, so did the nose, and underneath several layers of lipstick, so did the mouth – oh, my God. 'Hello, Thomas,' I said.

'It's Tasmin, now actually,' said Tommy the Trannie, my ex-boyfriend who had been an accountant, giggling girlishly. 'What do you think?'

I had been wrong: there were still things in life that could surprise me: first Bearded Bernie gets on the bloody blower, now Tommy the Trannie turns up like this. 'How's Price Waterhouse?' I enquired.

Tommy gurgled with laughter. 'Oh, them,' he said skittishly. 'No, Sophie, that's all behind me now, and I've never felt happier. I'm very unusual, actually, most transvestites aren't actually transsexuals, but guess what? I am! I always felt like a lesbian trapped inside a man's body, you know, so I thought, well why not go for the whole shebang? Become a lesbian trapped inside a woman's body!' (I didn't dare look at Penny at this point, but it was all right, Tommy still had more to contribute to the conversation.)

'Anyway, Sophie, I owe you such a lot,' he continued happily. 'It was you catching me out at Madame Jo Jo's that night that made me decide to go for it. If it wasn't for you, I'd just be a boring old wage slave, maybe married with children – ugh! Anyway,' he lowered his voice and leant forward confidentially, 'I haven't had the last op yet, so there's still a bit of me that's a man, but not for much longer. And what do you think of my boobs? Aren't they great? Would you like to touch?'

'Uh, no, thank you,' I said hastily. The lunchtime crowd at Joe's Café were a very sophisticated lot, but I felt that even they might draw the line at transsexual waitresses exposing themselves in public.

'It's been simply marvellous to see you again,' said Penny, very sweetly coming to the rescue, 'and we must have a drink some time, but look, Soph and I don't want to monopolize you. Great nails, by the way, where do you have them done?'

'Nails-R-Us,' said Tommy, looking at Penny with the respect that seriously well-dressed women reserve for one another. 'God, Penny, I must talk to you about shopping. I never realized it was this fun to be a woman, but listen, do you prefer slingbacks or mules?'

'Well, slingbacks are easier to walk in, but mules are sexier,' said Penny. 'Anyway, Tommy, sorry, Tasmin, it's been lovely. Here's my card. Give me a call.' She shoved a business card in his direction, and after a lot of air-kissing, Tommy wandered off. We sat in silence for a moment. 'So,' I said eventually, 'another successful episode in my love life draws to a close.'

I couldn't blame her: I'd have done the same in her position. Penny grabbed a napkin, stuffed it against her mouth, and sat, shoulders shaking with suppressed mirth, as the original waiter appeared, champagned us and walked off. She was so happy, she even forgot to be rude. 'All right, all right,' I said finally, 'it's not that funny.'

'Oh, yes it is,' said Penny, choking back a few last gasps. 'Oh, Sophie, you should have seen your face. That'll teach you not to be surprised when I tell you I have a girlfriend. Oh, Sophie!' She started off again, and suddenly the whole thing seemed so ridiculous, I couldn't help it, and joined in. We both sat there heaving with silent giggles, until the reappearance of the waiter, and a plea for an order, reminded us that more important matters were on the cards. 'We'll both have salade niçoise,' said Penny briskly, 'and two more glasses of champagne.' The waiter bobbed and raced off.

Penny sat back, looking more serious, produced a Dunhill, inserted it into a holder and expertly flashed a gold lighter. 'Now look, Sophie, we must get on to more important matters, I really can't stay out too long, so we haven't much time. I had a phone call from Charlotte this morning, and she told me something about Martin that I think you really ought to know.'

'What?' I said, tensing.

Penny sighed. 'Not good, I'm afraid,' she said, with genuine sympathy. 'And there's something else I'd better tell you as well. I've asked Michael to meet us here in a couple of minutes. I'm really sorry, Sophie, I know you and he didn't really get on, but we need his help. He's been a fund manager too, you know, and he'll know what to do. Oh, and I've told him about Charlotte as well, by the way.'

I looked at her in stunned silence. Michael? She wanted me to involve that horrible little man in business between me and Martin? I was hardly even thinking of Martin as my boyfriend any more, but this really was too much. I didn't know what to say, though: how do you tell your best friend that you hate her brother? 'Look, Penny,' I began rather hesitantly, 'you know how fond I am of you and I really appreciate Michael wanting to help. But don't you think this is a bit, well, private? I mean, I hardly know him and, well—'

'Here he is now,' said Penny brightly. I glanced up briefly and then glanced back again sharpish. My first thought was that I must be dreaming. My second was that this was just totally too much for a dream: I must have died and gone to Heaven. You have probably gathered by now that making his way through the tables, accompanied by a very attentive Tommy, was not the specimen I had met several years ago. No, it was someone quite different altogether – the chap who had been in Boom Boom last night, to be precise.

I blinked a couple of times and yes, it really was him. He had traded in the jeans and blazer for a dark grey business suit and grey and yellow tie, but it was indisputably him: tall, slim, with olive skin, black hair, black eyes and a very full mouth. In fact, height and hairstyle apart, the resemblance between him and Penny was unmistakable, and at this point, my friend herself stepped in. 'Sophie, Michael, I believe you've met?'

14

Michael, or whoever he was – events were leaving me behind, as usual – was looking as taken aback as I was. 'Sophie?' he said, turning to me after kissing his sister. 'You're Sophie? I thought, I mean, *you* are Sophie Brackenbury?'

'Of course she's Sophie,' said Penny slightly irritably. 'What's got into you, Michael? Do sit down, for Heaven's sakes. Sophie—' at this point she turned to me and saw the expression on my face. 'What on earth are you both so astonished about? I thought you'd met before.'

'What a sensational surprise,' said Michael, sitting down and beaming at both of us as the waiter appeared bearing two plates of salade niçoise. 'No, thank you, just a glass of your scrummiest champagne for me.' The waiter, now really regretting not putting us centre stage, grovelled and left. 'Amazing,' he went on. 'Simply amazing. Congratulations on your splendid lunchtime revelation, Penny. Did it take you long to plan?'

'Michael,' said Penny in complete exasperation, 'even for you this is going it a bit. Sophie is not used to your eccentric little ways and frankly you're beginning to sound certifiable. Just what am I supposed to have planned?'

'Don't tell me it was a coincidence,' said Michael, sipping the champagne that had appeared pronto and beaming at me again. 'You deliberately drop it into the conversation that you're going to Boom Boom last night, I turn up to surprise you and voilà! I bump into a marvellous girl who turns out to be the mysterious Sophie Brackenbury. Couldn't have planned it better myself. Cheers.' He drained his glass and beckoned for another.

'But you weren't in Boom Boom last night,' said Penny blankly. 'Have you been at the wacky baccy again?'

'What a hurtful accusation,' said Michael, who was looking anything but upset. Rather, he seemed to be in the highest of spirits. 'Those days are but a hazy memory in the dim and distant past. Tell her, Sophie, be my alibi, I was there, wasn't I?'

'Yes, you were,' I said blankly. 'We bumped into one another at Boom Boom last night, before you got there, Penny. Then Michael's bleeper bleeped and he had to go.'

'Never turn it off,' said Michael with a melodramatic sigh. 'I am constantly available day and night for the unreasonable and yet financially rewarding demands of my dear Papa. So it really was a coincidence then? I love it! Written any more poems?'

'My word, you must have been getting on well,' said Penny, her lips twitching with amusement. 'Sophie usually waits at least a week after meeting someone to reveal her hidden talents.'

'Don't be rude, it was a sensational poem,' said

Michael. 'All about twentieth-century alienation and I'm very much looking forward to reading some more.'

'But I don't understand!' I said. It was only gradually beginning to dawn on me that this character was actually Penny's brother. 'You can't be Michael Tang! No-one could have changed that much!'

The Tangs exchanged a glance of bewilderment. 'He's been like this for years, I'm afraid,' said Penny, 'although you're certainly not alone in wondering if he comes from a different planet. But I don't understand, either. I thought you'd met years ago.'

'We did, or at least I thought we had,' I said, wondering briefly if the other chap had been an impostor. I told you that the whole world was out to get me. 'I mean, at your parents' anniversary party, I met someone who said he was Michael Tang, but he wasn't a bit like, er, you. He had an American accent for a start.'

'Ha, ha!' snorted Michael, looking positively delighted. 'I always knew this would happen one day! Allow me to disabuse you of your terrible mix-up. You must have met our personality-challenged cousin, who is also called Michael Tang. We have an Uncle Andy, you see, who lives in Vancouver, and who is Papa's younger brother. He's always, quite understandably, doted on my father, so when I was born and named Michael, Uncle Andy followed suit when he had a son. The whole family came over for that party, so you must have met him. Not to worry, though. Easy mistake. Anyone could have made it. Cheers.' He lifted the glass of champagne the waiter had just put down, and took a hefty gulp.

'Good heavens,' I said. That certainly explained a

lot, and to think that all this time Penny had this absolute dish of a brother, eccentric though he was proving to be, and hadn't introduced us – well. I was miffed, that's all I can say.

'Blimey O'Reilly, it never occurred to me you could have met t'other,' said Penny. 'I thought the reason you hadn't got on was a perfectly understandable critique of Michael's personality. So you were hanging around Boom Boom picking up strange women, were you?'

'Sophie's not in the slightest bit strange,' said Michael indignantly, shooting me a sideways glance. 'And I resent that remark about my personality, I've always thought I was remarkably well adjusted, all things considered. Splendid outcome though, now we can all relax or rather, not relax. What's been going on around here? Come on you two, share and build, share and build.'

'Well, it's like this,' began Penny, downing some more champagne herself. 'We should really have got a bottle. Anyway, Sophie, you see, has really excelled herself in the romance stakes this time, and got herself involved with a chap whose main hobby seems to be fraudulent dealing.'

'Penn-ee,' I complained. 'You don't have to put it like that, I didn't know about him, you know. And at least I'm not going out with his estranged wife, in fact I'm not going out with him at all, I've decided. I've just got to let him know that.'

'No, don't apologize,' said Michael. 'Congratulations on such an interesting choice of boyfriend, although I can see it must be a little difficult when people ask you at cocktail parties what he does for a living. Perhaps you could say he pretended to have had some diamonds stolen, and then claimed on the insurance, that's so much more socially acceptable, these days. You can write books about it, and move in the highest circles in the land, you know.'

'Children, can we get on with it?' asked Penny. 'You know he went to New York about six years ago?'

'Yup.'

'OK, so that's when he met Charlotte, and they got married right away. It seems they went to Las Vegas for the weekend, the ceremony was officiated over by an Elvis impersonator and they were serenaded by half a dozen Dolly Parton lookalikes.'

'How eighties,' sniffed Michael. 'Really, if they had any sense of style, it would be some kind of New Age bonding ceremony carried out in the presence of dolphins. Anyway, don't let me interrupt you.'

'OK,' said Penny, glaring at her brother, 'so both were and remained interested in other women, the way of all flesh won through, and when the happy couple discovered that they had both been cheating on the other with the same secretary, they decided to call it a day.'

'I can't wait to meet this delightful wife,' said Michael, suppressing a grin. 'Trust Penny to go not only for the London look but the London lifestyle as well. Did she ever tell you about that sensational occasion she came home from Roedean with her hair dyed bright pink? Papa went ballistic until she pulled it off that night in the middle of a very formal dinner party and it turned out to be a wig.'

'I'm beginning to regret asking you to come along,' grumbled Penny. 'Well, listen to this. You'll never guess what – Martin's already been in trouble with his business dealings before now!'

'No!' I said.

'I do approve of a chap who works on perfecting his skills,' commented Michael. 'Well done him. But is there any actual proof of this, or did Martin just make an announcement to the local newspapers and sit back and wait to sell the film rights?'

'Will you stop being so flippant?' enquired Penny. 'Of course he didn't make an announcement, but unfortunately there wasn't any proof either. That's why nothing was ever done.'

'How do you know about it then?' I asked. Much as I was prepared to believe just about anything of Martin now, I rather felt we needed a bit more here than just speculation.

'Because he told Charlie, of course,' said Penny, in the patient kind of tone that you would use to calm a fractious and rather backward five year old. 'They had separated but stayed in touch, and late one night, Martin rushed round to her flat, well and truly in his cups, and said there was trouble brewing at work. Apparently he'd stumbled across some highly confidential information when he went to play racquet ball with a business chum.'

'Racquet ball?' I interrupted. 'Martin's idea of exercise is to run for a taxi. What was he doing playing racquet ball?'

'Apparently it's the in thing to do rather than having lunch in New York circles these days,' said Penny. 'Anyway, that is not the important bit. The important bit is that the chum went off to make a phone call, Martin just happened to knock the chum's briefcase open, and saw that a company called Herbert Manufacturing was thinking of buying another company called Sprocketts Inc. So guess who bought quite a few shares in Sprocketts Inc. that very afternoon and, a week later when the bid was announced, made an absolute killing by selling them on after the price rocketed.'

'What's wrong with that?' I demanded. 'Sounds quite sensible to me.'

'Shocking story,' said Michael, butting in as Penny paused to chomp a bit of tuna and shaking his head sadly. 'It may be sensible, but it's also illegal. That's what insider dealing is. You're not supposed to buy shares on the back of information that hasn't been made public.'

'Blimey!' I exclaimed. I couldn't believe that just for once, even if it was accidentally, I had got it right. I was looking forward to crowing about this with Little Ant. That would teach him to call me a fantasist. 'But what happened? Was he arrested?'

'Nothing happened,' said Penny calmly. 'Nothing was ever done about this little episode because no-one could prove anything and everyone denied everything. Martin said that he had never seen any papers, that he couldn't help it if his market antennae were so acute that he was five steps ahead of the game, and that his firm should be pleased to have a brilliant fund manager like him on board rather than moan about it.'

'Well, what about the other bloke?' I asked. 'Wouldn't he say something?'

'Oh, yes, and lose his job for his pains?' said Penny. 'Can you imagine what his bosses would have said if they knew he'd left confidential papers all over his local gym? Come on, be sensible.'

'But what about Charlotte?' I asked. 'She knew.'

'I know,' said Penny bitterly. 'Just think, she could

have nailed the little bastard there and then. But she was married to him and the next day, when he'd sobered up, he rang her and begged her not to tell. Said he was going to bluff it out and promised he'd never do anything so stupid again, and so she hasn't breathed a word about it to anyone until she met me.'

'So crime does pay after all,' said Michael gravely. 'Terrible indictment on twentieth-century society. Oh, well. Shall I get some more champagne?'

'Yes, but hurry,' said Penny. 'Actually, it didn't totally pay, because eyebrows had been raised, he never got promoted, and he finally decided to hot foot it back to these shores, and now the silly ass has done it again.'

'I still don't understand,' I said petulantly.

'Perfectly simple,' said Penny. 'For a while Martin is good as the gold he was awarded in bonuses by poor old Sir Jeremy. But Charlie and I think he and Mr van Trocken must have known one another for a while, and Martin must have found out that your boss was in talks with Molehill Magazines about selling *Food for Thought*. See, Molehill would have to make Mr van T party to their financial standing to prove they could afford to buy the magazine. Yesterday, they announced enormous losses, but it was only because the pound was strong against the dollar or vice versa, or something. Actually, their finances are so strong that they're in the middle of linking up with an American CD-Rom manufacturer, and indeed, just that information came out this morning. Mr van T would have known these announcements were going to be made, and he'd know what this was going to do to the share price. Yesterday it collapsed: today it soared, and anyone who had bought the shares at their low point would have made an absolute fortune.'

'Would have made an absolute fortune if they'd been able to sell them again,' said Michael. 'Just before I came out, I saw the Stock Exchange had suspended trading in them earlier since news of the DTI investigation's leaked out. Sneaky plot on Martin's part, but unless he sold this morning, I'm afraid he's going to be rather out of pocket.'

I still didn't really understand, but whatever. I had been scrabbling in my handbag: I now produced the picture frame and the note, which I placed between Michael and Penny. 'Read that,' I said.

Penny looked at it, raised an eyebrow, and said nothing.

'Of course, it's an act of terrible treachery for you to show us an incriminating note from your ex-boyfriend,' said Michael after doing likewise, 'but I like it.' He reached across the table and picked up the picture frame. 'Is that Martin?' he enquired.

'Uh, yes,' I said blushing. 'But honestly, he looks much better than that usually. Anyway, what should we do now?'

'Bin the bastard,' advised Michael, who had been studying the picture closely. 'Doesn't he know you never wear a wing collar with black tie? Shocking sartorial sense on his part, you must instantly find someone far more worthy of your sensational taste in clothes.'

'Oh, thank you,' I said, blushing more deeply.

'With your permission, I'd like to show this to Sir Jeremy,' said Penny briskly. She obviously felt we should get on to more serious matters. 'He'll know how to deal with Martin. May I?'

I nodded, and Penny whisked the note into her handbag. 'Listen,' I asked anxiously, 'they won't think I'm caught up in it will they?'

'Of course not,' said Penny reassuringly. She glanced at her wrist – today she was wearing the Love-watch by Yves Saint Laurent – and gasped. 'Oh my word,' she said, 'Sir Jeremy is going to think I'm up to no good too if I don't make a move. I'm going to have to miss out on more champagne.' She leapt to her feet and grabbed her handbag. 'Michael, could you settle up and take Sophie back to her office? You brought the Jag, I assume?'

'It's waiting outside,' said Michael. 'Absolutely nothing in the world would make me happier.'

'A million mercies,' said Penny showering kisses. 'I'll call you later Sophie. Oh, I can't wait to see that specimen's face when he hears about this. *A plus tard!*

15

I was in complete turmoil as I shoved my way through the front door of van Trocken and Co., having been dropped off by Michael – he also had a chauffeur-driven car, although it was a red Jaguar as opposed to Penny's blue Merc. First, there was Martin. I simply couldn't believe what I had just heard. It was one thing to realize that a relationship was over, but to find out that your boyfriend is not only a philanderer but a downright crook? It was just totally astonishing. I plodded up the hall, bunged my coat under my desk and sat down. Mr van Trocken smirked down from the wall beside me, but I was too overcome to care.

Even I couldn't have come up with a fantasy scenario like that one. There I'd been, day-dreaming away for months (well, OK, years) now, and all along this had been happening under my nose. Whatever next? I sighed dramatically, and in doing so sniffed a faint charred smell in the air. Oh bugger, I thought, not again. I nipped up to the kitchen on the next floor, where the third coffee machine I'd destroyed in the last six months was in its last moments, used a towel to click the off switch, and looked at the lump of melting plastic that had once been the coffee jug. It seems that I'd forgotten to turn it off after Mrs van Trocken had left earlier, although that now seemed a lifetime ago. A couple of days ago I'd have been worried about being sacked: that now seemed the least of my problems.

That one could be dealt with later. I went back downstairs to my desk, nodded to Jim and Sam, who had just come in and were giggling at one another (goodness knows where Henry had got to) and sat down. The pile of page proofs stared at me reprovingly. I picked up one by Walt Lemming, a highly fashionable young novelist who did a bit of journalism in his spare time, and tried to concentrate. 'The first time I took drugs was when I was nine years old,' I read wearily. 'It was child's play, the plaything of a child, an adult child, a childish adult, that advanced state of experience where the aged returns to second childhood and becomes the second birth, the born again, the new born. And in my newly-born state of experience, ecstasy was my rattle, dope, dumb me, my dummy, speed, oh speedy bliss, my teddy and heroin my cradle. And as I watched my girlfriend doing the washing up the other night, pulling on those long, erotic, exotic plastic gloves, a splash of colour in the filth of the sink, the association – plastic, rubber, rubber sheet, bedwetting, acid dreams – rose in me again and I . . .' There was pages more of this drivel, but I really didn't have the strength to get through it. I gathered that the gist of what Walter was saying was that he took loads of drugs when he was younger (and indeed still did, if what Petrushka told me was true) and sometimes it still gave him nightmares.

I sighed and pushed the pile of papers aside. Try as I might to concentrate, I couldn't stop mulling over everything that seemed to be happening at the moment, on top of which, I have to admit that my mind kept returning to Michael. All right, so he was obviously barking mad, but I liked him. In fact, I liked him enormously. And it was funny, he was a real mixture of East and West: when he was animated and chatting he did indeed look Southern European, but when his face was in repose, with those large oval eyes and full mouth, he looked like one of those Oriental statues I'd seen in the Metropolitan Museum last year during a trip to New York. It must have been the result of having a Chinese father and an English mother, I thought, and if that's what miscegenation did for you, then it was highly to be recommended.

Something was bothering me, though. Although he had continued to be extremely charming and friendly in the car on the way back, that was all he had been. None of the interest he had seemed to be on the verge of showing last night was apparent and there was absolutely no mention of meeting again when he dropped me off, except to say that he was sure he'd see me again with Penny. The evening next week in Boom Boom hadn't even been referred to. In fact, he hadn't even kissed me goodbye when we parted, just shook hands.

I sighed melodramatically. It wasn't often that you met someone with both looks and personality, apart from Little Ant, of course, except that he didn't count, but unfortunately this one was looking horribly like a non-starter. It was so unfair, after a lifetime of duds I felt it was my turn to hit the jackpot in the romance stakes, especially after the Martin revelations, but it seemed that life just didn't work out like that. Worse still, I couldn't even confide in Penny about it – or in Little Ant, now I came to think about it, as I'd just remembered that he'd met Michael as well. I sighed again and began to hum 'Goodbye to Love', as the phone rang. 'Van Trocken and Co.,' I said automatically.

'OK, look,' gurgled a voice. 'This is great, just great. You really are a receptionist, aren't you, Sophie? Amazing, look, how are you? It's Tiffany.'

I knew damn well who it was. 'Fine, and you?' I asked wearily. I couldn't even be bothered to correct the job description.

'Great, really great,' repeated the cow. 'God, Sophie, it was so amazing to bump in to you yesterday, we should never have lost touch. One of the boys thought you were quite cute, but then he had got through two bottles of this really amazing claret earlier! No really, just kidding. So look, Sophie, you'll never guess who's just called me.'

I had a funny idea that I could guess pretty accurately who had just called her, but I also couldn't be bothered to start game playing. 'Go on, tell,' I said.

'Martin!' crowed Tiffany. 'He wants to take me out to dinner tomorrow! Isn't that great? It's really strange, isn't it Sophie, that so many of your boyfriends have wanted to get to know me! I could never understand why you were so upset about me modelling for Alan, it was really totally innocent. Well, not totally maybe, but you never liked him that much anyway, did you? Anyway, I promise you that I'll slap Martin down if he gets too frisky! I think he's just great for you, though, I really do, and you know what they say. Beggars can't be choosers! No really, just kidding.'

I was silent. Well, what would you have said?

'Anyway,' continued Tiffany, who was not through with point scoring yet, 'he was just so sweet. He said I should choose the restaurant as he just wanted me to be just totally happy, but to make it somewhat discreet, so we could chat away without anyone interrupting us, which is why I called you. I thought "Sophie would know where he likes to go, so why not call her!" So I did! So where do you suggest?'

I was thinking fast. She could do what she liked with Martin, as far as I was concerned as I'd just met the world's dishiest Anglo-Oriental, even if he wasn't interested in me, and my desire to hang on to two-timing little insider dealers was zero. All the same, I was beginning to think that Mrs van Trocken wasn't the only one who wanted a bit of revenge, and Tiffany obviously had no idea what Martin had got himself caught up in. His name hadn't appeared in any of the newspaper reports, after all. 'What about Sonny's?' I said.

'Sonny's?' said Tiffany blankly. I don't think she'd been expecting that response.

'Yes, Sonny's,' I repeated. 'It's a really nice place in Barnes, well away from the centre of town, so it's nice and discreet. I know Martin likes it, we've been there several times before. Why not go there?'

'Oh, right,' said Tiffany, sounding slightly more uncertain. She recovered immediately, however. 'Ya, look, that'll be great. Amazing. OK, Sophie, you're just taking this so well. Look, we've got to meet up, and don't worry about Martin, I'm just not in the mood for a fling, though you never know. Things change! No really, just kidding. If he makes a greasy little lunge, I know how to handle it. *Ciao.*'

She hung up. I did likewise, and then dialled again immediately. 'Hi, Penny, it's me,' I said. 'You'll never guess what I've just heard. If Sir Jeremy still wants to have a chat with Martin, I think I might be able to help.'

About fifteen minutes later, having filled Penny in on the latest, I sat back with exhaustion. That smell of burning was still in the air. I shut my eyes, leapt out of bed, and swung down the huge pole in the middle of the room. The fire engine's sirens were revving up. 'Right boys,' I cried, leaping into my fire suit, 'we're off!' I and about half a dozen of the hunkiest firefighters in town leapt to our positions, the huge doors of the station were rolled back, and we drove out. 'Sophie to base, Sophie to base,' I said as we thundered through the streets, bells and sirens clanging away like mad. 'Yes, I can see the blaze now. Oh no! It's the head office of van Trocken and Co. in Poland Street and it's being burnt to the ground. Get the hose boys, easy does it boys—' I practically leapt out of my skin as a huge ringing sound filled the air, which I thought at first was the fire engine, and suddenly realized was the front-door bell. Rather unwisely, I pressed the buzzer.

'Where is he!' roared Rory, leaping into the hall. 'Where is he! He can try to frighten me but it's far too late now!'

He raced up the hall. I looked at him in distaste – he was sporting his usual militant khaki outfit, his hair looked just that little bit lankier than before, and now both sides of the black NHS spectacles were held together with Sellotape rather than just the one – and attempted to be as imperious as my employer would have wanted. 'I'm afraid you can't

178

go in there,' I said, as Rory headed for the study. 'That is Mr van Trocken's private room and visitors are not allowed.' Ignoring me totally, Rory shot in, with me following at speed after him. 'Oh, for Heaven's sakes, Rory, he's out,' I panted, returning to normal as Rory skidded to a halt on the vast Turkish rug in the middle of the room. 'Look, please go away, you'll get us both into the most terrible trouble.'

'Is he really out or are you just protecting him?' demanded Rory. His shoulders, which normally adopted the concave position, were thrown back, and there was a look on his face that I suspected Rory felt was heroism, and which actually made him look as if he were suffering from a particularly bad case of indigestion.

'Of course he's out,' I said crossly. 'Why in Heaven's name would I try to protect him? I loathe him as much as you do.'

'Yes, but he could have bought your loyalty,' said Rory in a sinister tone. I was beginning to think he was either drunk or had overdosed on one too many action movies over the summer. 'He could have won you over and purchased your silence just like he did to Tony.'

'Tony?' I demanded. 'What on earth has Tony got to do with this? Look, Rory, will you please tell me what is going on?'

'I can't tell you,' said Rory, beginning to edge backwards towards the door, all the while keeping his eyes fixed firmly on my face. I was beginning to think that if this went on much longer I was going to have to call the police. 'For all I know, you're with him now. Are you? Well are you?'

'Of course I'm bloody not,' I said irritably. 'Look, Rory, are you all right?'

'Yes, but no thanks to that evil bastard,' said Rory. He was continuing to edge backwards, and I was following him, which meant we were now halfway down the stairs. 'I know how I can tell if you're his. Sniff.'

'What?' I said blankly.

'Sniff,' said Rory, coming to a halt. 'Go on, sniff.'

Well, I had no idea what he was going on about, he was being just totally peculiar, but as it seemed to mean so much to him, I sniffed as hard as I could. It wasn't very impressive: my regular autumn cold hadn't started yet and I'd already blown my nose on getting up this morning, but it seemed to satisfy Rory. 'Well, maybe not,' he said in a slightly more concili-atory tone. 'I didn't think you would be, but you never can tell.'

'What do you mean?' I demanded. 'How could he buy me like Tony? Rory, please tell me, what do you mean?'

'Coke,' said Rory, coming to a halt. 'Didn't you know? I would have thought it was obvious. Tony's hooked on Charlie, and Vladimir keeps him supplied.'

For a second I thought he was talking about Charlotte before it clicked. I gazed at him in disbelief. Good Heavens, I thought, I had been right – entirely inadvertently – there too. 'Why?' I asked after a moment.

'Well, it's obvious, isn't it?' said Rory, peering at me myopically. 'Vladimir gives him what he wants and he'll do anything in return, just like last night.'

'What about last night?' I demanded.

'Vladimir set Tony and the boys on me last night,'

said Rory, beginning to edge down the hall again. 'But I'm too clever for him. I got away and it's too late to stop it now!'

'Stop what?' I cried in desperation. 'Please Rory, tell me, what's going on?'

Rory had got to the top of the hall. 'It's all going to come out,' he hissed. 'The women and the drugs – everyone's going to know, and he's brought it all on himself! No-one would have cared if he hadn't been so dead set on becoming Sir Vladimir.'

'*Sir Vladimir?*' I demanded.

'What else do you think that Tory Party donation was for?' asked Rory. 'You think he did it for the good of the country? No, it's not enough to make millions out of ordinary working people and treat them like slaves' – I decided it would be better not to break Barbara van Trocken's bit of news at that moment – 'no, he's got to lord it over us even more. He's obsessed with mixing with the aristocracy – even thinks he can become one. Ha! Well, not after this weekend, and it's all his own fault. If he'd stuck to running his business, rather than running around with Marcus Aimsworthy, no-one would have cared what he got up to with Apricot and Irina and God knows who else.'

'What about this weekend?' I asked. I had no idea what Rory was talking about, but it didn't sound like this insider-dealing business.

'You'll see!' cried Rory, beginning to bound down the hall. 'Whatever you do, buy a copy of the *News of the World* on Sunday. Just you wait and you'll see!'

The door banged behind him. What in Heaven's name is happening round here now, I thought. I went back to my desk and wondered whether to alert

Penny, but thought this might confuse the issue still more. Leave her to deal with the insider dealers and the rest, whatever it was, would sort itself out.

I looked around me. The office had that calm before the storm feeling and indeed, about one second later, a bang worthy of a bolt of thunder ricocheted through the air, and Mr van Trocken strode through the front door. Thank Heavens Rory had left. 'This is worse than I thought, Sophie!' he cried as he bounded up the hall. 'Don't try to bother me with trivia you idiot girl' – this was as I attempted to give him several more messages from newspapers – 'I have far more important things to see to. That fool of a wife of mine has closed down three of our bank accounts. What in Heaven's name does she think she's playing at?' The study door banged behind him and by a click on the wires I gathered he had started making phone calls. Gosh, I thought with increasing respect. Mrs van Trocken certainly wasn't messing around this time.

It was at this point, I confess, that I got a bit nosey. Well, wouldn't you? Mr van Trocken wasn't the quietest of men at the best of times, and I could hear a distinct rumbling from his office door. I crept up the stairs, and pressed my ear against the wooden panel.

'Can't you get a bloody injunction?' I heard him demanding. 'What do you think I'm paying you for? And why should I, Vladimir van Trocken, have to put up with these lies? I deny everything! How dare they suggest such things! Of course I haven't! Who? I've never heard of Martin Silverspoon!'

I held my breath. There was a short pause and then Mr van Trocken began yelling again. 'It must be Karel

Klimova spreading these lies! He has never forgiven me for beating him to that export contract with Outer Mongolia! Tell them all I will sue if they print a word of this!'

He banged the phone down and I crept back to my desk just in the nick of time. 'Sophie!' roared a voice. 'Get your ass in here immediately!' Oh no, I thought with horror, leaping up and speeding up the stairs to my boss's room, he's discovered that Mrs van Trocken has been here and taken something, and what am I going to do now?

As ever, though, when it came to the affairs of van Trocken and Co., I was wrong. 'Just what in Heaven's name is this!' thundered Mr van Trocken, as I skidded to a halt in front of his large desk. I nearly had a heart attack when I realized he was holding aloft Rory's scarf, a remarkably unpleasant piece of material covered in black and yellow stripes. You could see it was almost oozing grease.

'Er,' I said, thinking fast, 'that's mine.'

'Yours?' thundered Mr van Trocken suspiciously. 'I must say Sophie, I've always felt you had remarkably bad taste when it comes to clothes, but even you wouldn't wear something like this.'

'It was a present,' I said, thinking faster. 'From my flatmate.' I felt a bit guilty about attributing Little Ant with such appalling taste, but you know how it is, needs must.

'In that case,' said Mr van Trocken softly, rather in the manner of an executioner asking after the last wish, 'just what is it doing in my office?'

Oh, how totally awful. I didn't want to be accused of meddling in Mr van Trocken's affairs, but I was going to have to tell at least one bit of the truth to get out of this one. It went entirely against the habits of a lifetime – rather like Richard Nixon, I sometimes felt like lying even when I didn't need to, just to keep in practice. Anyway, here goes. 'After you left this morning,' I began in a shaky voice, 'I was just on my way upstairs to make some coffee, and I heard the sounds of shouting. I thought you might be having a problem or something, so I came in here and looked out of the window, but you and Tony seemed to have everything under control.'

Mr van Trocken paused and breathed fast. 'And?' he enquired.

'Well, that's it,' I said lamely. 'I mean I must have dropped the scarf then.'

'And just why,' began Mr van Trocken in the soft voice that he used when he wanted to be particularly unpleasant, 'were you leaving your desk to make a cup of coffee? I have very important friends, Sophie. What if one of them had called when you were away and there was no-one to answer? Well, Sophie? Have you got an answer to that?'

'I was listening very carefully and I could have got back to my desk in seconds,' I said defiantly. 'And anyway, loads of important people rang and I noted them all down. Can I get any of them on the phone for you now?'

Wrong question. 'Now?' bellowed Mr van Trocken. '*Now?* You mean you have kept me waiting all this time before reminding me to answer some extremely important telephone calls? I cannot believe the behaviour of the staff in this company! First that, that insolent insect, that deranged and degraded specimen of humanity, that repulsive, repellent, repugnant traitor Rory, and now you? You're fired!'

'Rory has nothing to do with me,' I protested. 'And I tried to remind you, but you wouldn't let me.'

Mr van Trocken paused while he tried to control his feelings. 'All right, Sophie,' he said eventually, glaring at me. 'I will give you one last second chance. But if I find you have had anything to do with that traitor Rory, I would advise you to attend to your last will and testament. Tell me now Sophie, and pray to the Gods for mercy if you attempt to lie to me, have you seen Rory since he left!'

'Absolutely not,' I said heartily. 'Wouldn't dream of it. Really. I've no idea where he is or anything, really.'

'I hope for your own sake that is true,' said Mr van Trocken, giving me a beady glance, and going back round the desk to his chair. He sat down. 'You may get Marcus Aimsworthy on the telephone now,' he said.

I padded sullenly back down the stairs to my desk and dialled the appropriate number. 'I have a telephone caller for Mr Aimsworthy,' I said.

'I'm sorry,' said a snooty voice, 'Mr Aimsworthy is very tied up in meetings. May I take a message?'

'Vladimir van Trocken would like to speak to him.'

There was a gasp at the other end of the line. 'Please hang on a minute, I think Mr Aimsworthy has just come back into the office,' said the voice. There was a bit more wittering before Marcus Aimsworthy suddenly miraculously became available to take telephone calls, and I put Mr van Trocken on the line. 'Marcus, my friend, how are you!' bellowed a voice from up the hall. 'What? No, there's absolutely nothing to worry about. I, Vladimir van Trocken, am a man of my word!' His study door banged shut, and I, Sophie Brackenbury, settled back to start typing Walter Lemmings' nonsense into our computer system.

16

All in all, I was feeling pretty dejected as I pulled
the doors of *Food for Thought* closed behind me
later that afternoon and set off for home. Very, very
unusually for him, Mr van Trocken had suddenly
decided to let us all leave early, which meant I had
plenty of time to go home before meeting Little Ant
and Mrs van Trocken in The Collection tonight, and
in fact I was intensely hoping that Little Ant would be
in so he could take me there in a taxi.

I had absolutely no money left in my purse at
all, and less than no chance of getting some out of
the cashpoint. Mr van Trocken's temper had not
improved during the course of the afternoon,
however: before I left I was variously berated for the
non-appearance of Petrushka – she had phoned and
said that as a protest about proprietorial interference
in the magazine, she would be spending the afternoon at the Groucho Club – the lousy copy submitted
by our contributors and the work-shy attitude of Sam,
Henry and Jim.

The way back home was mercifully uneventful. I
could have taken the bus – thank Heavens my pass
hadn't run out – but I felt like a walk and there was no

better place in the world to revive fallen spirits than Kensington High Street. As I walked along, I saw taxis disgorging rich tourists and businessmen outside the towering Royal Garden Hotel across the road, before entering the swarm of heroin chic-clad trendies emerging from a hard day's shopping and smoking behind the black portals of Kensington Market.

Then there was retail heaven on my left – Barkers department store, Warehouse, Karen Millen and Hobbs, all still heaving with excited shoppers – and further on, Marks and Spencer loomed reassuringly out of the dusk. I often amused myself by creating little histories for all these individuals as I passed by, but this afternoon was content just to soak in the bright lights of the shops, the roar of the traffic and the combination of wage slaves, tourists and shoppers streaming towards the tube. Each of them has their own past and their own life, I thought self-pityingly, and none of them work for van Trocken and Co. One day I, too, might reach that nirvana.

I walked on down the street, past a garage adorned with the sign 'This door is permanently alarmed' – it and me both, I thought – past Waterstones and the Odeon cinema and turned left into Edwardes Square, which looked lovelier than ever at this time of the year. With its small houses, little bigger than cottages, green gardens and flower-festooned pub, it looked more like a village than one of the most expensive residential locations in West London. I adored peering through the brightly lit windows at the still-life scenarios within – think antiques, Sotheby-style, and you get the picture – and wondering what was going on inside. In one very smart sitting-room a middle-aged man was pouring a glass of sherry and handing it to his wife, in another, a young couple seemed to be preparing for a drinks party as their furniture was pushed back against the walls and they were deep in discussion with a woman dressed in a black skirt and white apron.

I walked on, up to The Scarsdale, and turned right at the top of the square, where I paused to jump into a pile of leaves that had been swept off the pavement and on to the street. I had always loved the autumn: the sharp bite in the air that made you think of warm rooms and roaring fires, the way buildings stood out against the dark blue sky, the colour of the trees as the leaves turned first yellow and then red, and the ever-pervading sense of anticipation. I had always felt that the year really started hotting up at this late stage – a leftover from my school days, I supposed, where September heralded the start of a new phase in life.

I shivered as I remembered school. I had been exactly the same even then – 'A bit of a dreamer,' had been the comment on every single school report up until the year I left, usually alongside some tart remarks about more attention to detail being needed, and a slightly firmer grasp of the facts. I had never had a really awful time of it, like some of my fellow pupils, but neither had I ever been particularly happy: I had always wanted to join the world of adults, with its fun and excitement and certainties. All the big questions will be answered when I'm grown up, I remember thinking at the age of about eight, like why are we here and what should we do, and who would be our ultimate life partner. I was intensely relieved that no-one had told me the horrible truth about being an adult back then, but also slightly resentful that it all seemed so much more difficult than I had thought it was going to be.

Anyway, I was coming finally to at least one firm conclusion about my life: I really did want to be a journalist on a magazine. That had been why I went to *Food for Thought* in the first place and, all the other little local difficulties that were currently brewing aside, it was why I was now desperate to leave. I had begun to realize some time ago that Mr van Trocken was never going to allow me to contribute one word to his precious journal – I didn't have the right surname or connections, I hadn't been to Oxbridge and I didn't have a Class A narcotics addiction – but I knew I could write features. Well, I hoped I could, anyway – I'd already tried just about everything else.

I turned right again, walked up to our house and inserted my key in the front door. I had just turned the lock, when there was a sound right behind me. I whirled round to see – oh please, God no. Hadn't I suffered enough for one day?

'Hello, Sophie,' said Desperate Dan, the chap who had proposed to me on our first date, and who had just popped out from behind a nearby bush. He smiled sadly. 'Long time no see.'

'Oh, hello,' I said, hoping I didn't sound as dismayed as I felt. 'What are you doing here?'

'Waiting for you,' said Desperate Dan, peering deep in to my eyes. 'I've been here for hours. Look, Sophie, I've been doing a lot of thinking and we've just got to talk. Can I come in?'

As far as I was concerned, we needed to do no such thing. Dinner, about two months ago, had been a disaster, and I had either ignored subsequent messages on the answering machine or got Little Ant to say I was out on the numerous occasions that Dan rang. The calls had finally dried up a few weeks ago, and I had thought that had been the last of him but I had, as ever, been wrong. How totally horrible. 'Oh, all right,' I said with very bad grace, stomping in to the hall. 'It's up here.'

We made our way up to the first floor, and I opened the door to the flat. A second later what looked like a streak of ginger lightning appeared as Albert shot past with a very guilty look on his face, which meant he had been prowling around on the work surfaces in the kitchen, an area that was strictly forbidden. 'Yes, I'm coming home early to check up on you,' I called after him. 'Little Ant? Are you home?'

Silence. I reluctantly ushered Dan in to the long narrow hall, which was painted dark red and decorated with a series of eighteenth-century hunting prints, which he made a point of looking at with strong disapproval. By the front door was a little whatnot table, with a pile of unopened post. I led my visitor to the sitting-room, where Albert was pretending to be asleep on one of the sofas. 'Make yourself at home,' I said, rather unnecessarily, as Dan had already chucked his denim jacket on the floor and settled into an armchair. 'Would you like a drink?'

'Gin and tonic, please,' said Dan firmly, picking up a magazine from an overstocked mahogany holder on the floor beside him, and beginning to browse through the pages. 'You should wear something like this, Sophie,' he added, holding up a picture of a model dressed in grey rags, with black make-up around her eyes, and what looked like pin pricks on her arms. 'It would make you seem, you know, less aggressive?'

Seething inwardly, I marched back up the hall to the little kitchen, ransacked Little Ant's drinks cupboard for the necessaries and prepared a drink for Dan and a cup of tea for myself. It was wet of me, I know, but it wasn't yet six o'clock and I wanted to save myself for later. Anyway, I suspected that if I had a drink, too, it would encourage Dan to stay. Then I went back to the sitting-room, where I plonked the drinks down on a table between us. Dan threw the magazine onto the floor and gave me another sad smile. 'So,' I said, attempting not to sound too furious, 'how are you?'

'Really, really bad,' said Dan, putting his feet, which were clad in exceptionally dirty trainers, up on the table and taking a very large slurp of gin and tonic. 'I've just, like, been to Warsaw, you know? And this friend of mine had, like, had a breakdown and I had to get him sectioned? I've been back for three days and I've just, like, spent the whole time writing to the Polish authorities to see what the situation is. It's, like, a nightmare, I mean it's just Kafka.'

'Well at least your friend hasn't turned into a cockroach,' I said unsympathetically, looking at him in distaste. Dan had not been dressed snappily when we first met, and he was now looking downright appalling: he was wearing horrible old jeans, which had a rip just below the bum, and which had exposed a revolting glimpse of skeletal pink thigh when he had walked before me up the hall. This was supplemented with several baggy grey sweatshirts. Neither was the raw material of his appearance much to boast about: Dan had lanky brown hair, a gap between the two front teeth, greasy complexion and a ghastly, slobbery mouth. Albert seemed to share my opinion: he opened an eye, looked quizzically at our guest, turned round and then shoved one leg in the air and started his ablutions. From long experience I knew that this was my cat's way of saying, 'Bugger off.'

'I just, like, think that's a really uncaring thing to say?' said Desperate Dan. He had an extremely irritating habit of finishing off his sentences with question marks. 'I mean, Sophie, you've got to care about other people a little bit more. It's not just all about you, you know. It's like yoo-hoo, there are other people out there too-oo.' He waved a limp hand in the air.

'So I gather,' I snapped. I was getting increasingly irritable. I had wanted to have a bath and spend some time looking through all the other clothes I'd bought at Kensington Market over the weekend before deciding which to wear. And this was exactly what he had done the evening we'd met before: spent all night telling me about friends who were ill, or dying, or redundant, or shortly to be repossessed, or who had seriously lost out in the love stakes, moved on to a spot of personal criticism and then expected me to want to see him again. As a matter of fact, he'd expected more than that, he actually suggested we have a pagan love celebration, confirm our commitment by binding ourselves together in mistletoe and move into an underground tunnel peopled with chums of his who were protesting against the construction of a new cycling path across Regents Park. I was usually as sympathetic as the next woman, but really. 'What happened then?' I asked wearily.

'Got him sectioned,' said Dan, shaking his head in

despair and taking another very large gulp of his drink. 'OK, but that's over, now I'm back here again, just got to sort out my life now. It's just, like, AAAAAAAAGH!'

I jumped and whirled round, assuming that an intruder had suddenly appeared, before realizing that this was Desperate Dan's way of summing up the human condition. Then it got worse. 'I need a hug!' he yelled, leaping up.

Well, what could I do? I allowed myself to be pinned to the grey sweatshirts, avoided – with difficulty – that horrid slobbery mouth and disengaged myself as fast as I could. 'So, like, I just came here because I really needed to be with someone who doesn't know Isaac?' continued Dan, settling down in the chair again. 'I really needed to talk to you, Sophie, even though you're not a very empathetic person? It's like, maybe the two of us should take a look at what's going on with you?'

At this precise moment, that was the last thing I wanted to do. 'Yes, but um—' I began.

'So how have you been?' interrupted Desperate Dan, all thoughts of his tragic friend pushed to one side. 'What have you been up to?'

'Oh, this and that,' I said. 'Actually, um—'

'And what are you doing later? I thought we could, like, hang out, have a few drinks, maybe go out for dinner? And maybe we could talk through your problems with communication?'

'I'm sorry,' I said, increasingly irritably, 'but I'm already meeting friends tonight.'

'What are you doing?' Dan shot me a look from underneath his lanky fringe, and attempted to smile. He badly needed a good dentist.

'Going to a party,' I said. I don't know why, but I absolutely did not want to start telling Desperate Dan about my plans for the evening.

'Where is it?'

'Chiswick,' I said firmly.

'And what are you wearing?'

'Black Armani trousers, red Equipment shirt,' I said. Tragically my wardrobe included no such items, but as Desperate Dan lived in a squat in Hackney, I was hoping a bit of blatant consumerism might put him off.

'Sounds nice,' said my tormentor. 'Can I come too?'

'No!' I said. 'I mean, I'm really sorry, but it would be a bit difficult. I've already got plans.'

Desperate Dan looked deeply hurt. 'Why didn't you call?' he asked petulantly.

I would have thought the answer was blatantly obvious, but I couldn't be that cruel. 'I lost your number,' I said through clenched teeth. Albert felt no such reserve: shooting Dan a look of pure contempt, he leapt off the sofa and stalked out of the room with his tail in the air.

'But I left several messages.'

'I didn't get them.'

'I'll give my number to you again,' said Dan, fishing in his jacket for a torn up bit of paper and blunt pencil. He scribbled down a number, stood up to put it on the mantelpiece, and sat down again. 'So,' he said, 'I really like you, Sophie. Do you like me?'

'Oh, yes.'

'But you won't take me to the party,' said Dan quietly.

'Look,' I said, and frankly, I was nearing breaking point, 'I'm sure you can appreciate that's for about

195

10,000 other reasons that have absolutely nothing to do with you. Now it's been great to see you, but really—' and at that point my salvation finally arrived. There was the sound of a key in the lock. 'Little Ant!' I bellowed, as the door opened. 'We're in here!'

My absolutely fabulously wonderful flatmate appeared a moment later. He, too, was wearing jeans, but there the resemblance ended: he was in brown suede desert boots and a light blue linen shirt that showed off his tan. His blond hair gleamed in the half light of the room, his blue eyes were glittering wickedly, and you could have used those cheek-bones as a bread knife. 'Hello,' he said bustling round turning on lights, 'I'm Anthony Hurlingham. I don't think we've met.' He strode over and proffered a hand.

'Dan,' said the desperate one, who was not looking at all pleased at this interruption. He also, very rudely, ignored Little Ant's outstretched hand. 'I think we've spoken on the phone. I asked you to pass on a few messages, but, like, you didn't?'

Little Ant stepped back, saw me looking imploringly at him and took in the situation at a glance. 'Ah!' he said. 'Ah! Well, there's a reason for that, you see. I really don't like Sophie seeing other men.'

Dan and I looked equally dumbfounded.

'You see,' continued Little Ant, walking back to me and throwing an arm around my shoulders, 'I know I shouldn't be jealous, I know Sophie would never be unfaithful, but, man to man, you know how it is.'

'What?' cried Desperate Dan. I didn't trust myself to speak, but then again, Little Ant seemed to be doing fine for both of us.

'Yes,' said Little Ant happily, 'and now that Sophie's

accepted my proposal, I just don't think it would be right for her to see other men on her own. You do see my point, don't you, darling?'

'What? Oh yes,' I said hastily, as Little Ant squeezed my shoulder.

'Proposal?' asked Desperate Dan, aghast. 'You mean, you, and Sophie?'

'Yes, and in fact we're going out for a celebration, just the two of us, later on,' said Little Ant, keeping a firm grip on me. 'I'm really looking forward to it, aren't you, darling?'

'Oh, yes.'

'But she said she was going to a party!' cried Dan. 'Why didn't you tell me?'

'I expect she didn't want to hurt your feelings,' said Little Ant, releasing me. 'She's very kind, you know, doesn't have the heart to tell everyone she's already taken. Now we mustn't keep you, but you must come and visit us after we're married. We thought a discreet little ceremony in the Seychelles or something like that. It's been great to meet you.' He picked up Dan's denim jacket, and handed it to him.

'Right,' said Dan. 'Uh, right.' He came over to me and hugged me again before I could get out of the way but thankfully, under the watchful gaze of Little Ant, didn't go on too long. 'If it breaks up,' he hissed, 'you've got my number.'

'Oh, yes,' I said.

Dan released me. 'See you, Sophie,' he said and, escorted by Little Ant, who was now talking about our honeymoon plans, disappeared into the hall. I heard the front door click, and a second later Little Ant reappeared, with Albert in tow. 'What in God's name was that?' he enquired.

'A loony!' I yelled, jumping up and down and flailing my arms wildly. 'Oh, Little Ant, thank Heavens you turned up! It was that ghastly Desperate Dan person, and I never want to see him again and I hate him! I hate him! How dare he waltz in here like this and tell me I have problems communicating with other people just because if I said anything I'd tell him how horrible he is. Ugh!'

'So you don't want me to ask him to be best man, then?' enquired Little Ant, shooting me a sideways glance.

'Ugh! I hate him! But that was so brilliant of you, Little Ant,' I went on, rushing over and throwing my arms round him, 'I owe you one, no, I owe you about a thousand for that.'

Little Ant laughed and embraced me in return. 'You are hopeless,' he said. 'Poor old Sophie, first Martin and then that.'

'And Bearded Bernie and Tommy the Trannie, but I really can not bore you with them,' I said, continuing to hold on to my flatmate. For some strange reason, I didn't particularly want to let go, and Little Ant showed no signs of wanting to break away either. 'Oh, you do not know the day I've had,' I went on. 'It's been one past mistake after another rearing their ugly heads again. But one good thing did happen. I met Michael Tang! You know the chap I met before, he was Penny's cousin, not her brother! The real one is massively dishier.'

Little Ant released me abruptly. 'Well, I couldn't judge, I'm a man too, remember,' he said, slightly coldly. 'There's some post for you outside.'

'Oh, thanks,' I said, rather bewildered by the change of tone. I went into the hall, collected the letters, and came back to find Little Ant lighting the fire. It was a real one, he had to use ridiculous smoke-free logs or something, but it was terribly cheering on cold autumn evenings.

'Well, that can go in there,' I said, marching over and throwing Desperate Dan's number in to the flames. Albert, who had settled beside the fire, began to purr. I opened the first letter. 'Dear Miss Brackenbury, It is with regret that I must inform you that we are unable to offer you a post on *Metropolitan* magazine,' I read. You know *Metro*, it's that magazine that tells you how to have six impossible orgasms before breakfast, and I had recently applied for a job there. 'We do not feel that your experience is sufficient to cater for the needs of our readership, but we wish you every luck in your future career,' it went on. It was pp-d by the feature editor's secretary.

There were two more letters along these lines: one from *Snobs and Snobbery* (well, that wasn't its real name, but I'm sure you can guess what it is) and the other from *Pret à Porter*, a sort of down market *Vogue*, for those who couldn't even afford the latter's cover price, let alone the clothes inside. I sighed and handed them to Little Ant, who took a glance and threw all three in the fire. 'Come on, you don't have time to be gloomy,' he said, sounding rather more friendly again. 'We're going out tonight, remember?'

'I know,' I said. 'Hang on a sec.' I took down a photograph of Martin that I'd stuck on the mantel-piece, and after a moment's hesitation, threw that in the fire too.

'Well done,' said Little Ant, looking at me slightly

curiously. 'So it really is totally over between you two?'

'Yes, although I'm not sure if Martin realizes that yet,' I said. 'Oh, God, Little Ant, what is it about me? Why do only losers, louts, lechers and leeches want to go out with me?'

'Very good,' said Little Ant, sounding impressed. 'A line from one of your poems?'

'No, I thought it up on the spot.'

'Don't worry, my darling, your time will come. Now go to your room, decide what to wear, and I'll bring you a gin and tonic,' said Little Ant soothingly. 'Come on, do as Little Ant says.'

I obediently walked up the hall, accompanied by Albert, and threw open the door of my bedroom. Chaos confronted my eyes. Clothes lay in heaps on the floor, on the chairs, on the rather nice mahogany bed, which was my pride and joy, and from the handles of my wardrobe. All around me lay reminders of my various previous careers: notes on grandfathers who had run off with their step grandchildren from my time as a television researcher for an afternoon chat show, huge piles of worthy tomes that I had not yet read, but had acquired at a staff discount when I worked in a book shop as a shop assistant and a very expensive camera that my father had bought me when I decided I wanted to be a photographer. That would-be career went out of the window when I discovered I'd shot a whole roll of film without removing the lens cap.

On the mantelpiece, for sentimental reasons, I kept the glass I used to put tips in when I was a waitress, while the top of my chest of drawers was covered with needles for acupuncture and bottles of paint stripper from when I decided to be a furniture restorer. Peeping out from under the bed was my tool box, bought when I decided to be an electrician's apprentice. I'm going to get rid of all of this right now, I thought, before realizing the bin was too full to take anything more. Honestly, if I couldn't even keep my bedroom in a reasonable condition, how was I supposed to sort my life out? I turned as Little Ant appeared at the door, bearing a brimming glass of the necessaries. 'My word, it looks better in here,' he said brightly, handing it over. 'Been doing some tidying up?'

17

As usual, though, I managed to rescue something rela-
tively decent from the chaos, and spent the taxi
journey over to The Collection day-dreaming about
being Emma Peel – I was wearing some of my latest
acquisitions, an Avengers-style short black dress,
made of viscose, with no collar and a white stripe
down each arm, and a pair of knee-length black boots.
Little Ant, meanwhile, wittered on about how awful
Martin and my crowd of exes had been, and how it
was time that I found someone decent. We were
certainly in agreement there.

The drink with Barbara was brief but fab. Little Ant
had changed as well, and put on a black suit and
collarless white shirt, which emphasized his slim
physique and very blond hair. He looked quite as
glamorous as the occasion required as we walked
past the bouncers at the door – all the fashionable
restaurants these days need bouncers, it seems – and
towards the huge barn of a room that housed the bar
and the restaurant. To get there you had to go over a
sort of catwalk – Collection, geddit? – which was lit
from underneath, and which I always rather worried
about skidding over as it looked as if it should be

slippery. It wasn't, of course, or the restaurant would have resembled a casualty ward at chucking out time.

Inside, the massive arena was buzzing. The walls were bare brick, which somehow worked because of the size of the place, to the right was a staircase, which led up to the restaurant, and straight ahead of us was a huge bar that ran down the full length of the room. It was filled with all the usual suspects: groups of glamorous, pretty twenty-somethings, almost all blond, huddled in groups and keeping an eye out for chat-up material, a selection of male Eurotrash, Middle Eastern types and Tory MPs doing pretty much the same, and the fashionable London set who had picked on this venue for tonight's entertainment. Tomorrow it would be Daphne's, and the day after would be Le Caprice. You know the type.

We pushed our way through the scrum and looked around. I must say, I had been wondering how poor, pale, frail Mrs van Trocken would be able to cope with this lot, and so at first I didn't even notice the staggeringly beautiful woman sitting with a professional looking chap at one of the tables at the side of the room and motioning in our direction. It was Little Ant who nudged me. 'I think someone's trying to get your attention,' he said.

I turned and to be honest, it took me a moment. The stunning creature who had leapt up and run over to kiss me was about the last thing I was expecting. 'Oh Barbara,' I burst out tactlessly, 'I would never have recognized you.'

'I'm very pleased to hear it,' said Mrs van Trocken, shaking hands with Little Ant and leading us back to the table. 'My lawyers very kindly agreed to meet me at my hairdresser's this afternoon.'

She really did look quite amazing. The grey clothing had been swapped for a brilliant red silk sheath dress, which made her look slim rather than malnourished. The grey in her hair had disappeared as well, and been replaced by auburn highlights, which were cut into a very chic bob. Simple pearl earrings and a slim gold watch were the only jewellery, while her face had been carefully made up to conceal the worry lines. She had also had a French manicure and was sporting red Manolo Blahnik mules with kitten heels – I might not have been able to afford them, but I could certainly recognize them – in exactly the same shade as her dress. In short, she looked sensational, and from the look on Little Ant's face, I could tell he thought so too – in fact, he was looking quite overcome. Do you know, when I saw his expression, I quite suddenly had a bit of a pang.

'Meet Edmund Wilson,' said Barbara, as we got to the table. The professional type, a tall distinguished looking man in his fifties, got up and shook hands. 'Edmund's my lawyer,' she continued, 'and I tell you Sophie, if you ever find yourself caught up in a messy divorce case, he's the man to go to. Champagne, everyone?'

'Yes, please,' said Little Ant and I simultaneously.

Edmund splashed the sparkly into four glasses and passed them around. 'To freedom,' said Barbara, raising her glass. 'Sophie has been so sweet, Edmund, she looked after me when I had to go into Vladimir's office today, and now here she is, consorting with the enemy.'

I looked around nervously – that joke was a bit close to the bone for my liking. 'Don't you worry,' said Edmund reassuringly, 'he's not here now,

Sophie. In fact, I strongly suspect he's locked up with his own lawyers. Barbara and I have been pretty busy today.'

'Oh, do tell,' I said.

'Those papers I got from the study today,' said Barbara happily, 'are the ones that confirm ownership of the firm is mine. Then we've attended to a few other matters' – from that I assumed she was referring to the bank accounts her husband had been shouting about earlier – 'and at some point during this evening he's going to get served with the divorce papers. I intensely hope he's with Apricot when that happens.'

'How on earth did he persuade you to marry him?' asked Little Ant, gazing at her with undisguised admiration.

'Youth and folly – in both cases mine – were on his side,' said Barbara. 'And he does have a very strong personality.'

'I'll say,' I said with feeling.

'You poor girl,' said Barbara, turning to me. 'I must say, Sophie, I haven't taken to many of Vladimir's employees, but you're quite different from the rest of them, and it must have been awful for you. Do you know, a most peculiar young man who used to work for Vladimir has been bombarding me with telephone calls about something that he says is going to appear in the *News of the World*, "to warn me," apparently. Most odd. Never mind, Sophie dear, it's not for much longer. Now Anthony,' she beamed at him as she said this, 'you will look after Sophie until all this is sorted out?'

'It will be my pleasure,' said Little Ant, beaming back.

'Barbara,' I said anxiously, 'I think I know who you

mean. A chap called Rory walked out yesterday, and I have a feeling something really will be in the papers.'

'Jolly good,' said Barbara calmly, 'it will be all the more ammunition for the divorce. I must thank Rory the next time we speak. Anyway,' she continued, 'we won't keep you, I know the two of you are having dinner, and we don't want to intrude. But next week, why don't we all have a proper celebration? Dinner for four?'

'I'd like nothing better,' said Little Ant standing up. We both kissed her and shook hands with Edmund, who was looking positively paternal towards his client, and made our way upstairs to the restaurant. 'I must say,' said Little Ant as the waiter ushered us to a table, 'your employer must be mad.'

'I know,' I said. 'But honestly Little Ant, you wouldn't believe the difference since this morning. Really, she looked just totally ill, then.'

'Well, she certainly looks fine now,' said Little Ant as we sat down. He waited until the head waiter had moved off and leant towards me. 'Now look, Sophie,' he began, when he was interrupted by the appearance of the second in command. 'Would you like to – you again!' cried our new companion.

I looked up sharply, and a second later recognized my friend from last night. How totally unexpected. 'Hello,' I said warmly. 'Little Ant, this is the very nice barman who was looking after me last night. You know, I told you, in Boom Boom.'

'Little Ant?' demanded the barman turned waiter. 'That's a very funny name. Your parents had a good sense of humour, did they?'

'No, no it's a joke,' said Little Ant hastily. 'Everyone calls me that because I'm quite tall. My name's actually Anthony. So you work in two places do you?'

'Yeah, sometimes I work here on me nights off when they need extra people,' said the waiter, giving Little Ant a dubious look. 'Now you look after this young lady, she was wiv a very funny bloke last night. Want a drink, either of you?'

'Yes,' said Little Ant and I simultaneously. I was slightly wishing that my new friend would get a move on, actually. I didn't want him to start telling Little Ant about Michael being in the bar too. Although I had filled him in on the details of everything else that had happened, I had left that bit out, wasn't quite sure why.

'Let me guess,' said the waiter consideringly. 'Kir for you?' I nodded. 'Make that two,' said Little Ant. The waiter moved off.

'So you were saying,' I said, picking at a bit of bread.

'Yeah,' said Little Ant, beginning to get up. 'Look, Soph, sorry about this, but I've got to go to the cigarette machine. I won't be a minute, then we can talk about this.'

He scooted off. The waiter reappeared a minute later, plonked down the drinks, the menus and the wine list, cheerfully told me to take my time and moved off. I lit a cigarette and looked around. All the tables were full, as per usual, and smoke and chatter were rising above the well-dressed throng and bouncing off the cheerful brick walls.

When I say well-dressed, I mean well-dressed except for a table on the opposite side of the room. There were two young men dressed in black trousers and black T-shirts, engaged in intense conversation. I must have been gazing a bit too intently, because after a minute one of them looked up and caught my eye.

The other followed her gaze. Yes her, because I suddenly realized they were Henry and Sam. There was no sign of Jim. Both ignored my weak grin, looked me up and down, and resumed their conversation. I was beginning to think I couldn't move around this city without a couple from that little trio appearing to haunt me. To my intense relief Little Ant then reappeared and sat down. 'Actually, let's choose our supper first and then talk,' he said.

Nosh sorted out, Little Ant fished out a packet of Silk Cut, offered me one and we both inhaled deeply. 'Now, this is a bit difficult to say,' he began.

'Oh, what is it?' I asked petulantly. Little Ant, possibly feeling responsible for me by virtue of his great age, was sometimes prone to the odd lecture about my lifestyle.

'Listen,' said Little Ant. 'It's nothing bad, at least I hope not. You and Martin really are through, aren't you?'

'Yes, I told you,' I said, taking a gulp from the glass of wine the waiter had poured out and trying not to think of the two glasses of champagne I'd had at lunchtime, the gin and tonic earlier, champagne with Barbara van Trocken, a kir and now this. I was beginning to think I'd have to put off my resolution to have only one hangover a week for another day or so and, most alarmingly of all, I didn't feel in the slightest bit woozy at the moment. In fact, I felt alarmingly lucid.

'I see.' Little Ant paused.

'Little Ant, what is this about?' I enquired. 'You've been acting funny ever since you got back. What's wrong?'

'Nothing's wrong,' said Little Ant hesitantly. 'It's just that this is difficult to say, but I've been thinking, and I've got to tell you. Listen, Sophie, we've known one another for a long time.'

'I know.'

'And you see, I suppose I've always taken you a bit for granted in a way. I mean, it felt a bit as though you were my sister when you first moved in. But you're not.'

'I know I'm not,' I said blankly, taking another gulp, and noticing Little Ant had hardly touched his wine. My glass was nearly empty. 'What's that got to do with the price of fish?'

'Everything,' said Little Ant, stubbing out his cigarette and lighting another immediately. 'I mean, the thing is, do you look on me as a brother?'

'Well, I guess not,' I said, catching his glance for a second and then looking away. I had thought I did, but for some reason, Little Ant had never seemed less like a brother – of mine, at least – in his life. 'Why?'

'Because—'

'Teriyaki?' enquired a voice. We both jumped. 'Teriyaki?' repeated our friend the waiter. 'For you, wasn't it?' he placed a plate in front of Little Ant, and put a salad in front of me. I picked up my fork and toyed with it. I had totally lost my appetite.

Little Ant waited until the coast was clear and then started again. He took a few deep breaths. 'The thing is,' he began, 'I did a lot of thinking while I was away.'

'Yes, me too,' I said, rather wishing he'd get on with it. I didn't like it when the one stable element of my life started acting so strangely. 'I've been thinking, and I've definitely decided our sitting-room needs repainting.'

'What?' said Little Ant abstractedly. 'Yes, but we'll talk about that another time. I mean I've decided that

I just really think it's time you got together with a decent chap, who does not cheat on you with his students, and who does not turn out to be a transsexual and who does not want to go through a pagan bonding ceremony and above all, who is not an adulterous fraudster.'

'Well you and me both,' I said, gratefully taking another slurp from my newly refilled glass. I was, however, concerned that Little Ant was paying no attention to what I quite suddenly had realized was an extremely important issue. 'But look, Little Ant, the sitting-room really, really does need repainting. I mean, it really, really does.'

'I quite agree,' said Little Ant, sounding rather tense. 'But look, Sophie, please do concentrate, I'm talking about something important. I have someone in mind for you.' He took rather a large gulp of wine.

'Anyone I know?' I enquired raffishly.

'You're talking to him,' said Little Ant.

Well, you could have knocked me down with a feather. For a moment I sat gazing at him in stunned silence, and then burst out, 'You?'

'Why not?' asked Little Ant slightly indignantly. 'OK, so I'm ageing a bit, but so, God knows, is Martin. And I'm happy to assure you that there are no other women lurking in the background, that I do not fancy that dreadful woman Belinda, or Tiffany, or whatever you said her name is now. I have not dabbled illicitly on the stockmarket, I have no desire to turn into a woman, I have a good job, sound prospects and your parents like me. And believe it or not, some people even think I'm quite attractive.'

'Oh, you are,' I said gazing at Little Ant, before polishing off my glass of wine, which was instantly refilled by our friend the waiter, who had been lurking suspiciously closely nearby. 'But I mean, well, this is so unexpected. I don't understand.' Indeed, I don't think I've ever felt so confused in my life.

'I'm in love with you, Sophie,' said Little Ant simply. 'And it was when I went away that I realized I've been in love with you for years. That's why I didn't like all your exes – that and the fact they were awful, of course – and that's why I was pissed off by Martin and that dreadful man earlier and that's why I've been acting a bit strange. I've so wanted to tell you, and the time's never been right, but I've got to tell you now. I love you.'

'Oh, my word,' I said, finishing off another glass.

'Is that it?' asked Little Ant, beckoning for a second bottle. 'Oh, my word?'

'But I mean,' I began, bewildered, 'but I thought, I mean, you see, I don't know what to say.' My emotions were, in fact, in total chaos: a picture of Michael Tang flitted briefly through my mind – but he's not interested in me, I thought – followed by a parade of exes, each vying with the next for the highest score in the unacceptability stakes. And then sitting opposite me, gazing at me intensely, was lovely, reliable Little Ant, who looked after me when Mr van Trocken was being horrible, and who had never let me down and who had even forgiven me when I set his flat on fire.

Why on earth hadn't I realized how handsome he is before? I thought. And I'd been living with him for three years so I knew he didn't leave toenail clippings in the bath or tea bags in the sink or let the milk run out or the drinks cabinet run dry. And what I wanted, more than ever after the last couple of days, was a settled relationship. I'd been far too flighty in the past, and I wanted to settle down. 'Gosh,' I said, trying not to hiccup.

We paused as the second bottle appeared and plates were cleared – I'd hardly touched any of mine – before lighting inter-course cigarettes and settling back. 'Gosh,' I said again.

'Translation?' enquired Little Ant. He was beginning to smile.

'Well, you know,' I said. I looked up and began to smile back. Little Ant looked at me very consideringly, and then leaned over and kissed me, very briefly, on the lips. I went beetroot.

'Food,' said an abrupt voice behind me. We both jumped and looked up. Our friend the waiter was standing behind us with the second course, and behind him, a middle-aged couple sitting across the room were waving at Little Ant.

'So sorry,' said Little Ant looking embarrassed, 'that's my new boss. I must just go and say hello.' He shot off. The waiter put both plates down on the table and looked at me consideringly. 'Gettin' on well wiv him, aren't cha?' he enquired.

'Yes,' I said. I was feeling rather nonplussed. 'Aren't you pleased? You told him to look after me.'

'I didn't mean like that,' said the waiter crossly. He was looking increasingly annoyed. 'What about that uvver bloke, last night?'

'Oh, him,' I said appalled. 'We've split up, he just doesn't know it yet.'

'I don't mean him,' snapped the waiter. 'The uvver one earlier. I thought you liked him, did'n I. He liked you.'

'No, no, no, no, no, he didn't,' I said equally firmly,

trying not to hiccup again. 'I've met him again and he was just being polite.'

'That's not what it looked like from where I was standing,' said the waiter. 'And what was going on wiv you two just then?'

'I've known him for years,' I said mistily. 'And tonight, well, we've just decided to take things a step further.'

'You're makin' a mistake, right,' said the waiter. 'I saw the way you looked at that uvver bloke last night, did'n I, and it's him you like.'

'How do you know?' I said, suddenly indignant, knocking back some more wine. It was a bit much to go out for a quiet supper and find that even the waiter is intent on lecturing you about your love life. 'I don't even know him, although you know what? His sister is my best friend! Isn't that spooky? She's going out with a woman, you know.'

'Is she,' said the waiter, displaying a hurtful lack of interest in Penny's life and times. 'But I'm talking about you an' that uvver bloke, it can happen just like that. Happened wiv me and my bloke, right? He just came in to the bar one night and that was that.'

'And there's never been anyone since?'

'Well I wouldn't say that,' said the waiter, looking bashful. 'But no-one important. Look, gel, you're making a mistake. This one tonight, he's a nice-looking bloke, I can see what you see in him, but he's not right for you. Hang on for the uvver one.'

'Well thanks for the advice,' I said haughtily, 'but I know do, I mean, I do know what I'm doing.' Little Ant was threading his way back through the tables: he looked about a million times more attractive than anyone else there, and the way he was looking at me quite took my breath away. I felt overwhelmed by love. Why on earth hadn't we got together years ago? I wondered. 'Honestly,' I said to the waiter, 'I'm right. At long last I've met the right chap.' The waiter, looking dubious, moved off. 'Little Ant,' I said fondly as he returned to the table, 'darling Little Ant. You've been away so long. I've missed you. I love you. How have you been?'

18

Of course I wasn't right. Why should I, Sophie
Brackenbury, after a career of unerringly making the
wrong choice about jobs, men, the gender of my cat
– Albert was actually a girl, as we discovered when he
unexpectedly became a mother last year, but we still
referred to him as he, if you see what I mean – you
name it, why should I suddenly start changing the
habits of a lifetime? It must have been a combination
of all the wine we'd drunk and Martin and the
momentous events at work and goodness knows
what else, but I knew even before I opened my eyes
in Little Ant's capacious wrought iron four poster the
next morning that this time I had got it horribly,
hideously, horrifically badly wrong.

And who knows why it should have been so
wrong? On paper, I know, it looks fine: we'd known
one another for years, known one another's little
faults and foibles, the best relationships are based on
friendship and all that jazz and still it wasn't right. To
be honest, I think we knew one another too well. Yes,
I know, familiarity is a brilliant foundation, but I don't
think that's what some people, including, alas, yours

truly, really want. They, or rather we, want a relationship built on mystery. And with Little Ant, the mystery just wasn't there.

Little Ant, star that he was, realized straight away that something was wrong, from the moment he put a hand on my shoulder, and I tensed and pretended to be asleep. He got out of bed, padded down the corridor, and returned a few minutes later with a tray bearing coffee and orange juice. 'It's all right Sophie, it doesn't matter,' he said, sitting down on the bed beside me.

'Oh, yes it does,' I said in agony. I'd pulled on one of his old rugger shirts when he was out of the room, and now sat up straight. I winced as I caught sight of myself in the mirror on top of his chest of drawers: my hair was sticking straight up on end, and the remnants of my make-up were all over the place. And I felt even worse than I looked, my head was pounding, my throat was dry and now I was going to lose the person who I suddenly realized was really my best friend. I was terribly fond of Penny, but Little Ant came first, and now I'd ruined it. I burst into tears.

Little Ant hastily put the tray down on the floor, and moved over to hug me. 'Now come on, this isn't like you,' he said, smoothing down my hair. 'Come on, Sophie, nothing's that terrible.'

'Yes it is,' I said between sobs. 'Oh, Little Ant, I utterly adore you, I really really do, but just not in that way.' By now I was crying so hard I could hardly make myself understood. 'And I can't believe I've messed it all up, you saying all those things to me, but it's just not possible between us. I've known you too long, you really are like my brother, and it just couldn't work. I'll move out tonight.'

'You will do no such thing,' said Little Ant, hugging me tighter. 'It was my fault, I should have realized you were all wrought up about everything that's been happening, and I should never have come out with it all like that. Come on, Sophie, it will be like it was before, and I positively forbid you to move out.'

I sniffled and wiped my cheeks with the collar of Little Ant's dressing gown. 'You're just saying that,' I said. 'You'll change your mind and decide you hate me.'

'You do say the silliest things,' said Little Ant, helping me with the wiping process. 'You are the last person I could ever hate, and I couldn't ask for a nicer flatmate. I'm just angry at myself, not you. Come on, Sophie, have a gulp of coffee, and then we'll run you a bath.'

I accepted the mug, gulped, and caught sight of myself in the mirror again. I now had bright red puffy eyes to add to the general impression. 'Honestly,' I said in agony, 'how can you bear to see me looking like this?'

Little Ant laughed. 'Very easily,' he said. 'Now come on, Sophie, I think you need extra rations of bubble bath.'

Little Ant didn't confine his heroics to this. 'Would you like a lift into the office?' he asked, after I'd emerged from the bathroom, having slapped on about half a tonne of make-up.

'The office?' I said blankly.

'Well, yes,' said Little Ant. 'It's Friday, and you're still working there, aren't you? Unless they've shut it down, or something.'

'I suppose so,' I said. It hadn't actually occurred to me that I had to go into work that day, but he was right, no-one had actually done anything yet. 'Yes, I'd love a lift. I'll go and get my coat.'

Little Ant was waiting for me at the front door of our communal hall, when I came down the stairs. Feeling that today was going to be a momentous one, I had dressed for the occasion: white trousers that I'd bought from French Connection last summer, a black polo neck, black ankle boots and my mother's white coat. It was more in the style of *The Persuaders* than *The Avengers*, but at least the boots would enable me to make a speedy getaway if Mr van Trocken totally flipped.

'You look lovely,' said Little Ant smiling at me. 'This is for you.' He handed over a note with 'Delivered by hand' in Martin's handwriting on the envelope. I opened it with a decidedly sinking feeling, and began to read.

> 'Sweetest love, I do not go,
> For weariness of thee,
> Nor in the hope the world can show
> A fitter Love for me . . .

> 'Well, maybe I do, just a bit. It's been fun but it's time to move on, dear little dollop of sunshine. I know you'll get over me one day and try not to suffer too much. 'You're in my heart, you're in my soul' as a more modern poet put it!
> Lots of love, Martin.
> P.S. Tell Vladimir I've gone abroad. M.'

'Bastard!' I shouted, passing the note to Little Ant. 'Bastard! How dare he finish with me before I've finished with him! I'll show him! I'll, I'll, I'll . . .'

I paused. I couldn't think quite what I'd do.

'What a complete wanker,' said Little Ant, who had just finished reading. 'Write a poem in return. Go on, Soph, I know you can.'

'Yeah, yeah,' I said. 'Oh Little Ant, what an utter louse.'

'I know,' said my flatmate. 'I know. Where do you think he's gone?'

'Well, he was supposed to be having dinner tonight with bloody Tiffany,' I said fretfully, as we walked to the car. 'I bet he won't go anywhere before that.'

'Do you know where they're going?' asked Little Ant, opening the door for me.

'Yes, Sonny's, in Barnes. I've already told Penny, so she can tell Sir Jeremy.'

'Hm,' said Little Ant. He walked round to his side of the car, climbed in and gave me a quizzical look. 'Fancy supper, maybe at a quiet restaurant some way out of the centre of town?' he asked.

About ten minutes later, the car pulled up on Kensington Gore, and I jumped out. We weren't quite there, but Little Ant was going to Simpsons to buy a new suit, so I suggested he drop me off early. 'See you later,' called Little Ant, and zoomed off.

He really is a hero, I thought, beginning to make my way up Gloucester Road. No more reference at all had been made to last night, and he had been making an effort to be downright chatty. I intensely wished it could have been him, but - oh, well. Michael wasn't even interested anyway, so I really had cut my nose off to spite my own face. I wonder what it would be like to be a plastic surgeon? I thought dreamily. I donned my white coat and stepped into the consulting room. 'Yes, nurse, show Mrs

Fotheringay-Fishkettle through,' I said. 'We will be redesigning her nose, cheeks, chin, forehead, mouth, ears and eyebrows – what we call the full "Wacko Jacko" round here – after which we will be discussing breast augmentation, stomach reduction, thigh sculpture, wrinkle elimination and toenail replacement therapy. We shall then—' 'Watch it, darlin', look where you're goin'!' roared a voice.

I skidded to a halt and looked wildly around. At first I thought I'd taken a wrong turn and ended up at Kensington Palace, but no, this was Gloucester Road, and I was standing outside the offices of van Trocken and Co. About twenty other people were standing there as well, however, some, including the chap who had yelled at me, carrying really heavy-duty cameras and some holding notebooks. Pushing aside a sudden picture of myself as an award-winning photographer in the front line of battle, I approached one of the more civilized looking specimens present, who was dressed in a trench coat and carrying a pile of newspapers. 'What's going on?' I asked.

'Oh, it's the bloke who runs this place,' said the chap, pushing his glasses up his nose. 'We've all been waiting for him to turn up for hours, but no-one's there yet. Look, I'll show you.' He rummaged in the pile of newspapers, and produced a very dogeared copy of the *Daily Telegraph*.

I took it and gasped. There on the front page was a huge picture of Mr van Trocken, with the headline 'Concern grows over Czech tycoon'. There was lots of guff about *Food for Thought* and Molehill, as well as stuff about the Tory Party donation. 'We are very concerned about the allegations, and of course we will reconsider accepting a donation from anyone under suspicion of fraud, whomsoever they may be,' a highly embarrassed Marcus Aimsworthy was quoted as saying.

Then there was a bit about Mr van Trocken's 'highly colourful' personal life, about which 'further allegations were thought to be appearing in a Sunday newspaper,' and a line saying Barbara had filed for divorce. 'How on earth do they know all this?' I asked, handing back the paper.

'Oh, you'd be surprised at the number of friends who are prepared to start squealing when they know someone is in trouble,' said the chap, who I had by now gathered was a journalist. 'Not that this chap seems to have made many friends.'

'No-one in their right mind would want to be a friend of Mr van Trocken,' I said with feeling.

'What,' said the chap, 'do you know him? My name's Christopher Jenkinson from *The Times*, by the way.'

'Sophie Brackenbury,' I said, shaking hands. 'Yes I do, actually, I work for him.'

My words seemed to have an electrifying effect. 'No!' said Christopher. 'You work for him! What's he like? Have you any idea what's been going on? Has he ever made a pass at you? How many mistresses does he have?'

'Er,' I said. A whole group was gathering around me. I could hear murmurs of 'She knows him!' 'She works for him!' 'She's the one who bought the shares!' 'She's his mistress!' A very tall woman placed a hand on my arm. 'Don't say anything,' she hissed in a Welsh accent. 'I represent a very well known newspaper – look at the sky and you'll get it – and we're very interested in your story. We're prepared to pay.'

'Look this way, darlin'!' shouted a voice. I looked round and a camera flashed, then another and another. 'Look,' I cried, 'I don't know anything about it! I only work for him!'

This did nothing to dispel the crowd. They all pressed closer, some shoving microphones in my direction, and shouting more and more questions. 'What's he done with the money?' yelled one. 'Where's his wife?' yelled another. 'What's your name, how old are you, how long have you worked there and how much do you earn?' shouted a third. And then, 'Leave her alone!' someone bellowed above the scrum.

Everyone, me included, stopped shouting and whirled round. And there, standing a few paces away, was the tall dark figure of Michael Tang. With that black hair and olive skin, for about one second he looked like a figure from Chinese mythology – not that I knew anything about Chinese mythology, I might add – and I half expected him to start brandishing a curved sword until I blinked and he turned into a pinstripes and Hermes-clad Western type again. 'Sophie, what a joy to see you!' he continued, forcing his way through to me. 'Fancy bumping into you like this. Sensational story, isn't it,' he added to the throng, 'but to Sophie, it's all just a load of tantalizing,' he paused for a second, 'gobbledygook. She knows nothing about it.' He reached me, put an arm around my shoulders, and began forcibly pulling me away through the crowd. 'Wait!' cried various members of the ratpack, some of whom were looking rather confused at this outpouring. 'We haven't finished talking to her!'

'Make it all up!' yelled Michael cheerfully. 'Say how

hideous the whole experience has been for her, detail her suffering and say she only wants to be left in peace! Or alternatively, wait till van Trocken gets here and ask him, he's the one who knows what's been going on. Come on, Sophie, this way, onwards and upwards. Are you all right?'

'Yes fine,' I said rather shakily, 'this was just totally unexpected.' Despite the best efforts of the crowd, which had been following us and shouting out more questions, we got to Michael's car, today *sans* chauffeur, and he shoved me inside. 'What are you doing here?' I asked after he'd nipped round and got in the other side.

Michael started the engine and, narrowly avoiding a hack or two, pulled out. 'Welcome to the sleaze-free zone, i.e. my car,' he said. 'I'll just drive round the corner and come back in a minute, when that lot have calmed down. Sophie, congratulations. You are in the unique position of being able to talk about your terrible trauma at the hands of the biggest bounder since Robert Maxwell, without being in the least bit implicated yourself. I can't wait to read it. You'll be a star! It's going to be a very good, very powerful, very scary story, complete with full details of Mr van Trocken's terrible acts of treachery to his company and his wife. Very, very shocking.' He shook his head sadly.

I giggled in spite of myself. 'Actually, it wasn't really like that,' I said. 'I mean it was quite scary working for him, but only because he shouted such a lot, and to be honest, there are a couple of other innocents in there as well.'

'That's simple, make it up,' said Michael brightly.

'What, you mean *lie*?' I demanded.

'I prefer to think of it as a creative approach to the truth. Oh well, maybe not. Shame, though, it would have made a sensational story.' He grinned at me again.

'Yes, well,' I said. 'Anyway, you haven't told me, what are you doing here?'

'Oh, just happened to be passing by,' said Michael airily. He shot me a sideways look. 'Well actually, I don't live that far away, I'm just on the Old Brompton Road, and when I was taking my morning tabloid, it occurred to me something like this might happen. We had a similar situation in Hong Kong a couple of years back, splendid story, did you know that history is supposed to repeat itself first as tragedy and then as farce? It looks as if it's skipped a stage back there. Anyway, then I thought you probably hadn't had much experience of dealing with the gentlemen of the press when they've scented blood and are going in for the kill, so I thought I'd pop in to see what was happening.' He swerved sharply to avoid a passing pedestrian and beamed at me.

'You came by because of me?' I asked.

'Indeed I did,' said Michael. He had the same slightly clipped tone as Penny, English, but with just the slightest Oriental twang to it. 'No point in seeing you caught up in these sensational events more than you have to be, a fresh and fragrant flower like you trapped in the middle of all those old and hairy hacks. I expect you'll be writing a poem about it any minute now.' He turned a corner and began circling back.

'Thank you,' I said. I couldn't think of anything else to say, and anyway, was feeling ludicrously tongue-tied. We were both quiet for a few minutes until we got back on to Gloucester Road, where Michael stopped the car. This time we were on the other side of the road and the hacks, who were now all lounging against trees and lamp posts and talking feverishly into mobile telephones, ignored us.

'Where do you think your devious employer is?' asked Michael. 'On a slow boat to China? I hope not, for the sake of the old country. Or hiding in some corner of South America if the resident criminal fraternity hasn't used up all the appropriate space?'

'I've no idea. Do you think I should try to get in to the office?'

'Good God, no,' said Michael firmly, looking at the crowd, 'they'd all just try to follow you in. Much better to wait until he arrives.'

We lapsed into silence again, and then both started talking at once. 'No really, you first, I insist,' said Michael. It might have been my imagination, but he seemed to be slightly less sure of himself than before.

'No, you.'

'No really, you.'

'No really, I've forgotten what I was about to say.'

'I was just going to say,' said Michael clearing his throat, 'that was an amazing coincidence.'

'What was?'

'Our ships passing in the night encounter in Boom Boom and you turning out to be Sophie. Did the barman give you my message, by the way?'

'Um, yes he did.'

There was another short pause. 'And were you going to pop along, or was I going to be left standing at the altar?' asked Michael after a moment, examining his hands as he spoke. They were long and brown, with slim fingers and short, clean nails.

'I thought I might pop along,' I said, looking firmly out of the window by my side.

'I've met your flatmate, you know,' said Michael rather cautiously. 'When we were both travelling around Europe. Splendid chap. Took on the highly dangerous role of communicating with our Gallic friends and actually managed to impress the waitress so much that she let us stay on for an hour after the café closed. Couldn't have done better myself.'

'Yes, I know, he told me. How did you know he was my flatmate?'

'Penny was telling me about you yesterday morning, on the phone. Name, rank and serial number, and she mentioned his name. He,' Michael shot me a sideways look out of those long oval eyes, 'he said he was going to talk to you about something when he got back.'

'Really?'

'Yes, some quite serious stuff, I think he said.'

I took a deep breath. For some reason I sensed my reply was going to be very important indeed. 'We did have a very quick chat, but it was nothing serious on either side, you know, he was probably just feeling sentimental because he was away. He's a brilliant friend.'

'Splendid,' said Michael, still sounding cautious. 'Just a friend?'

'Yes, yes, well you know all about Martin and Little Ant was just giving me a shoulder to cry on and everything,' I said. 'That was it.'

'Marvellous,' said Michael. He suddenly seemed in an excellent mood. 'Absolutely marvellous! Lovely day for a stake-out,' he added.

'I know, it's gorgeous,' I said, admiring the way the

sun was glinting off the red of the Jaguar. 'But I feel bad keeping you here, shouldn't you be at work?'

'That's no problem at all,' said Michael. 'I am, after all, wired for sound: I have my bleeper on me and am able to communicate with my estimable Papa at any hour of the day or night. Not that I've got a lot to communicate about yet, I've left the firm I was working for in Hong Kong – you know I was in fund management too? – partly because things have changed a lot there and anyway, good old Papa thinks it's time I started learning the ropes in the family business. Penny and I are expected to run it eventually, in the unlikely circumstances that he ever decides to retire, so the time had come for the prodigal son to come home. My first task is to oversee that all our executives are wired up to the Internet, although at their age I'd have thought being wired up to dialysis machines would be a lot more sensible. Never mind, the burdens of high office and all that.'

'Gosh,' I said, impressed. 'My father once let me work in his antiques shop to see if I'd be any good at it, but I broke an eighteenth-century vase within the first half hour and he didn't seem so keen after that. Anyway – oh, look!'

We both scrambled out of the car and watched as an enormous black Rolls Royce drew up outside the building. Tony, wearing a very smart chauffeur's uniform, leapt out of the front, battled his way through the press, who were swarming all around the motor and opened the rear door for his master. A very familiar roar filled the air. 'Get out of the way, you fools! How dare you shove that camera in my face! I, Vladimir van Trocken, will make you pay for this!'

Michael and I walked over, and stood at the back of

the crowd. Mr van Trocken, today sporting a black woollen two-breasted suit and black and silver tie, and holding a silver-topped cane, emerged with some difficulty and, using the cane as a kind of machete, began to clear a path through the throng. There were a few howls of pain as he swatted his way to the steps, mounted them, and then turned round to face his accusers. 'I hope the hacks are getting paid danger money,' hissed Michael. 'Hideously risky, tackling him in this mood. What on earth is he doing?'

'Believe it or not, I think he's going to make a speech.'

I was right. Mr van Trocken raised his hands for silence and such was his sheer physical presence that, even now, a hush began to fall on the onlookers. 'Quiet!' he roared. 'I demand that you be quiet! I, Vladimir van Trocken, will speak!' He paused. A car roared by, and you could hear the traffic in the distance on Kensington Gore, but otherwise all was silent.

Mr van Trocken filled his lungs and started again. 'I come to you in sorrow, not in anger,' he began. (You could have fooled me, from the expression of fury on that mottled face, still sporting a livid black eye, anger was the mildest term available for his emotions. Even his beard looked as if it would spring off his face at any moment and start attacking the crowd.)

'I am a man more sinned against than sinning!' he cried. 'I, a humble boy from the streets of Prague, came to your great country nearly thirty years ago, and in return you have shown me the greatest generosity. You allowed me to build up my businesses, you granted me British nationality, you accepted my hospitality – yes, you! And you! And you!' He jabbed his fingers sharply in the direction of specific members of his audience at this point, who started looking at their feet and muttering about corporate hospitality not being the same as accepting bribes.

'You gave me much! But I gave to you in return. I have been a great and generous employer of thousands of our fellow British citizens,' (I couldn't control a snort at that point), 'I have paid millions in taxes to this great government of ours and the many who have gone before and I have made a huge contribution to the cultural life of this country. I, Vladimir van Trocken, not only mix with the great and good, I am the great and good! And it is for this reason that I am being persecuted. My friends, there is one terrible canker at the heart of the British soul.' His voice dropped nearly to a whisper. 'Envy.

'Yes, envy! For, why else should I be treated in this way? I have done nothing wrong. I have been honest and upright in my business dealings, and I have been a faithful and true husband to my dear wife Barbara. I have worked for the British people and suffered for the British people, and what is to be my reward? I am bound upon a wheel of fire, that mine own tears do scald like molten lead!' He threw out his arms dramatically.

'Gosh, that's good,' I hissed to Michael.

'Sensational,' he hissed back. 'It's Shakespeare.'

Mr van Trocken was obviously beginning to enjoy himself. The circumstances might not have been all that he would wish for, but he was well and truly centre stage, his favourite position in the world, and he was milking it for all he was worth. 'It is not for myself that I mind these terrible accusations that have been levelled against me,' he boomed. ('Oh, not much,' I snorted.) 'I am an innocent man. Innocent! And the whispers and the gossip and the lies will all prove to be nothing more than the filth in the gutter that I, Vladimir van Trocken, step over every morning in the streets of this great capital city that I have come to call my home! No, I suffer for those around me. I suffer for my friends and colleagues at Molehill Magazines. Why should they become the subject of scurrilous rumour and attack just because they want to buy a great and worthy magazine?'

'Like it,' murmured Michael. 'Going for the sympathy vote.'

'I suffer for my dear friend Marcus Aimsworthy and his estimable colleagues in the Conservative Party, many of whom I have entertained at length in my home in Wiltshire and on my yacht in the Caribbean,' Mr van Trocken went on. (It may have been my imagination, but I rather felt he emphasized that bit.) 'But most of all, I suffer for you, the British people. Yes, you! For it is an insult to your generosity and, yes, your intelligence that my detractors say that I have in any way deceived you. How could I deceive you? You are very smart people, you would know if I had done anything wrong.'

'Well yes, you've got a point there, Vladimir,' called a voice from the crowd. I stood on tiptoe, and saw it was Christopher Jenkinson, the chap from earlier. 'I mean, we've always been led to believe you built this company up out of nothing.'

'Yes, my friend, I have,' said Mr van Trocken, glaring at him. 'Quite an achievement for a humble boy from the streets of Prague, don't you think?'

'Yes, indeed,' said Christopher. 'There's just one

thing. I went down to Companies House yesterday to look at the accounts, and it seems to be entirely owned by your wife. She's the only shareholder. Why is that?'

'A mere detail,' said Mr van Trocken grandly. 'For legal reasons, it is easier that way. A triviality. What's hers is mine and what's mine is mine.' He roared with laughter, revealing that set of great, shark-like teeth.

His audience, however, did not seem to get the joke. Always a bad idea, I mused, to tell people that they would have to be incredibly stupid not to rumble you, and then make it obvious you've been lying through your teeth. 'What about your wife?' called another voice. 'We've heard she's left you. Is that right?'

'She is taking a few days holiday,' said Mr van Trocken through clenched teeth. 'My dear Barbara and I are as happy as ever.'

'Well, what about these rumours about Apricot Bellissimo?' shouted another voice. 'And Irina Scatterdust,' shouted a third.

'Lies!' cried Mr van Trocken. 'All lies! Now I have been kind and generous with my time, but I have a business to run! Go forth, tell your readers I am a simple, honest man, and that no more of these things should be printed. *Adieu!*'

With a great flourish, he whipped the keys to the office door out of his pocket, inserted one and waggled. Nothing happened. He waggled again, but there was still no movement. The crowd started muttering. Mr van Trocken withdrew the key furiously, inspected it, and shoved it back in the lock. Still nothing happened. A murmur was beginning to go through the crowd when, to my absolute horror, Mr van Trocken suddenly spotted me. 'Sophie!' he bellowed. 'Come here, you idiot girl!'

As everyone turned in my direction, I looked at Michael in panic. 'Come on,' he said, putting a guiding hand on my shoulder, 'I'll go with you. Marvellous opportunity for you, Sophie. You'll be able to dine out on accounts of this for at least a year afterwards.'

Slowly we made our way through the crowd and up the steps. When we reached the top, I could also see Jim, Henry and Sam were huddled together at the back. They made no move to come forward. 'Who in God's name is this?' demanded Mr van Trocken as Michael and I reached him. 'Never mind. Give me your keys, you idiot girl.'

I scrabbled in my handbag and produced my set. Mr van Trocken grabbed them and shoved them in the lock, but equally to no avail. It was gradually beginning to dawn on us that someone must have changed the locks. Cool, I thought with respect, she really has been working fast.

Similar thoughts were passing through the mind of Mr van Trocken. 'I will make her pay for this,' he hissed. 'Tony! Come and deal with this immediately!'

Tony, who had also been watching the proceedings from the back of the crowd, seemed to be prepared for all eventualities. Throwing open the boot of the Rolls, he produced an enormous axe. The crowd hastily fell back, as he bounded up the steps and to the door, where he gave a tremendous sniff and prepared for action.

It only took four blows, but in that time I have never seen so many cameras start snapping in my life. Michael had grabbed my arm and pulled me out of the way, so when all the pictures appeared in the papers the next morning it was just the two of them: the enormous and enraged figure of Mr van Trocken and the slight, lithe figure of Tony as he broke down the door. And then the fun really began.

19

Pausing only to tell the assembled hacks that he would sue them for trespass if they entered the building, Mr van Trocken stormed through the front door with Tony in tow. I followed, as did Michael, and as did Jim, Henry and Sam a few moments later. My employer was in such a rage that if he actually noticed Michael was still here, he was too beside himself to wonder what he was doing in the office. Accompanied by Tony, he charged into his study and even forgot to bang the door.

The five of us grouped round my desk. Michael was greatly amused by the picture of the leering Zeus. 'Delusions of grandeur!' he said. 'Love it! Those whom the gods destroy, they first make mad.'

'Oh, he's always been like this,' I said wearily. 'It's just a bit more concentrated now.' I smiled at Jim, Henry and Sam, who for the first time in my entire acquaintanceship with them, were looking downright friendly. 'Want to see our tattoo, Soph?' asked Henry.

I nodded. The three of them rolled up their matching black T-shirts, having discarded their matching black denim jackets behind my desk, to show three muscly upper arms decorated with the legend ℋ+𝒥+𝒮. A heart was drawn around it. 'Oh, how lovely,' I said uncertainly. 'When did you get that done?'

'Last night,' said Jim. 'We went to a tattoo party, and decided we couldn't choose between one another, so all three of us are going to be a couple instead.'

'How very reasonable,' I said.

Sam turned to Michael and looked coy. 'You her boyfriend?' she asked.

'Sam!' said Henry and Jim in unison, but Michael didn't look unduly perturbed. 'No, unfortunately, I'm not,' he said.

Unfortunately? I didn't dare look at him, but at that point we all jumped as a blast erupted from up the hall. 'I don't believe it,' bellowed Mr van Trocken, who seemed to be speaking on the telephone. 'She's closed down all of the accounts? *All of them?*'

The study door banged shut. We all looked at one another in awe. 'She always looked so meek before,' said Jim in astonishment.

'You should have seen her last night,' I said.

'Seen who?' demanded a deep gravelly voice from the bottom of the hall. I looked down in astonishment. It was another first for the entire time I had been working here: I had never once seen Petrushka coming into the office before lunchtime, and now here she was, climbing in through the wreckage of the front door, wearing her trademark black and sunglasses. 'Were you talking about me?' she continued, staggering up the hall. 'All that stuff that appeared about me in the papers this morning is all lies, darling, bloody bastard lies. I did not knock over that dinosaur's skeleton in the Natural History

235

Museum last night, darling, I just happened to be standing beside it when it fell. Can't see what they made such a fuss about, they can put it back together again, and anyway, that ghastly little Bolshoi ballet lot shouldn't hold receptions there if they're not prepared for a bit of wear and tear. Got any aspirin, darling?'

I scrabbled in my desk – I had already taken my morning dose at home – and handed over the bottle. 'God, thanks, darling,' said Petrushka, having washed a couple down with the contents of her hip flask. 'Seen this?' She slammed down a copy of the *Evening Standard* on the desk.

We all leapt on it. 'Astonishing picture,' said Michael gravely. 'Glamorous wife shrugs off tragedy and has night on the tiles. Like it.'

'You were not telling porkies,' said Henry, as we gawped at the cover, for there on the front page was a picture of Barbara herself, glowing with beauty and confidence, leaving The Collection with Edmund last night. 'Barbara van Trocken, wife of the controversial tycoon at the centre of the growing row over Molehill Magazines, leaves a fashionable London restaurant with a mystery companion,' read the caption. 'Full story: Page 3.'

Inside the newspaper was a lot more of the stuff we already knew: the share price row and Haverstock and Weybridge (I noticed Martin's name had still not been mentioned), plus a bit more about home life chez van Trocken. There was one picture of my boss and his wife which must have been taken years ago – she looked pretty much as she had last night, but he was much thinner and beardless – talking to Princess Michael at a party, and then there was the much more recent one of the monster and Apricot. As if on cue, there was a shriek from the bottom of the stairs.

'What on earth is going on?' cried an exceptionally glamorous looking woman, who bore an uncanny resemblance to Irina, stepping through the ruins of the door and threading her way through the debris lying on the floor. Behind her, I could see about a million cameras snapping away. 'Where's Vladimir? I demand to see him now!'

I gazed at her as she made her way up the hall. It was unquestionably Apricot, I recognized her from the photograph in the newspaper, but I also quite suddenly realized she was the same woman I had seen talking on her mobile phone in Hyde Park two days ago. So much had happened since then, it felt like another lifetime. Judging by the voice, I also gathered that it was she who had been making all those tear-stricken telephone calls.

But although I could see what chaps saw in her – dressed in a powder blue two-piece suit and fawn high heels, she was very, very thin, immaculately made up, and had acres of tumbling blond curls – she just wasn't in the same class as Barbara van Trocken. There was a little bit too much make-up actually, her voice was just a touch shrill, and someone should have told her that women over thirty shouldn't wear frosted pink nail polish. 'Tramp,' muttered Petrushka, who had heaved herself onto the desk and was now shakily lighting a cigarette. 'Never knew what he saw in all those women, anyway.'

Apricot, mercifully, didn't hear this. 'Vladimir,' she called as she reached the top of the hall. 'Where is he?'

We all pointed mutely in the direction of the study.

Apricot tottered towards the door, and threw the door open. 'How dare – Apricot, my darling, why are you here?' boomed Mr van Trocken from inside.

Apricot was not an actress for nothing. Righteous indignation was flooding from every pore, her blond tresses were quivering with emotion, and she had managed to arrange her face into an expression of pain and anger, with just a touch of indigestion thrown in. 'Vladimir van Trocken,' she began. 'You have cost me my career!' A tiny delicate lace handkerchief appeared from somewhere, and she began to weep.

'Oh puleeze,' said Petrushka, 'spare me the sob story. Some of us have got a lot more to cry about round here.' She took a gulp from her hip flask, and passed it to Michael.

'What a star,' said Michael, taking a gulp. 'Sophie? No? What a racy thingummy you work in, I wish my dear Papa would condone this sort of behaviour at his place.'

'Apricot,' said Mr van Trocken hastily appearing at the door of his study, and casting a ferocious glance in the direction of our little group, 'come inside. This is no place to discuss our private matters.'

'No, let the world know,' cried Apricot, pressing her hands to her bosom. She might have been crying but her make-up was looking suspiciously unsmudged. I was impressed: she could teach even Mr van Trocken a thing or two about making a drama out of a crisis. 'I want the world to hear! My agent rang me this morning and said the BBC had withdrawn the offer for *WestEnders* because' – she took the opportunity to emit a particularly large sob – 'they were concerned that I would bring the Corporation into disrepute! They don't want to employ someone who is associated with a drug-taking liar and a cheat!'

I really thought that Mr van Trocken was going to put himself out of our misery there and then: he looked as if he was going to internally combust. Great waves of red were washing over his face and neck, and his eyes bulged so much that they looked like red-veined tennis balls. 'Drugs?' he cried. 'Who said anything about drugs?'

'They know about Buckingham Palace,' said Apricot, weeping more loudly still. 'Some little runt called Melvin Micklemouse has been on to me, and they're going to publish everything. We are undone, Vladimir, undone.' She began retreating backwards to where I sat. All of we onlookers, Michael and Petrushka included, hastily retreated behind my desk.

'But Apricot,' said Mr van Trocken casting a beady eye in our direction and advancing down the hall after her, 'I will not allow them to say such things. I will have my lawyers on to them immediately. And is the BBC mad? Does it not realize that all publicity is good publicity?'

'Not any more,' said Apricot, who had now reached my desk. 'It's signed a Moral Manifesto, saying that it will no longer portray anti-social behaviour such as drug-taking and,' she sniffed tremulously, 'my agent says that if it won't show it on screen, it would be the height of hypocrisy to employ actors who are known users. Now the part is to go to some little upstart called Tiffany Day, who was just to have had a supporting role. Oh Vladimir, it was a bad day for me when I first set eyes on you! Don't call! Don't write! I never want to have anything to do with you ever again!'

With that she really did burst into tears, and rushed off, down the hall and through the broken door. A huge clicking sound started from outside, as all the cameras reared into action again. How typical, I thought. The only time actresses ever displayed any real emotion was when their career looked as if it was heading skidswards, and as for that bit about Tiffany – well, it didn't bear thinking about.

I didn't have time to brood on that now, though: the drama happening in front of my very eyes was proceeding apace. Mr van Trocken had followed her only as far as my desk, where his eyes fell on the copy of the *Evening Standard*, and the picture of his wife. 'What in Heaven's name?' he cried. 'How dare she! I – answer the phone at once, you idiot girl.'

Old habits die hard. The phone was indeed ringing: I picked it up. 'Van Trocken and Co.,' I said automatically.

'Put me through to Vladimir immediately,' said a woman's voice.

I handed over the receiver.

'Yes?' barked Mr van Trocken. 'Caprice, my darling! How – what? What letter? How dare you tell me to destroy my own post. Now look, darling, don't be hasty. We can – hello? Hello?'

In silence he handed the receiver back to me. I replaced it: it rang again immediately. 'Van Trocken and Co.,' I said.

'OK, look,' said a voice. 'This is Tamara. I have a message for Vladimir van Trocken: tell him never to ring me ever again. Got that?' She hung up. I did likewise, and decided to delay delivering the message, not least because Henry, Jim and Sam, who had been whispering between themselves in the background,

240

had something to say. 'Mr van Trocken,' said Jim, 'I speak for all of us. We resign!'

Open mouthed, Mr van Trocken watched as they picked up their denim jackets, looked him up and down, waved goodbye to me and made their way out of the building. Petrushka took another swig from the hip flask, summoned her resources and spoke. 'I resign too, darling,' she said in that deep, gravelly voice. 'I can no longer tolerate this level of proprietorial interference in the magazine!'

Now it was my turn. 'Mr van Trocken,' I began.

'You're fired!' yelled my employer.

Did absolutely everyone have to get their retaliation in first? First Martin and now the monster. How totally annoying. It was at this point, though, that the fates finally decided to give me a helping hand. 'Oh no she's not,' said a very clear, firm voice from the bottom of the hall.

We all looked down. As knights in shining armour go, mine had arrived in an unusual form: that of a Home Counties heiress who really had had enough of her errant and crooked husband. Looking quite imperious in a navy Armani trouser suit, cream silk T-shirt and navy loafers (I couldn't help it – even in times of crisis I noticed these things), Barbara van Trocken made her way towards us. Behind her were Edmund, two more men in suits who I later learned were accountants, two policemen and about five thousand members of the press – or that's what it seemed like, anyway. There were probably only about twenty.

'In fact,' continued Barbara, reaching my desk, 'she's promoted. Vladimir, it's you who is fired. Goodbye.'

'Like it, like it,' murmured Michael in the background.

'I take back my resignation,' said Petrushka hastily.

Mr van Trocken looked at his wife. I very much doubt that he had ever been speechless at any point in his life before, but you know how it is: there's a first time for everything.

'In fact,' continued Barbara, 'you are also fired as chief executive of van Trocken and Co. on grounds of severe professional misconduct. My accountants have been going through both sets of accounts, the ones you file in Companies House and the real ones, and we will shortly be contacting the Inland Revenue to discuss backpayment of taxes. We will also be giving our full cooperation to the Stock Exchange in its investigation into share dealings in the stock of Molehill Magazines. I would appreciate it if you would vacate the premises immediately.' She stood back to allow him to pass.

I didn't think that this was the end of it – and indeed, I was right – but Mr van Trocken obviously knew there was no point in fighting this particular battle. With an expression on his face that was well-nigh murderous, he began making his way down the hall, with the ever faithful Tony behind him. The crowd of journalists pressed against the walls as he passed, and no-one said a word until he reached the front door. He stepped into the sunlight – someone had unlocked the battered door and pulled it open – then looked back in. 'You haven't heard the last of me Barbara,' he said in a tone of controlled fury. 'I will not be treated like this! I am Vladimir van Trocken and I'll be revenged on the whole pack of you!' He disappeared.

'Gosh,' I whispered to Michael, who had been sitting on the window sill and watching quietly as the whole drama unfolded, 'good exit.'

Michael chuckled, and produced a packet of cigarettes from his pocket. 'Shakespeare,' he said.

20

I shuffled restlessly in the corridor. Petrushka had been in with Barbara for over half an hour, now, and it took every bit of concentration I had to be able to eavesdrop. 'So you see darl, er, Mrs van Trocken, I've been so desperately unhappy here,' I heard her say in that deep voice. I pressed as close to the door as I could without being noticed – I was sitting on a chair outside – and listened harder. 'I've been telling Vlad that I just couldn't edit the magazine if he interfered so much, but what could I do? Just what could I do? I thank Heaven that you've finally taken over, you're the saviour we all so desperately need.'

'Am I now,' said Barbara, not sounding at all convinced. 'All right, look Petrushka, there's a lot to sort out, but we'll all talk again in a day or so. Could you ask Sophie to come in now?'

I hastily straightened up and began studying my fingernails intensely. A moment later Petrushka appeared, announced, 'Your turn, darling,' with very bad grace, and flounced off down the hall. I went into the study.

It was a couple of hours since Barbara's coup and Mr van Trocken's study – or to be more accurate, Mrs van Trocken's study – looked exactly the same as it had before, except that all the pictures of her soon to be ex-husband had been taken down and piled in a heap on the floor. The picture on the mantelpiece of my erstwhile employer shaking hands with Prince Charles had also disappeared – in fact, come to think of it, I hadn't seen it since Rory burst in the day before.

The press had largely dispersed, Edmund having told them that there was to be no more drama that day, and that he would be issuing a press release summing up all the changes in the company later, Michael had gone off to his office and a carpenter was mending the broken front door. One of the accountants was on phone answering duty: the other one had gone off with Edmund to the main offices on Poland Street to start ringing the changes in there.

'Well, well,' said Barbara, grinning at me as I sat down. 'I gather I'm the office saviour. I wouldn't object to doing a bit of saving so much if that irritating woman wasn't his daughter.'

'Whose daughter?' I said blankly.

'Vladimir's, of course,' said Barbara wearily. 'She was born some years before I met him.'

'But what,' I began. 'I mean, who? I mean it's not possible, she's never treated him like a father and she, well I mean, just now she was saying, I mean she was always complaining about proprietorial interference and she was never in the office and I mean, well, I don't understand. I mean, she resigned earlier.'

'Yes, I thought that was a fine display of filial loyalty back there,' said Barbara dryly. 'Obviously runs in the family. Oh yes, she's his daughter all right, can you imagine him letting anyone else get away with behaving like that? He's never officially recognized her of course, as her mother was married to someone else at the time and even Vladimir didn't want to weather that particular storm, but he's always looked after her – to an extent, anyway.'

'Blimey,' I said in amazement. 'Does she know?' This was turning out even better than I'd expected – Barbara might have had only one thing in common with her soon-to-be-ex-husband, but happily for me, anyway, it was indiscretion.

'Yes, although she doesn't know that I know. Actually,' said Barbara, suddenly looking downright mischievous, 'I bet it would really annoy him if I started to look after her. Anyway, we'll see.'

'Oh, right,' I said. This had cleared up another mystery as well: I had always wondered why, alone of all the glamorous women he surrounded himself with, Petrushka had never been the subject of Mr van Trocken's revolting attentions. Now I understood.

'Tee hee,' said Barbara, who had been scribbling a few notes. 'Anyway, Sophie, it's your turn. Now tell me what's been happening with you.'

'My ex-boyfriend's on the verge of running off with a soap star,' I said through gritted teeth.

'*What?*' demanded Barbara. 'Sophie, I can't believe it. He didn't try it on with you, too, did he?'

'Oh, he tries it on with everyone,' I said mournfully.

'Well, I know,' said Barbara. 'Sophie, you poor child, why didn't you tell me? Are you all right? You know, this might have made me angry a few months ago, but now I just feel concerned about you. He didn't force you to do anything you didn't want to, did he? Oh, you poor girl, all this must have been even more upsetting than I'd realized. You should have come to me before. Do you want to speak to the police? You're not still harbouring feelings for him, are you?'

'I most certainly am not,' I said, wondering vaguely why on earth Barbara would be angry about Martin. Maybe she thought I should have stood up for myself more. 'No, I don't want to talk to the police, I'm sure they're already on to him. But honestly, you know what I found out the other day? He's married! And the bastard never told me.'

'No dear, he does tend to keep it a secret when he meets someone he likes,' said Barbara sadly. 'But I thought you knew he was married before.'

'No, I never had a clue,' I said, now wondering how Barbara seemed to know so much about Martin. 'But I met his wife the other day for the first time, and then I found out.'

'But Sophie, dear, we'd met before,' said Barbara very gently. 'You must have forgotten.'

'What?' I said blankly. 'I hadn't forgotten, I know we'd met.' I was beginning to wonder if the strain of all this was getting to her.

'But you said you didn't realize he was married.'

We stared at each other for a moment, until the mist began to clear. 'Oh, Barbara,' I said after a second. I was just totally horrified. 'You can't have thought, I mean you didn't think, I mean Mr van Trocken? Urgh! I mean sorry, I know you're married to him, but oh, no. No, no, no, no, no. No, the chap I was seeing is called Martin Silverspoon, you know the chap who works at Haverstock and Weybridge. Penny, my best friend, she thinks he bought all the shares.'

Barbara looked at me for a moment, and then began to laugh. 'Oh, Sophie, I do apologize,' she said after a moment. 'Oh, how could I have thought such a thing of you. Oh my dear child, we do seem to have a lot in common, you know. Your description made him sound just like Vladimir.'

'Gosh, yes it did,' I said, feeling quite spooky. 'I hadn't realized. But you see, you confronted Mr van Trocken, and I want to have it out with Martin. He's running after Tiffany Day.'

'You say he was involved with buying the shares?' asked Barbara, suddenly looking very serious and ignoring what I felt to be the real bone of contention.

'Yes, but Penny, my best friend, she works at Haverstock and Weybridge too, and she's told Sir Jeremy Haverstock.'

'Hmm,' said Barbara dubiously. 'I hate to tell you this, but you might find you have to have a quick word with the police anyway. And Penny, how does she come in to all this?'

'Oh, she's going out with Martin's ex-wife,' I explained.

Barbara began to look a bit confused. 'And the young man I met with you last night?' she asked. 'Does he play a role in this too?'

I thought for a second. Barbara van Trocken was turning out to be a seriously decent type, and I felt the need to confide in someone. 'Well, please don't tell anyone, but I spent the night with him last night, but it was a big mistake,' I said. 'I think I like someone else.'

'Tricky,' said Barbara sympathetically. 'The chap who was here earlier?'

'How did you know?' I demanded.

'Good guess,' said Barbara. 'Who is he, he's not involved in share buying too, is he?'

'No, he's Penny's brother,' I said. 'I don't know if he likes me too, though.'

'I wouldn't worry too much about that,' said Barbara, grinning at me. 'Anyway, back to Martin. Yes, I do see that you want to have a word, but from what you tell me, Martin is bound to be in very serious trouble anyway. You say Sir Jeremy Haverstock knows about this?'

'Yes, Penny's told him everything. Look, this is the picture he hid the note behind.' I still had the photograph in my handbag, and after a bit of scrabbling, I handed it over.

'Well, well, well,' said Barbara, after she had inspected it. 'Do you know where this was taken, Sophie?'

'No.'

'At our house in Wiltshire,' said Barbara. 'At a party we held there about a year ago. They must have known one another for some time, although I must say, I'd had no idea he was there. I didn't meet him myself, but then Vladimir was always throwing parties and failing to introduce me to his business contacts. It was his way of keeping power over the company, I suppose. Do you mind if I keep this in the safe, Sophie? I don't know if it will be of interest to the authorities, but it may well be, and don't worry, I've had the lock changed. It will be quite secure.'

'Yes, of course,' I said. I felt quite pleased to think that I might be helping the little drama along.

'And is it really worth you speaking to Martin personally?'

'I want to!' I burst out. 'I find out without any warning at all that he's married, then he waltzes off with bloody Belinda right under my nose. He's having dinner with her in Barnes this evening, she told me, and now to cap it all he's been in cahoots with your horrible husband all along. Er, sorry.'

'Don't worry about it,' said Barbara, smoothing a bit of runaway auburn hair behind her ear and beaming at me, 'I feel just the same about my horrible husband. Belinda? I thought you said she was called Tiffany.'

'Her real name's Belinda Cuttlesnipe, but the Beeb have asked her to change it. And now she's going to get the leading role in *WestEnders*! I want to go and meet them in the restaurant tonight!'

'Very galling,' agreed Barbara. 'Well, I do see why you want to talk to him, but I insist on coming too. I don't want you going in there on your own.'

'Oh, really? Are you sure you wouldn't mind?' I asked, more convinced than ever that Barbara was seriously good news.

'Of course I wouldn't, you helped me so I'd love to help you.'

'Cool,' I said. I was delighted. 'Little Ant's coming too.'

'Anthony's coming too, is he?' asked Barbara. 'He's certainly being a very good friend, and most men wouldn't be, you know, if you turn them down. I must say, I liked him very much. Are you really sure – no. I can see you are really sure.'

'Little Ant's brill,' I said. 'But I just don't feel that way about him.'

'That's settled, then,' said Barbara. 'Now Sophie, we must just have a quick word about your job. I've been looking through the company records, and you don't seem to have been paid this month.'

'No, I haven't been.'

Barbara looked around cautiously, and then withdrew a brown envelope from her handbag. 'It was in the safe,' she said. 'I have no idea what he was going to use it for, although I have an idea it might have been to feed Tony's little habit, so I think it would be much better off with you. I think you'll find it makes up for back pay, and a bit of a bonus besides.'

'Oh, I can't,' I said, horrified. 'I mean, *it's in a brown envelope*.'

Barbara laughed, pulled out a wodge of notes and handed them to me. 'Sophie, it's not a bribe, it's payment for working here,' she said. 'It's the company's money, not his. Believe me, I know, I've been through everything thoroughly enough. I don't know what Vladimir's been playing at, but the books are in chaos.'

'Gosh, thanks,' I said, trousering the dosh.

'One last thing,' said Barbara. 'Are you interested in fashion?'

'Yes,' I said rather emphatically. 'I am.'

'I somehow thought you were. Now Sophie, I've decided to revamp the mag, widen its scope and so on, and we'll be writing about fashion. Would you like to be a researcher? It would be rather dogsbodyish for six months or so, but once you've got a bit of experience, we could put you on to some writing.'

I stared at her for a moment without speaking.

'Sophie?' said Barbara anxiously. 'Aren't you pleased? I thought it might appeal to you.'

'Oh, Barbara!' I burst out at last. 'Pleased? Oh, you can't imagine. Oh, this is fantastic. It's fabulous. It's incredible. I mean, it's just totally, totally,' I searched for the right word, 'cool!'

Barbara beamed at me. 'Well at least I've got one

251

satisfied customer,' she said. 'Now don't get too excited, there'll be a lot of running around in circles to begin with. Look dear, it's been a tiring week. Why don't you take the rest of the day off. We'll have a chat on Monday about your new role, but I think you deserve a bit of a rest, especially if you're going to see Martin tonight.'

'Oh, Barbara,' I burst out again, 'this is just totally unbelievable. I thought I was never going to have a proper job on the magazine, and I thought I'd be working for him for the rest of my life.'

'I thought I'd be married to him for the rest of my life,' said Barbara shuddering. 'Now where shall we meet tonight?'

'Why don't you come to our flat for a drink at about seven,' I said rather shyly. I wasn't used to entertaining my employer. 'It's in Edwardes Square, not far from here at all.'

'I've got the address, it's in your personnel records,' said Barbara. 'That would be lovely. Now you go off and have a lovely afternoon. Buy yourself something nice.'

21

Well, I did. After all, who was I to disobey my new
boss? The retailers of Kensington High Street did well
out of me that afternoon: my first stop was Hobbs,
where I invested in a rust red trouser suit, then on to
Russell & Bromley where I got a fabulous pair of
black patent leather mock croc court shoes, and
then I went to Waterstones, where I bought a lovely
coffee table book about changing fashions through
the centuries. Had to prepare for my new job, after
all, I thought, turning in to a new and extremely
avant garde art gallery that had recently opened up
on the street.

The gallery was painted in stark white, so the
objects on display would all show up more clearly
against the walls. Almost everything seemed to be
some kind of furniture: there was a chair with a
vicious spike in the middle of the seat, a table painted
in bright red, which had an upside down pyramid
shape where the surface should be, a huge cande-
labra, which on closer examination seemed to have
severed hands crawling up it (very reassuring for
those quiet nights in, I thought), and a bright yellow
wishing well, which was covered up and adorned

with a sign saying, 'Dream on, darling.' None of it was quite to my taste.

Still, if I wanted to be cultured, I had to take an interest in these things. I wandered over to the centre of the room to look at the central exhibition: entitled 'Everything but . . .', it was a 1950s kitchen sink painted in matt black. That was it: there was nothing else. Two creatures of indeterminate sex, both dressed in black, one with short cropped hair and the other with a long black ponytail hanging down its back, stood in front of me examining it. 'I mean it's so post modern, so ironic,' the one with the ponytail was saying. 'It's a statement. It's like, a represent-ational iconographic reality, a piece of its time and yet apart, a household utility elevated to the shrine of post-nihilist philosophy.'

'I'm sorry,' the other member of the couple argued, 'but to me it still looks like a sink.'

'It's great, isn't it,' said a voice behind me. I turned round to see a tall, beautifully dressed girl, strongly resembling a pedigree mare – all long, bronzed limbs and a mane of auburn hair – who was holding a price list. She was obviously looking after the place. 'The artists, Stig and Druid, found it in a skip in Clapham,' she continued.

'Oh, right,' I said, taken aback. 'It's very interesting. How much is it?'

The girl handed me the price list. I found 'Exhibit 12,' on the sheet of paper: next to it was a figure that could have bought a nice little one-bedroom flat just round the corner from here. 'Er, I'll think about it,' I said, and hastily made for the door.

Once outside, my good humour returned. I had a new job! I leaped into the air and whooped, much to the consternation of passing shoppers, but I didn't care. I was finally going to be a real, live journalist! Swinging my bags of shopping in the early afternoon sun, I blurred my eyes. Kensington High Street faded around me, and I stepped into a minimalist chrome and steel office, decorated entirely in black and white. 'Oh, invitations, invitations,' I said to Debbie, my secretary, as I spread out a pile of gold embossed cards on my perspex glass desk. 'Look, here's one from Prada, and there's one from dear Christian, and a nice little note from Giorgio, and it's dinner with Vivienne tomorrow and supper with Donna in New York the day after that.'

'You deserve it, Miss Brackenbury,' said Debbie respectfully. 'They say you can make or break a designer's new collection with just one article, and your writing is as fine as the gossamer threads on a Catherine Walker dress. Oh, I wish I could be like you, Miss Brackenbury! I wish I had your taste, your style, your poise and your talent.'

'One day, one day,' I said kindly. 'I started off like you, you know, I was a welcoming agent and telephone intermediary once, a long time ago. You won't know the name Vladimir van Trocken, he's been in Broadmoor for, oh, a good fifteen years now, but I used to work for him a long time ago. He owned this magazine once, before it changed its name to *Chic*.'

I giggled, tripped over a paving stone and refocused on the street. Just for once it really was going to happen, I really was going to fulfil the stuff of my daydreams, even if not in quite such an elevated position as that. *Pret à Porter*, eat your heart out. I was in such a good mood that I wasn't even remotely looking where I was going, and ran slap bang into a very well dressed man in his late twenties walking down the street.

'Oh, do excuse me,' said the chap politely, in the way that well bred Englishmen do when the fault is yours and not theirs. 'I do apologize – Sophie? Sophie Brackenbury? Is that really you?'

'Will?' I demanded, looking at him wildly. Weirdo Will had been my ex from the French Foreign Legion, but the last I heard had been that spot of bother with the mercenaries. And he couldn't have looked more different from the last time we'd met, then he had been in khaki combat gear, and here he was in a Savile Row suit and brogues. 'We— Will? What are you doing here? Someone told me you were in Africa.'

'I was, but got myself into a spot of bother,' said Will with a self-deprecating laugh. 'Decided to come back to the jolly old motherland. Got myself a job in Borings merchant bank, much rougher stuff than when I was with the Legion. Ha, ha!'

'Oh right,' I said. It was a great relief to see that at least one ex of mine had actually improved with the passage of time, rather than becoming even more peculiar than before. Then I felt miffed. How dare he not be pining for me like Desperate Dan?

'Anyway, mustn't keep you,' said Will. 'I'm meeting my cousin for drinks, super girl, though her parents despair of her. They gave her a lovely name like Jemima, and she insists on being called Jim! No accounting for tastes, eh? I'm thinking of introducing her to a chum of mine at Borings, very eligible chap.'

'Excellent idea, I'm sure she'll appreciate it,' I said heartily. 'Fab to see you again, tara.'

'Toodle-oo,' said Will, kissing me on both cheeks and rushing off. I wonder if she'll take Henry and Sam along with her, too? I thought. Poor old Will, I rather felt he was on to a loser there.

The flat was empty when I let myself in a couple of minutes later, but the answering machine was flashing away like nobody's business. I pressed the relevant button, and leant down to tickle Albert under the chin. 'Hello, Sophie, what on earth has been happening?' said Penny's clipped tones. 'I tried you at the office, but someone said you'd been promoted and given the day off. How marvellous. Oh, and by the way, I went to a tattoo party last night, and I've now got an amazing Chinese dragon on my upper arm. I can't wait to show Dad. Give me a call, I'm at work.' The machine bleeped.

'Hello, Sophie,' said Desperate Dan, 'I'm, like, feeling really, really miserable? I'm just, like, having this existential crisis about my life? Let me tell you all about it. I—' I pressed the fast forward button until the next bleep.

'Hello, Sophie,' said Jane, my sister who was a teacher, 'what on earth's going on? We've been reading all about your Mr van Trocken in the papers, are you involved too? Joke! Give us a call.' The machine bleeped.

'Hi, gorgeous, it's Tasmin here,' said Tommy the Trannie. 'It was great to see you two yesterday. Fancy a girls' night out? Let's get Penny to come too, I could do with some style tips.'

'Hi, kiddo, it's Bernard,' said the next one. 'I don't want to set your heart fluttering too fast, but I'm a free man again. Cordelia told me last night that marriage is just a legalized form of prostitution, and, hey, you know what? She's right. So we've decided to have a committed but open relationship, in which we both respect each other's privacy and individuality, and in which we are free to bond with past and potential partners. Also, she's going to India next week, which means I've got some spare time. Drink? Call me.'

It was the last one, though, that really gripped me. 'Hello Anthony, it's Michael Tang here,' said a voice. 'Could you give me a call? It's important. Thanks.' He rang off and the machine told me I had no more messages. Feeling slightly peculiar, I went off to have a bath.

The feeling of peculiarity grew as the afternoon wore on. First I tried to write a goodbye poem to Martin:

I've had a fatal accident,
My love for you has died.
But now you're as spent as a tent with a rent
Though you've taken us all for a ride.

I've seen at last you're just a cheat
In business and in leisure,
And now I just hope that they'll turn up the heat
As you rest at Her Majesty's pleasure.

It didn't quite scan, but whatever. Trust Martin to be an unreliable muse. Then I made contact with Penny and told her about this morning's goings on. 'Well that's fantastic, I can't wait to tell Charlotte,' she said. 'Oh, how the mighty are fallen. I'd love to say let's meet tonight for a celebration, but Charlotte and I are going to the opening of Leo Tickell's new jewellery store.'

'Gosh,' I said impressed. 'Who else will be there?' Leo Tickell was a fabulous jeweller, who was now almost as famous as his celebrity clients, and far better looking than most of them, including the women. He was a close friend of the Tang family, who regularly popped in to purchase something of the 24-carat variety, and was opening a new branch in Knightsbridge.

'Oh, just the usuals,' said Penny cheerily. 'It's going to be quite a big party, actually, Joan Collins is the guest of honour. I've got the most fabulous dress to wear, which will really set off my tattoo. Do you think my father will be pleased? We've all been invited, including Michael.'

'I should imagine his reaction will exceed your wildest dreams,' I said truthfully. 'Look, Penny, why do you feel the need to wind him up like this?'

'Who said anything about winding up?' said Penny haughtily. 'Well, maybe I do a bit, but it's all his fault for being so rich and established. It means that whatever I do in life, people will just say it's down to him.'

'Well, you could always tell him you don't want to inherit a bean,' I said.

'You must be joking,' said Penny. I could almost see her shuddering over the phone. 'No, if he's decided to inflict wealth and privilege on me, I'll just have to shoulder the burden as well as I can. Anyway, I'm allowed to, I'm the younger child, and they always rebel against the status quo. Must go, Sir Jeremy's just come in.' She hung up. I did too, and attempted to banish a sudden stab of jealousy at the news that Michael would be out partying with a whole load of rich and glamorous women that night.

Next on the list was a chat with my sister Jane, in which I explained that no, I had not bought any shares I shouldn't have and neither was I one of

Mr van Trocken's girlfriends. 'Speaking of which,' I added, 'Martin and I have split up.'

'Yes!' cried Jane. 'Oh, well done, infant, none of us could ever see what you saw in him. Anyone else on the horizon?'

'I don't know.'

'Which means yes. Who is he?'

'Uh, no-one.'

'Look, infant, you could do a lot worse than go for Little Ant, Mummy's always said so,' said Jane. 'Why don't you start making a few suggestive glances in his direction?'

'No,' I said firmly. 'He's the brother I should have had to protect me from you two, nothing more. Must you keep calling me infant?'

'OK, embryo, if that's what you say,' said Jane, sounding disappointed. 'It's just that your past choices haven't always been totally ideal either, you know.'

'I know, I know, but I'm turning a new leaf. I saw Tommy the Trannie yesterday, by the way.'

'Really? How is he?'

'She,' I said. 'He's turned into a she. He's not just a transvestite: he's a transsexual too. Honestly, Jane, how did you and Rosie do it?' Both my sisters were happily married and, courtesy of the one I was speaking to, I was three months away from becoming an aunt.

'Determination and application, oh glint in the milkman's eye,' said Jane. 'Don't worry, little sis, there's someone out there for you, there really is, it's just a case of waiting for him. I'm just glad it wasn't Martin. Look, I must dash, I've got thirty essays to mark about the importance of drug addiction to the narrative thread, but don't fret. Go and buy something.'

'I already have,' I said. '*Drug addiction?*'

'Yes, you know, *Confessions of an Opium Eater*, *The Moonstone*, *Trainspotting*, that kind of thing,' said Jane vaguely. 'A good number of my students, I might add, are writing about this far more knowledgeably than they did last week, when the subject was the romantic hero. That's fabulous news about the job, by the way. Catch you later.'

'Bye,' I said, and put the phone down. A second later there was the sound of a key in the lock. 'Little Ant?' I called. 'Is that you?'

'None other,' said Little Ant, coming into the room accompanied by Albert. The latter leapt up on my knee and started purring: the former threw himself into a chair and ran a hand through his silvery blond locks. 'Quite a day, I hear.'

'It certainly was,' I said with feeling. 'How did you know about it?'

'There was something on the lunchtime news, and also, I've just been having a coffee with Michael Tang,' said Little Ant, shooting me a glance.

'Anything interesting?' I asked, trying to sound nonchalant.

'Yes, very. Just something we had to sort out.' He came over to where I was sitting, ruffled my hair for just a second, and went to start building a fire. 'He's a very nice bloke,' he continued, with his back to me. 'You like him, don't you?'

'Yes, he's fine,' I said, plonking down a protesting Albert, and hastily tried to change the subject. 'Now look, Little Ant, Barbara van Trocken is coming here tonight to give me moral support on the Martin

261

front. Fancy a trip to Oddbins to stock up?'

'Is she?' said Little Ant, turning round and noticeably brightening up. 'Oh good, I like her. No, don't worry about Oddbins, we've got loads of wine in stock. Anyway, she's not the only one coming along, Michael's turning up too.'

'*Michael?*' I said, feeling an equally abrupt stab of elation. 'I thought he was going to a party.'

'He may be later, but he's coming with us first. Would you like to know what we were talking about?'

'Yes,' I said uncertainly.

'You,' said Little Ant. 'When I met him in Paris, I told him about, well, you know, what I said last night. Don't worry, Sophie, it really doesn't matter. Anyway, it was just one of those things when you start talking to people you hardly know and it all comes out. Well, he seemed to want an update, and I told him I'd made a mistake. We really are just good friends.'

'Oh,' I said. 'Look, Little Ant—'

'I mean it,' said Little Ant gently but firmly. 'I made a mistake. Last night was lovely, Sophie, but you were right. We work best as friends and that's the end of it, we don't need to mention it ever again. Now update me, what's going on with you?'

'I got promoted and I went shopping,' I said. 'Want to see my new clothes?'

Little Ant laughed. 'Indeed I do,' he said.

22

'Why don't I go in the back with Barbara, and you sit in the front with Michael,' suggested Little Ant. It was just before eight, and after a discussion about which car the four of us would take, we had plumped for Michael's Jag, not least because it was the biggest car available. Although Barbara had spent the afternoon reclaiming the van Trocken assets, she was exceedingly annoyed that the Rolls, along with her husband and Tony, had vanished. No-one seemed to know where they were.

I obediently climbed into the front of the car, blushed when I bumped against Michael's knee, and the other two clambered into the back. 'Excellent stuff,' said Michael, who appeared to be in a better mood than ever. He started the ignition and set off. 'A stake-out this morning and a confrontation in the evening, thank Heavens I'm back from Hong Kong! Life's been so boring there with nothing but a dull old total change of political regime to distract everyone. Congratulations, Barbara, on your sensational take-over of the company. I'm thinking of trying the same thing myself if my dear Papa decides to stay in situ for ever.'

'That's very kind of you, but I did have the enormous advantage of being married to a crook,' said Barbara. 'From what I hear tell, your father is the epitome of corporate rectitude.'

'Yes, he is,' said Michael, sighing deeply. 'Penny and I were certainly dealt a tough hand in life. Oh well, can't be helped. Now, what's the form for this evening? Do we all rush in, beat Silverspoon over the head with bagfuls of illicit share certificates and make for the hills? Sophie, I hope you've been preparing yourself for a very dramatic, very turbulent, very emotional scenario this evening.'

'Don't alarm the poor girl,' protested Little Ant from the back. 'Actually, I've booked a table at the restaurant and I've specifically asked for a table as close as possible to a couple who will be made up of a short fat man and an even shorter anorexic woman. Said we were going to give them a surprise.'

'Like it!' said Michael. 'Devious and yet truthful. Personally, I can't wait to surprise Silverspoon. He reminds me of a chap who used to work for my father, the late, demented Harold Wilberforce. Used to be our butler. After his untimely demise, Papa found most of the Tang family cutlery hidden away in shoeboxes under Wilberforce's bed, and a will leaving the lot to his mistress, who was called Little Bit. Good Heavens, she wouldn't be related to you would she, Little Ant?'

'Not as far as I know,' said Little Ant regretfully. 'It would be rather fun to have an ancestor called Little Bit, I must remember that when and if I get round to the children naming stage. How are you doing, Sophie, you OK?'

'You don't think he'll do anything silly, do you?' I

asked anxiously. Now that it was actually coming down to it I was beginning to feel rather nervous. 'I mean, Martin's very prone to overreacting.'

'Of course he'll do something silly, why do you think he'd change the habits of a lifetime now?' said Little Ant cheerfully. 'Don't worry, Soph, it will be fine.'

'I wonder if he'll be charged with anything,' said Barbara thoughtfully. 'The police told me they've got a warrant for Vladimir's arrest.'

'If nothing else, he should be charged with being the biggest berk in Britain,' said Michael. 'Not only does he not realize that in Sophie he had found the very flower of British womanhood – apart from you, of course, Barbara – but he's not even a very competent crook. Imagine leaving written evidence all over the place in your girlfriend's handbag and then running off with another woman!'

'He didn't dump me, I dumped him,' I said defensively.

'And about time, too,' said Little Ant. 'Oh, look, you just turn left here, and it's just on the right.'

'I've been looking forward to this all afternoon,' said Michael as we pulled up on Church Road. 'I say, I've never been part of a lynch mob before. Are you sure we can't hoist him from his own petard?'

'Or enmesh him in his own web of deceits and lies?' added Little Ant.

'Or bury his head in a bucket of sleaze?' suggested Barbara.

'Children, please!' I said, forgetting I was speaking to my new employer, to say nothing of the fact that I was, by a factor of at least half a decade, the youngest person in the car. 'This is serious!'

'I know,' said Barbara, leaning forward and patting me reassuringly on the shoulder. 'We're just trying to bolster your confidence. Come on everyone, let's get this over with.'

We all scrambled out of the car and headed for the restaurant. It was a bit idiotic, actually, making such a fuss about going into a quiet but fashionable eaterie in the south London suburbs, but I must admit, I did feel a bit nervy as I pushed open the glass door of Sonny's and stepped inside, with the others in tow. What would Emma Peel have done in a situation like this? I wondered. Probably a few karate chops to disable the restaurant staff, followed by a learned discourse on whatever wine Martin was drinking before frogmarching him off to the authorities. I didn't really feel up to that, a few mental high kicks would have to do. A casually dressed chap approached. 'Do you have a reservation?' he asked.

'Yes, Hurlingham, as in the club,' said Little Ant, pushing his way to the fore.

The waiter gathered up menus and began to lead us to the back of the restaurant. I could already see them, actually: they were sitting at a table in the back on long cushioned benches, and so engrossed in conversation, that they didn't actually notice us until we reached the table opposite. Martin looked as if he was about to have a heart attack when he looked up. It was time to start Operation Silverspoon.

'What a lovely surprise!' I cried brightly, sliding in beside Martin before either had a chance to say anything. The man in question, I am happy to say, blanched visibly as I sat down, while my chums seated themselves opposite, ordered a bottle of wine and settled back to watch. 'Honestly Martin, fancy seeing you here, and while half of London is looking for you, too.'

'Sophie, my dear little ex, how lovely to see you,' said Martin, struggling to regain himself. 'What a co-incidence. I see you're with friends.' He shot my companions a nasty look.

'I am indeed,' I said, giving him the once over. As ever, he was in a loud navy blue pinstripe, today matched with a yellow and white striped shirt and yellow tie. He'd washed his hair for a change, but his complexion was as bright and moist as ever, and his little currant bun eyes were darting around nervously all over the place. What ever could I have seen in him? 'Very good friends, and it's a jolly good thing we're here, too, isn't it Tiffany? You see,' I confided in Martin, 'Tiffany said she was worried that you were going to make a greasy little lunge at her, so I expect she's greatly relieved. Don't blame you,' I added, turning to Tiffany, 'he lunges at everyone else. Good outcome all round, then. What are you having? The food here is delicious.'

'Yes it is,' called out Michael from the next table. 'I'd fill up if I were you, from what I've heard you're not going to be getting the chance to dine out in style for quite a while. Then again, I could be wrong, what with most prison staff making a nice little earner on the side by bringing in gourmet nosh for their charges.'

'You said what?' demanded Martin, glaring at Tiffany and pretending he hadn't heard Michael. 'Look, my dear girl, I'm not used to being spoken of in this way. Have you any idea who I am?'

'Not yet, but she soon will do,' I said cheerfully

accepting a glass from a waiter and helping myself to a splash from the wine bottle. 'In fact, the whole world soon will do. Mm, nice, Puligny Montrachet. He always orders that when he wants to impress, we had it on our first date, too.'

'Look, Sophie, great,' said Tiffany, who also didn't seem to be quite clear about how to handle the situation. 'But you know, OK, this is just not my bag. Martin, I never said anything—'

'Greasy little lunge?' repeated Martin, who did not seem to be making much progress in the conversation.

'I know, I thought that was an unkind way of putting it myself,' I commented. 'I'm sure she didn't mean it, though. Now Tiffany, how have the two of you been getting on? Has Martin told you about his wife, yet?'

Tiffany opened her mouth and shut it again. 'My wife?' asked Martin, who looked as if he still hadn't digested the greasy little lunge remark. 'What's she got to do with it? Anyway, she's a lesbian now, so it doesn't count.'

'Apparently she was bisexual until she met Martin,' I confided to Tiffany, who was looking just totally dumbstruck.

'Yes, and now she's going out with my sister,' called Michael. 'Lovely girl, you must meet her.'

I decided not to mention the fact that she already had. 'You know it's frightfully brave you being seen with Martin in public, the last person who was supposed to get the starring role in *WestEnders* lost it when the Beeb discovered who she'd been spending her time with,' I confided in Tiffany.

'Very true,' said Barbara, leaning across to Tiffany

and proffering a friendly hand. 'I'm Barbara van Trocken, by the way. I believe you know my husband?' she added to Martin.

'OK, look,' said Tiffany firmly. She might not have had a clue about what was going on, but she certainly was quick on the ball when any potential career setback was mentioned. 'What's that supposed to mean, Sophie? Apricot lost the part because the Beeb thought she wasn't up to it. What are you talking about?'

'Actually, she lost the part because she was having an affair with my husband,' said Barbara sweetly. 'I'm divorcing him on the grounds that he is a drug-taking crook. He is also, as it happens, a business associate of Martin's, isn't that right?'

'Yes, it is,' I chipped in. 'Honestly, Martin, I would have thought you would know better than to hang around with people like that after that unfortunate business about Sprocketts was it? – in New York. So much better if you tell Tiffany now, at least she'll be prepared for it when she hears about Molehill. Anyway, I'll leave you two alone to chat, now. Toodle-oo.'

I got up to go, and found myself prevented from doing so. Martin had my wrist in a vice-like grip, but just as I was on the point of losing my nerve, Little Ant leaned over. 'I say Martin, do let Sophie go,' he said. 'You don't want to add intimidation to the rest of your problems, do you? Especially in front of so many witnesses.'

Martin released me sharpish, and I regained my courage. 'This must be quite a nostalgic time for you, it's just like New York all over again,' I said sweetly.

Martin's face had gone the shade of red more commonly found on the features of Mr van Trocken. '*What?*' he demanded. 'How on, I mean why, what are you talking about, Sophie? This is outrageous. I demand an explanation at once.'

'Something to do with Sprocketts and buying shares you shouldn't have,' I said. 'His wife told me that,' I added to Tiffany, who was now fumbling in her handbag for her mobile phone.

'Sophie,' said Martin, dropping all attempts at charm, 'this is getting beyond a joke.'

'And now Molehill Magazines,' I said defiantly. 'We know it was you who bought the shares.'

'Utter nonsense,' said Martin.

'No it's not,' I said. 'We found that note behind the picture, and Penny's given it to Sir Jeremy. And the photo was taken at the van Trockens' a year ago, so you must have known him for ages.'

'Wild and irresponsible speculation,' said Martin. 'Really, Sophie, this is bordering on slander. I have no idea what you're talking about.'

'Sir Jeremy doesn't think so,' I said.

'Nor do I and I should know,' added Barbara.

Tiffany had dialled a number. 'Is Giles there?' she asked. 'It's Tiffany Day and I have to speak to him right away. I don't care if he's in the middle of dinner, he's supposed to be my agent, and I have to talk to him now!'

Martin, who had shot a horrified glance at Barbara, was obviously considering his options equally quickly. And if I knew anything about him after those six months together, of one thing I was sure: when the going got tough, Martin got going, usually out of the nearest exit point available. On this occasion, he didn't disappoint. 'Now look all of you,' he said, rising nimbly from his seat and pushing past me, 'this has gone quite far enough. What ever dear Charlotte told you is total fabrication, the poor dear girl never got over our separation, and I suspect this is some way of trying to get back at me. I, ah, I'm going to the loo and when I get back I would be grateful if you'd gone, Sophie. It's all a most entertaining fantasy, but I'd like a quiet evening. Tiffany, you mustn't listen to a word of this. Bye, darling. Lots of love.' He shot off towards the stairs at the front of the restaurant.

Believe it or not, that last bit was aimed at me, probably force of habit. I got up too. 'You know,' I said to Tiffany, who was tapping her fingers on the table increasingly urgently, as she hung on the phone, 'I've probably just done you a big favour.'

'Yah, OK, great,' said Tiffany, shooting me a filthy look. 'Giles? Is that you? Yah, OK, look. I'm having dinner with a guy called Martin Silverspoon, and it seems he's done something heavy, I don't know what. Is that going to ruin my career?'

I could hear an eruption of fury from the other end of the line – agents didn't like having their own dinners disrupted by ludicrous questions, it seems – and deemed this as good a moment to make a getaway as any. I moved across and sat down beside Michael.

'Sensational performance,' he whispered.

'Well done, Soph,' hissed Little Ant.

'Welcome to the wronged and now resuscitated women's club,' murmured Barbara.

'Oh, it was nothing,' I said modestly. Tiffany was now involved in a heated argument with her agent, and was point blank ignoring us. 'I just said my piece and – oh, look!' Two policemen had just come in, and were talking to the casually dressed chap at the bar, who was looking none too pleased at their appearance. He pointed up the stairs towards the loos.

'That's where Martin went,' whispered Barbara.

'I know,' I whispered back. 'Imagine being arrested in a loo! He'll never live this one down. I don't suppose anyone has a camera?'

A moment later there was a howl of fury from the direction of the stairs, worthy of Martin's partner in crime himself. 'Let me go!' he bellowed. 'There's been a terrible mistake! Have you any idea who I am?'

'Yes sir, we do sir,' replied a cheery voice. 'That's why we're here, sir. Now if you just pipe down a moment, I'm going to read you your rights.'

Well, I couldn't have asked for anything more – when we read about it afterwards, it seemed that the police broke down the loo door to find him trying to climb out of a window. At the time, though, we just had to be content with seeing him being frogmarched out of the place a few moments later in handcuffs, beetroot with rage, and demanding not just his lawyers, but a personal word with the Home Secretary.

'It's not the Home Office, sir, it's the Department of Trade and Industry who want to have a word with you, sir,' said the policeman happily, as he led him through the door. 'Do you know, sir, I've never arrested anyone in a restaurant before. Thank you, sir, for not having a quiet night in.' After that, unfortunately, I couldn't hear anything more as the door closed behind them, and Martin was led to a police car and driven off. The chap in charge of the place was having a quiet word of explanation with the other diners, who had been watching the proceedings in astonishment – 'Something to do with the City, I believe. Don't worry, he's not from round here' – and I am extremely happy to report that after another waiter had had a quiet word with her, Tiffany marched out with a face like thunder. She ignored my friendly 'Cheerio!' as she went.

There was a short pause, and then my three companions burst into a round of spontaneous applause. 'What a star!' cried Michael when they'd stopped. 'Sophie, I couldn't have done better myself. What a joy to watch. First you broke the terrible news that we all knew what the silly bugger's been playing at, and then Silverspoon is marched off in chains! Absolutely sensational! I could kiss you!'

'Oh, please do,' I said, forgetting myself.

Michael leant over, and planted a very gentle kiss on my cheek. He had extremely soft lips. I went absolutely crimson, until I realized that Little Ant and Barbara were also swapping smackers of appreciation, after which they both also insisted on kissing me. The waiters must have thought they were entertaining a table full of madmen. 'Are any of you ready to order yet?' asked one plaintively, coming over to the table.

'Oh, this definitely calls for more champagne,' said Barbara, beaming at the waiter. 'I couldn't be more pleased if it was Vladimir who had been arrested, although I expect we'll be hearing something about him soon. I'm free and you're free and Martin isn't!'

'I'm free, too,' added Little Ant.

'And so am I, in fact I'm extremely free,' said Michael cheerfully. 'Oh good, here's the champagne. Let's have a toast: to freedom and the fervent hope it won't last for very much longer!'

23

Do you know, I had absolutely gallons of champagne that night, though most of it wasn't at Sonny's – it was at Leo Tickell's bash. After we'd chatted about the events of the evening for ages, Michael told us he'd been invited and suggested that we all go along.

'That's very kind, but I'm exhausted,' said Barbara, beaming at him. 'I'm going to have to spend the weekend at the office sorting out Vladimir's mess, so I think I'll pass. You three go on, I'll get a cab back from here.'

'Actually, I'm quite tired too,' said Little Ant. 'I only got back a couple of days ago, and I've hardly even had time to unpack. You two go on, Barbara and I can share a cab back.'

'Come on, Sophie, I insist,' said Michael turning to me. 'It'll be a sensational party, and we really should celebrate in style.'

'Oh, I don't know,' I said bashfully. 'I won't know a soul there, except for Penny of course, and anyway, I haven't got a thing to wear.'

'You know me,' said Michael, 'and if you really haven't anything to wear, I've got some of my dear Mama's evening clothes at my flat. She sometimes uses it as a base to change, and you look about the same size as her.'

Well after that, unaccountably Barbara and Little Ant suddenly decided that they weren't totally exhausted after all and might stay on at Sonny's for a little supper, much to the relief of the poor waiters, who looked as if they had long given up on any proper orders from our table. And I ended up at one of the most glamorous parties of the year, dressed in a cream silk dress that looked very much like the one that I had dreamt about sporting in the South of France. I was, however, totally upstaged by Penny, who had turned up sporting not only a Chinese dragon on her upper arm, but metallic blue fingernails and a totally see-through pink lace dress, with extremely minimalist black lace bra and knickers underneath to preserve at least a bit of modesty.

It caused an uproar, not least because she spent the entire evening arm in arm with Charlotte, who was dressed in an officer's uniform. 'I don't think that picture shows enough of my tattoo,' she said petulantly, turning over a page of *The Sunday Times*, which had devoted a fair amount of space to the bash. 'Honestly, Sophie, I went to all that trouble, and you know what Dad said? He likes it!'

'Oh bad luck,' I said, dreamily taking a bite of croissant. It was Sunday morning and five of us – Penny, Charlotte, Little Ant, Michael and I – were grouped around our big mahogany table, having brunch and studying the newspapers. Albert was asleep in front of the fire, twitching his ear from time to time, and dreaming cat dreams. 'You're just going to have to take a leaf out of Mr van Trocken's book and snort loads of cocaine before going to a Buckingham Palace garden party,' I continued.

'It really is almost too sensational for words,' said Michael, putting down a copy of the *News of the World*. Splashed across the front was a huge headline, 'Charlied With Charlie!', above a strapline which read, 'Drugs shame of disgraced tycoon'. Inside was an extremely detailed in-depth account by Irina about how she and my ex-boss had indulged in Class A narcotic abuse before the garden party, alongside the picture that had been in Mr van Trocken's study of him shaking hands with Prince Charles. That must have been what Rory had been after when he burst in to the office a few days before. Apricot had also been there and, it seems, had met Mr van Trocken through Irina, which gave an added venom to Irina's description of the whole thing.

In total, there were pages of the stuff, with details of Mr van Trocken's past and present affairs, a brief description of what it was like to work for him by an 'unnamed source' (Rory again) and even several drafts of a letter in which he told Marcus Aimsworthy that a £1 million donation to the Tory Party would look so much better coming from Sir Vladimir van Trocken rather than plain old mister. It was unclear whether the letter had ever actually been sent, and an appalled Aimsworthy was quoted as denying all knowledge of it. Rory must have been rooting about in the rubbish bin for months to get the ammunition for that lot. 'I mean, really absolutely sensational, although I think Count Vladimir has a better ring to it than Sir,' continued Michael. 'What a dirty and sneaky thing for your ex-colleague to do. But I like it. Really, Sophie, I do think it's time for you to pen a

277

"my part in his downfall" piece yourself.'

'I just hope Barbara's not too upset by it all,' I said. Every single one of the Sundays had devoted reams of space to the whole affair, with the broadsheets concentrating on Martin's arrest and the business angle, and the tabloids going hell for leather over Mr van Trocken's personal life, with at least two bearing the headline, 'Bad Vlad is dangerous to know'. The only element that the lot of them left out was his current whereabouts – he seemed to have vanished without trace. 'I mean, it must be awful having all that stuff about your husband in the papers.'

'Oh, she didn't seem too upset when she saw the early editions last night,' said Little Ant, laying down a copy of the *Observer*. He had been reading a leader item entitled, 'When will they learn?' about the Tory Party accepting donations from dubious characters – not, it seems, that they were actually going to receive a penny of that £1 million. 'She said it would give her loads more ammunition for the divorce. What? What is it? Why are you all staring at me like that?'

'Last night?' enquired Penny, who had been examining the pictures of her, Charlotte and the tattoo in the *Mail on Sunday*. 'And just how, pray tell, did you find out her reactions last night?'

'Well, I was with her, wasn't I,' said Little Ant patiently, running a tanned hand through his sun-bleached blond hair. 'I took her out to dinner, thought someone should make sure that she was all right after the last few days.'

'Little Ant,' I said accusingly, 'you took her on a date!'

'It wasn't a date,' protested Little Ant. 'It was just a quiet supper at Le Caprice, and we took a walk through the West End afterwards and got the early editions. She's a very charming woman. Anyway, at least I don't go off to parties on Friday evening and not come home till Sunday morning.'

I went scarlet. Michael and I had got on so well on Friday night that we had sort of gone on getting on and, after rounding up the usual suspects, had not returned to Little Ant's flat until an hour earlier. I caught Michael's eye and went even more scarlet when he winked at me.

'Dirty stopout,' said Penny. A flash of diamond-inspired rainbow shot across the room as she rubbed a minuscule spot from her black leather trousers. 'And with my own brother, too. What's that you're reading, Charlie?'

'Och, just catching up on some background about ma ex,' said Charlotte, laying down a copy of the *Sunday Telegraph* and stretching. It had devoted a whole page to a piece entitled 'Fall of a fund manager'. 'The wee man's been a busy boy, I must institute some divorce proceedings myself. Don't have another croissant, Penny, it'll spoil your appetite for lunch.'

'My parents,' said Penny glumly, in response to my enquiring glance. 'Daddy and Charlie got on so well at the Leo Tickell party that he wants to get to know her better.'

'Oh, bad luck,' I said sympathetically. 'Why not tell him you bought some of the shares with Martin? You know, I'm sure he'll have something to say about that.'

Epilogue

Well, there you have it, an insider's view of the momentous events surrounding the spectacular downfall of my ex-boss and my ex-boyfriend. Not that Mr van Trocken ever looks likely to be really brought to justice. It seems he was a lot smarter than Martin, and, accompanied by Tony, left the country by private jet that very Friday when Barbara took over the company. There have been reported sightings of him all over the world, but personally I believe the rumour that he's now living in South America, probably in the lap of luxury.

Yes, you read that right. When Barbara and her team of accountants started going through the books, they discovered he'd been siphoning off money for years into an offshore account in Liechtenstein. From there it went off into various other offshore accounts, until it finally disappeared entirely from any prying eyes other than his own, although Rory, who has now become an investigative journalist, is determined to track it down one day. 'I suspect,' he muttered to me when I bumped into him in Oxford Street last week, 'he's in with the drug barons of Ecuador. He's taken so much of the stuff himself, he might as well put his knowledge to good use.'

Not that Barbara need worry. The divorce is due to come through any day now, and she's a rich woman in her own right. That is just as well, because another thing the accountants discovered is that van Trocken and Co. was on the verge of collapse, which must have been why Mr van Trocken was trying to sell his beloved *Food for Thought* to Molehill. It seems he'd used one bit of the company to lend to another, and then that bit to lend back again, until no-one had the faintest idea what the firm did and didn't own, and certainly not what it was really worth.

Barbara did what she could: she salvaged what could be salvaged, sold most of it off, and closed down the rest. The only bit she hung on to was *Food for Thought*, which has since been renamed *Stylish Living*, and turned in to a lifestyle magazine. A chastened Petrushka had been kept on as features editor, and displayed a lack of concern about her missing father that was entirely in keeping with the rest of her character, but finally, much to Barbara's relief, resigned last week as she was getting married to one of the advertisers on *Food for Thought* – the little soirée had gone ahead, after all.

'God darling, it'll be bloody bastard brilliant to be free,' she commented. 'I just can't be doing with getting into the office every day. Got any aspirin, darling? It was my engagement party last night, and my bloody, bastard head's about to fall off.'

Barbara is brilliant to work for. She was really relaxed about it when I accidentally closed down the computer network a while back and lost the copy from four of our most valuable contributors. 'Really, dear, don't worry about it at all,' she said. 'Anthony's coming to collect me in half an hour, and I'm sure he'll be able to get it back. He's marvellous with technology, you know.'

Yes, Barbara van Trocken and Anthony Hurlingham, aka my beloved Little Ant, are an item. She's only eight years older than him, after all, and having a toyboy is even more fashionable than being a lipstick lesbian, so why not? They seem terribly happy together, and last week he showed me the designs he's doing for their new house. 'Oh, and another thing,' he added, after I'd finished a stream of dutiful praise, 'how do you feel about being a godmother, Sophie?'

Penny and Charlotte, who is now divorced, are still together. It seems that just for once Penny wasn't pulling a publicity stunt to upset her father – just as well, really, as he wasn't upset – and they recently bought an enormous loft apartment in Clerkenwell, which they've filled with exotic paraphernalia from the Far East. 'Och, it's our own corner of a foreign land which is for ever China,' explained Charlotte. 'Anything to keep the wee girl happy.'

The wee girl is going from strength to strength. Her future at Haverstock and Weybridge looks more assured than ever, not least because her father has just bought the company. 'He insisted on coming along when Sir Jeremy took me out to dinner to thank me for giving him that note from Martin, and the two of them bonded within about two seconds,' said Penny wearily, when she told me about it afterwards.

'It seems they have a mutual love of golf and making money, and Daddy is keen to diversify away from the Hong Kong side of the business as it's all so changeable over there, so he needed a new toy to play with.

Honestly, Sophie, it's so unfair, now when I get promoted, everyone will think it's just because my father owns the company. You don't know how he's made me suffer.'

Martin, I am happy to report, really is a spent force. There's still no fixed date for his trial so, although he's out on bail, he can't actually work in the City until the whole business is cleared up. Not, I hasten to add, that he will probably ever work in the City again, though I've heard on the grapevine he's been making enquiries about moving to Saigon once all this is over. Poor old Vietnam, what did it ever do to deserve Martin?

WestEnders started its first run last week: did you see it? I thought it was hilarious, the Beeb's done it beautifully, and Camilla Duncan was brilliant in the leading role. Poor old Tiffany, such a shame that the Londoner's Diary in the *Evening Standard* ran that piece about her being with Martin on the night of his arrest. Even more surprisingly, they found out that her real name is Cuttlesnipe, I can't imagine how. Honestly, it wasn't me that leaked the story, although Barbara cackled in a way that wasn't like her at all when I showed her the piece. Anyway, Tiffany has finally made it to the small screen: she is currently appearing in an advertisement for a new brand of sanitary towel.

Well, that just about wraps up the cast list in our little drama – oh, except for one last thing. 'I've got a sensational idea, Sophie,' said Michael over dinner last week, when we'd finished discussing our forthcoming visit to meet his relatives in Hong Kong. 'You should move into my place. You've got to find somewhere else to live when Little Ant's sold his flat, so why not?'

'Certainly not,' I said loftily. 'I refuse to be a kept woman.'

'Oh, don't worry about that,' said Michael. 'You could earn your keep, you know, cooking, cleaning, ironing, just the usual sort of – Sophie, don't look at me like that. I was only joking. Actually, this is just a sneaky ploy on my part to get Albert to come and live with me and he agreed, but he said you had to be thrown in as part of the bargain. We had a recent one on one male bonding session, you see, in which we both went out and miaowed our hearts out together in the woods.'

'Actually, Albert's a girl.'

'All the more reason for you to move in. She's probably terribly confused about the nature of her sexuality, if you've been forcing her to deny her femininity and she needs the stability only two parents together can provide. Now, what do you say?'

'I'll think about it,' I said. I moved in last night.

Anyway, I must dash, I've got to get changed for the anniversary party Penny and Michael are throwing for their parents tonight. 'You won't believe what I've got to wear,' said Penny, when I spoke to her on the phone yesterday. 'It's a metallic sheath dress, which comes to just below my hips, and I've got these really amazing see through plastic platforms to go with them, from a shop Tasmin goes to. Oh Sophie, I just can't wait to see Daddy's face!'

As for me, I'm wearing a one-shouldered red silk cocktail dress, with matching red kitten-heeled sandals. No really, I am. I'm now a proper fashion writer on the magazine, and just about the first thing that I learned was that fashion houses give you a big discount on their clothes. The second thing I learned was that this doesn't apply to me as I'm still too unimportant to cultivate, and the third thing I learned was that I'm the same size as Barbara van Trocken, and she recently had a big clear out of all her designer clothes. They may say that day-dreams never come true, but you know what? Sometimes, life can turn out to be just totally cool!

THE END

BLONDE WITH ATTITUDE
by Virginia Blackburn

More at home with hangovers than takeovers? With a client more concerned with bedsheets than spreadsheets? It's not too much to handle when you're a blonde with attitude.

Emily, with a stressful job in a firm of City PR consultants, was finding her life out of control. Waking up once again in a strange bed, with little recollection of the night before, arriving late at work with laddered tights and roots in need of retouching, inadequately briefed for an important meeting with a new client – who turns out to be an all-too-dreadful reminder of the night before – her chosen career looks, to say the least, precarious. Her immaculate secretary Camilla is only too anxious to expose Emily's shortcomings to her boss, while her friends are all undergoing such acute personal crises that Emily requires frequent absences from work to sort out their problems in various City wine bars. Her gorgeous ex-boyfriend Jack seems more interested in blonde bimbos. And attempting to get her life back in control by escaping to her solitary flat proves difficult when Nigel, her track-suited social worker neighbour, is determined to forge a closer and more meaningful bond.

How Emily escapes from the toils of the City and learns to become a real human being again is told in this entrancing and witty story.

0 552 14514 9

MORE INNOCENT TIMES
by Imogen Parker

Two generations, two sisters, too many lies . . .

Sometimes the past won't let you love again . . . until you confront it.

Gemma is ready for a change of scene. Her self-imposed exile in America worked for a while, but now she is returning to England for a fresh start. A new job, a new house, a new life beckons, but there are old problems too, the same painful, raw problems she ran away from ten years ago.

Daisy stole Oliver from her. Her beloved sister just walked off with the love of her life. They never talked about it. They haven't talked about anything since. Not even the death of their father, Bertie, and the subsequent suicide of their beautiful mother Estella.

This is the story of two pairs of sisters – Gemma and Daisy, their mother Estella and her sister Shirley. It tells of love and passion, jealousy and secrets, and follows a family mystery back to its origins in the 1950s – to more innocent times.

A wonderfully woven tale of tangled relationships. I loved it'
Penny Vincenzi

0 552 14498 3

A SELECTED LIST OF FINE NOVELS
FROM CORGI BOOKS

14060 0	MERSEY BLUES	*Lyn Andrews*	£5.99
14049 X	THE JERICHO YEARS	*Aileen Armitage*	£5.99
14514 9	BLONDE WITH ATTITUDE	*Virginia Blackburn*	£4.99
14323 5	APPASSIONATA	*Jilly Cooper*	£4.99
13313 2	CATCH THE WIND	*Frances Donnelly*	£5.99
14261 1	INTIMATE	*Elizabeth Gage*	£4.99
14442 8	JUST LIKE A WOMAN	*Jill Gascoine*	£5.99
14096 1	THE WILD SEED	*Iris Gower*	£4.99
14537 8	APPLE BLOSSOM TIME	*Kathryn Haig*	£5.99
14385 5	THE BELLS OF SCOTLAND ROAD	*Ruth Hamilton*	£5.99
14529 7	LEAVES FROM THE VALLEY	*Caroline Harvey*	£5.99
14486 X	MARSH LIGHT	*Kate Hatfield*	£4.99
14220 4	CAPEL BELLS	*Joan Hessayon*	£4.99
14208 5	FATHER OF LIES	*Janet Inglis*	£5.99
14397 9	THE BLACK BOOK	*Sara Keays*	£5.99
14333 2	SOME OLD LOVER'S GHOST	*Judith Lennox*	£5.99
14320 0	MARGUERITE	*Elisabeth Luard*	£4.99
13910 6	BLUEBIRDS	*Margaret Mayhew*	£3.99
14498 3	MORE INNOCENT TIMES	*Imogen Parker*	£5.99
10375 6	CSARDAS	*Diane Pearson*	£5.99
14125 9	CORONATION SUMMER	*Margaret Pemberton*	£5.99
14400 2	THE MOUNTAIN	*Elvi Rhodes*	£4.99
14549 1	CHOICES	*Susan Sallis*	£4.99
14548 3	THE GHOST OF WHITECHAPEL	*Mary Jane Staples*	£4.99
14132 1	SILENT HONOUR	*Danielle Steel*	£4.99
14118 6	THE HUNGRY TIDE	*Valerie Wood*	£4.99